I0768958

First to Fall

BARTHOLOMEW SERIES
BOOK ONE

LANEY HATCHER

Copyright

This book is a work of fiction. Any resemblance to actual persons, living or dead or undead, events, locales is entirely coincidental.

Made in the United States of America

Developmental Edits: Emerald Edits
Editing: Write On Editing
Cover Illustration: Blythe Russo
Proofreading: Judy's Proofreading

One

AUGUSTUS

Hampshire, 1855

"Are you going to propose or shall I do it myself?"

Ah Christ.

Letting loose an aggrieved sigh, I regarded my oldest, dearest, and most meddlesome friend across the drawing room. Emery paused dramatically in the doorway after throwing down her gauntlet. Hands on hips, she gave me an impatient *what are you waiting for* glare.

"Well?" She emphasized her point by widening her already enormous eyes.

I still didn't answer, merely thumbed the newspaper in my hand and resumed reading about the latest bill currently being proposed in Parliament.

Three, two, one ...

"Augie!" exclaimed Emery as she abandoned her pose by the door and bustled determinedly into the room. Blond brows lowered over whiskey-colored eyes, my childhood friend Emery Bartholomew, middle daughter of the Marquess Northcutt, dropped onto the settee beside me. Grasping the newsprint, she attempted to garner my attention. "What are you waiting for? You need to ask me. Your family will be here any moment and we need to tell them we plan to marry."

I tapped my chin for emphasis. "I love how you've assumed I'm going along with this scheme as if it's a foregone conclusion. We have never once discussed marriage. I only arrived home from university yesterday."

"Yes, but I told you in my last letter that this is the perfect plan. You and I shall marry. It will alleviate the pressure from your mother and your brother to enter the military or the clergy. And it will get my mother off my back about London and the season and balls and so on and so forth."

I glared at Emery and her high-handed solution to our problems. Of course my outspoken friend of twenty years would take it upon herself to create a plan and simply expect me to fall in line. Granted, that was what I'd always done. As evidenced by the multitude of Emery plots over the course of our childhood and adolescence in which I'd ended up thrown from a horse, naked in a lake, and dressed in slippered dancing heels.

"You're thinking about that time I put you in Patty's shoes and forced you to waltz with me in the ballroom, aren't you?"

Dammit. "No." I flicked her forehead.

Emery squawked indelicately. "Will you let that go? I was five and you were eight and I'm sure no one remembers it anyway."

Rubbing her forehead she attempted once more, "But *this* plan is perfect, Augie. It solves all of our problems."

I considered her for a moment. Yes, she had written to me at Cambridge a fortnight ago and outlined her ludicrous strategy to wrangle our futures away from our respective families. While I appreciated Emery's efforts and her well-meaning strategizing, I just couldn't see making such a permanent decision at our ages. I was only five and twenty. Of course, *now* she thought she didn't care about London or life among the *ton*. She craved a quiet existence surrounded by horses and the English countryside. Emery wanted a comfortable life with companionship *right now*. But what if things changed in the future? What if she decided marrying her best friend was a mistake? What happened when she changed her mind and wanted children someday? What if she met someone else and fell in love? I rubbed absently at the unpleasant tightness behind my sternum.

I refused to condemn Emery to a contractual sham marriage just to save me from a life I didn't want. She said this harebrained plan suited her needs as well as my own, but I couldn't imagine that to be true. How much needling could the Marchioness Northcutt really inflict upon her daughter? Surely it wasn't so drastic as to require a fake marriage to one's best friend.

"I can't do that to you, Em," I said quietly, looking away toward the window.

"Do what?" she remarked, all confusion. "You're my oldest friend. You act like being forced to see your face every day would be punishment. No one understands me like you, Augie. No one makes me laugh like you. I could actually be myself. No proper union could make me as happy as a fake marriage to you. I know it."

At some point during her little speech, she'd released the newspaper and grasped my arm in earnest. I knew Emery believed what she was saying. This wasn't some misplaced effort on her part. She wasn't placating or sacrificing herself in any way … in her eyes.

But I knew better. I knew she *deserved* better. Better than some agreement, a plan cooked up as a last-ditch effort. She deserved a chance at happiness. A real chance with someone she could love. I knew love matches weren't typical among our set. The probability of a daughter of a marquess finding true love and settling into happily ever after was unlikely. There were dowries to consider and extended families were scrutinized for suitability. Love or affection rarely factored into the equation. But if Emery had even the slightest chance … I could never take that away from her.

And if she did find love with someone else, I didn't think I could stand by and watch.

I rolled my shoulders back, prepared to do battle, and turned on the settee to face Emery fully. "But what if that changes? You're only two and twenty. What if you go to London like your mother wants and meet someone you actually want to marry? You could miss out because you foolishly proposed to me before you even took a chance."

Her face scrunched up like she smelled something foul. "But that's what I'm trying to avoid. I don't want to go to London. I don't want to dance at balls or have tea with gossipy chits. I don't want to *promenade in the park*." This statement was accompanied by a mocking wave of her gloved hand complete with pretentious inflection in her tone.

I snorted a laugh. "You're ridiculous. Most girls live for that sort of thing."

"Well, not this girl." Tone serious and eyes sober, she continued, "You'd be saving me too." I started to protest but she forged onward. "I know you believe this proposed arrangement to be all one-sided. That I haven't considered the options or my future. That I'm only being impulsive. But that's not true. I … I can't live that life, Augustus. I won't."

I ruminated on Emery's words, and not just what she said but the way in which she said it. She was the fun one, the outgoing personality. Emery was magnetic and charming, occasionally outlandish. She wore a smile more often than her favorite riding boots. It was a rare thing to see her somber and serious. And rarer still to detect a hint of vulnerability.

Perhaps … perhaps we could …

Cursing myself for taking advantage of a weak moment, I firmed my resolve. Turning back to Emery, I opened my mouth to voice my final objection when she extended her fingers and covered my lips. I pulled in a startled breath as she spoke. "Just think about it, okay? I realize I was too hasty. You're home for months. A proposal doesn't have to happen tonight, at our first Bartholomew/Ward Disaster Dinner of the summer." As the pads of her fingers pressed gently against my mouth to still my impending interruption, Emery's gaze drifted to my lips and stayed there a beat longer than appropriate. Shaking herself, she met my eyes once more. "Besides, our families will need time to see us together, to believe that we want to marry. We can't just spring it on them. They'll never believe it."

I growled against her fingers. Oh, was that the plan? Pretend affection and infatuation in order to gain support from our families. My frustration grew unchecked, and I had only myself to blame.

Emery's eyes widened at my expression and she jerked her hand away before I snapped out, "What? You expect me to follow you around like a besotted fool?"

She paused, considering. "Well, I wouldn't say fool, but I can work with besotted."

"You want to lie to our families? Make them believe that we're in love, is that it?" I asked incredulously.

Her brows furrowed in confusion, matching her tone. "Why are you so upset?"

"I'm not upset. I didn't realize this plan involved a performance. And attempting to deceive everyone we know with ill intent."

Sighing dramatically, Emery attempted to do what Emery always did: wrestle control of a situation. "Our intent is not ill! This plan is best for everyone. Gads, you act like we're trying to swindle them out of their fortunes."

I narrowed my eyes at her short-sighted explanation. "So you're planning on lying to them for the rest of our lives?"

"Well … I …" She blustered and cleared her throat several times. I scrutinized her odd reaction as she coughed and reached for my dish of tea on the low table before us. I stiffened as she leaned across my lap and looked to the ceiling for patience and tolerance and whatever else might be up there.

After a fortifying slurp—ladylike as always—followed by a grimace, Emery replaced the teacup. "That could use some sugar."

Refusing to get pulled into a decade-old sweet tea debate, I merely raised a brow in her direction.

"Fine," she acknowledged in exasperation, while refusing to meet my gaze. "I hadn't planned that far ahead."

There we are.

I laughed without humor. "Em, I know you mean well. But let's just forget about this for now, survive the first dinner of the summer, and maybe we can sneak in a ride in the morning." I was attempting to distract her with the promise of her beloved horses.

Her elegant blond brow rose as she pursed her lips. "You're trying to distract me."

I rolled my eyes but a genuine laugh escaped. This girl—this woman—knew me so well. There was a comfort in being in the presence of friendship so profound. Someone who knew all your stories and instigated most of them. Emery was my home, my foundation. She knew me inside and out, could read my expressions and my intentions with unerring ease.

So I was continually surprised that she hadn't yet figured out I was hopelessly in love with her.

The Bartholomew/Ward Disaster Dinner was served promptly at eight o'clock on a mild June evening at Laurel Park. I was in attendance with my elder brother, John Ward, the current Duke of Kendrick, and my mother, Amelia Ward, the dowager duchess.

Emery was seated across from me, with Lionel Bartholomew, the Marquess Northcutt, at the head of the table and our mothers facing one another. Em's elder brother, Silas, was away on the continent for the summer and I'd heard Genevieve, the youngest Bartholomew, wasn't feeling well and wouldn't be joining us. She was probably faking it. I wished I had thought of that.

No matter the household hosting, main entrees could be counted upon to be lavish and over-the-top. Elaborate one-upmanship was the name of the game. Our intimate party of six had been seated for at least an hour with no end in sight.

With Harriet Bartholomew, Marchioness Northcutt, the hostess for this particular evening, one could expect a multitude of long and drawn-out courses featuring a plethora of meats, sauces, jellies, vegetables, and wines to choose from. Venison was fashionable currently and would undoubtedly show up later in the meal. Lady Northcutt always served roasted asparagus with breadcrumbs and made a great show of mentioning the dish to my mother as she was served by the footmen. "Amelia, I have your favorite!"

My mother detested asparagus. "Why, thank you, Harriet! Always so thoughtful and considerate." But she'd rather choke down four bites of asparagus than let our hostess know she'd landed a hit.

Ah, dining with friends. Always a lovely time.

Our families had been neighbors for decades. My late father had been friends with the Marquess Northcutt since boyhood. Their respective wives had reached their odd friendship through proximity and—mostly innocent—competition over the years.

Next was the fish course. Salmon, naturally. My brother, John, was allergic. Luckily he was too far in his cups to consider the food being served nearby.

Apparently Emery hadn't eaten all day judging by the speed and intensity with which she was consuming nearly everything. My friend must have caught my mother's disgusted sneer as Emery slathered a comical amount of mint jelly on her lamb because she looked over and shot me a wink before continuing her path of destruction. I hid my silent laugh and mirthful expression behind my wineglass.

These dinners had become commonplace over the years. Monthly during the summer months, almost always a holiday gathering near Christmas for the Bartholomews and Wards, with the standard house party attendance once a year at my family's estate as well as Emery's, and finally a few spur-of-the-moment meals sprinkled throughout the year to celebrate someone's birthday or other such memorable occasion.

We were all used to the ridiculousness at this point. This overwhelming competition between our mothers was ludicrous. They endeavored to serve the most stylish and sought-after dishes while also striving to annoy the holy hell out of their guests with food choices that forced true ingenuity in order to avoid them and, in some cases, circumvent allergic poisoning.

While the women were friendly in most regards, they were also a perfect example of how nonsensical relationships were among the *ton*. Friends were not trusted confidantes but competitors. Any little reaction was deemed a win and the injured party must not show fear or disdain or any other negative emotion.

Gossip was rampant among aristocrats in England, and there seemed to be no loyalty, even between friends. No one was safe from the spread of tall tales and outright lies to improve one's position over another. I often detested our society and the utter absurdity of it all. Seeing this display so often between our families rarely garnered more than an eye roll from Emery or myself, but that was equally frightening for we'd obviously been conditioned to our surroundings. This was not normal and yet we behaved as if it were, and merely did our best to survive each encounter.

I'd known from an early age that these exchanges were unsettling and something other. And I'd been fortunate enough to receive kindness and healthy examples of relationships early in life from other sources.

Perhaps recognizing the irrationality seen between our mothers helped me appreciate my friendship with Emery. It was genuine and perhaps the only true thing in England. We knew our mothers' behavior was lunacy, but they kept playing the game. And we remained dismayed yet faithful spectators. Emery and I would likely review the events of the evening later and award fictional disaster dinner points to the parties involved. A winner would be named and we would once again question the sanity of our mothers.

But I found I couldn't completely regret the time wasted at these tragic affairs. Emery and I had first bonded across the dining room table and then solidified that bond through hours of amusement. We learned early on that one must maintain a sense of humor in the face of irrational dinner parties.

It was my ability to be honest and open with Emery that I prized most. Well, not that honest. If she knew about my feelings … I don't know what would happen. But it was too risky a scenario to contemplate. I refused to lose her.

Change was a frightening concept. The unknown was equally worrisome. And the combination of the two was unfathomable. If Emery found out I loved her, desperately and hopelessly, that knowledge could potentially wreak havoc on our friendship. I couldn't allow that. It was another reason why Emery's proposal and the very idea of marriage had my heart racing inside my chest. There were so many variables and I couldn't plan for any of them.

Determined to focus on getting through dinner, I took a deep breath and looked to Emery once more. She glanced up from her plate with a smile aimed my way, but it was quickly replaced by a frown. I don't know what expression she read on my face but I imagined it was some reflection of the utter panic I felt at the idea of losing her in any way, even if she were to become my wife. Her latest scheme had the capacity for spectacular failure. If we were to wed, and I'm not saying I'd agree to it, could we still remain friends as we were right now?

I didn't know. And it was going to give me hives.

My mother cleared her throat delicately. "Did you hear about the Viscountess Westbrooke?"

Lady Northcutt's brows furrowed as she was forced to reply in the negative. "I'm afraid I did not."

One point to Mother.

"Well, she was quite proud of herself for adding to her collection. She recently acquired a new landscape by M. Barton." My mother's statement was met with murmurs of approval and interest around the table.

Anticipating forthcoming gossip, Lady Northcutt leaned forward. "Is that so?"

"Quite," replied Mother. "She was indulging in a bit of sherry at our last gathering and admitted she paid over nine hundred pounds for it."

M. Barton was a notable painter in the London art scene. Part of the appeal was the novelty of the artist. His work was outstanding to be sure, but it was the secrecy involving his fame and artistry that made the lords and ladies of the *ton* clamor for a commission.

"That's ridiculous. What a waste," came my brother's slurred response. No one paid him any mind.

Emery mumbled something under her breath.

And Lord Northcutt was nodding awkwardly, eyes glued to his salmon in white sauce. Odd.

In a very obvious effort to change the subject, Lord Northcutt began, "So, Augustus, are you looking forward to being home for the summer?"

I focused my attention on her father, but before I could respond, Emery spoke ahead of me, smiling brightly. "Of course he's happy to be home. He's spending the summer with me."

The marquess snorted at his middle daughter. "What kind of trouble has she cooked up for you this time, m'boy? Remember that time we found you waltzing in slippers just because Emery wanted a dancing partner and had demanded to lead?" He chuckled good-naturedly.

My stone-faced response aimed at Emery clearly said, *No one remembers, my ass*.

Her answering eye roll said she didn't care.

Both of us were on the verge of smiling. Hopefully someone would introduce a new topic before either one of us succumbed to our mirth.

Unfortunately it was my inebriated brother who spoke. "It won't matter what scheme or summer plan Lady Emery has for Augustus, he'll need to focus on his future and make a decision while he's here."

I cleared my throat uneasily as my brother's statement blanketed the room in awkward silence.

My mother attempted to soothe the tension and my brother's ruffled feathers, but unfortunately accomplished neither. "Have you considered which path you'd like to pursue, Augustus? The clergy? Or perhaps the military?"

One glance at Emery hurried my response. Nostrils flaring and fists white-knuckled on the table, she was preparing to defend my honor. With a tight smile for my mother, I rushed out, "No, Mother. I'm afraid I haven't yet decided."

My brother set his goblet down with a *thunk* on the oak surface, sloshing wine over the recently refilled brim. *Was that his seventh glass? No, eighth.* I watched the dark liquid seep into the bright tablecloth as John took up his familiar position. "Everyone has a purpose in life, little brother. I have responsibilities to the duke-dom. I'm Father's heir and working damn hard to make sure our legacy endures." *Debatable.* "Second sons have expectations as well. And the longer you avoid doing your duty to this family, the more of an embarrassment you become."

I wasn't predisposed to rage. It took quite a lot to rouse me to anger. And this was an old argument. John had been the Duke of Kendrick for over ten years, following the death of our father. I'd been getting some version of this little speech every time I was in his presence for ages now. But he rarely spoke to me in public this way. He was truly beyond his threshold for alcohol intake. My banked fury was causing a warm flush beneath my cravat.

My mother looked pained at the airing of our dirty bedlinens. She had a firm sense of responsibility and often pressured me to uphold my familial duties, but she loved me. And as any aristo-cratic lady, she eschewed scandal directed at her family. While this was verging on a public embarrassment for my mother, it undoubtedly rankled that the Bartholomews were witness to our internal squabbling. Despite the theatrics taking place at the dinner table, Lady Northcutt nor anyone else appeared pleased by the spectacle.

I made the mistake of looking to Emery. I could read the fury there as well as panic at the thought of my unhappiness at being forced into a future I didn't want. Her wide eyes and visible distress only spelled disaster. Then I watched a change come over her. My friend's fear and anger morphed into resolve and I knew what was coming.

I shook my head minutely, but she refused to acknowledge my silent plea. My brother was drunk. He didn't require a response. He merely wished to hear himself speak. And he definitely didn't need the reaction he was about to get from Emery. But her amber eyes were lit with a spark of indignation on my behalf. I knew there was no stopping her now.

Propping my elbow on the table, I rested my chin in my hand and waited for the words I knew were coming.

Emery straightened in her seat, wiped her mouth free of mint jelly with her cloth napkin, and then shocked the room into stunned silence with her next words. Well, shocked everyone save me. I knew Emery better than anyone; I had seen this runaway train derail from a mile away. "Augie won't need to fret over whether to join the clergy or the military, Your Grace. His future is rather handled. Because he'll soon be marrying me."

Two

EMERY

Complete and utter silence met my pronouncement.

One would assume that declarations of marriage would be met with felicitations. At the very least a gasp of excitement or some sign of having heard such joyous news spoken aloud. Well, perhaps that was how it worked in polite company. Unfortunately for Augie and myself, we were trapped in the dining hall of misfortune and disaster.

Sitting straight in my chair, I noticed that all eyes were on me. Well, almost all eyes. Augie had his head in his hand across the table, brown curls on full display. I knew we hadn't fully discussed this plan, and he wasn't completely on board. At least not just yet. But Augie always came around. He would eventually see my way of thinking … after days of internal fretting followed by list making to evaluate the advantages and disadvantages. And then another day of agonizing. I was merely speeding up the process.

While my methods could often be seen as high-handed and occasionally manipulative, I always meant well. And in this particular instance, I could not stand by and watch Augie suffer under the scrutiny of his family. His brother, the Duke of Kendrick, demeaning him and criticizing him whenever he got the chance made my blood boil. Augie was the best man—the best person—I knew. He didn't deserve his wastrel brother trying to force his hand. The fact that that drunkard held any sway over my Augie was unacceptable.

Augustus Ward held the courtesy title of Earl Barrington. By all accounts save birth order, Augie deserved to be his father's heir. Augie loved his family home and their adjoining lands. He wanted to honor his father's legacy and use his vast knowledge to support and enhance the estate his brother was neglecting. Life was not fair, I knew this. But it still burned that my dearest friend was treated this way.

I wasn't going to sit here one more second while my friend was condescended to. I had been gripped with panic at witnessing Augustus's easy acceptance. He seemed resigned to his future and that hopelessness more than anything spurred me into action. And then John had kept talking. It was too late by then.

When you're a woman, sometimes the only thing you have to offer is your hand.

Perhaps someone could muster up a smile for our good news.

Another glance at Augie. No help there unfortunately. I'd have to bluster through on my own.

Mama and Father stared incredulously. The dowager duchess and her son, the duke, seemed equally perplexed. Perhaps no smiling, then.

I met their gazes steadily and with confidence. Twenty-five percent of making a point was to stand by and support your convictions. The other seventy-five percent was merely appearing to do so.

I could do this. I would do this.

For Augie.

I looked once more to my friend. His head had finally come up, chin resting in his palm, elbow propped on the table. Augustus looked more grown up and handsome than I'd ever seen him. Blue eyes glowing … with fury? At me, probably. Had his shoulders always been so broad, his jaw so defined and masculine?

Augie arched an eyebrow imperiously high as if to say, *What now, Emery? How are you getting out of this one?*

Hadn't Augie learned in twenty years of friendship? I could get out of anything.

Emboldened by his challenge, I raised my chin in defiance. That got an eye roll out of him. And thank God for that. Augustus needed a spark, especially now when his family sucked all the good feelings from the room. I hated seeing my oldest friend lifeless in the presence of his overbearing brother. If my actions could jolt him out of whatever bored acceptance he'd resigned himself to … well, I'd call that a win.

Now, to speed dinner along so Augustus and I could escape and strategize in private.

I took that eye roll and gave him a little wink in return, but before I could address the room at large with engagement details completely invented on the spot, Augie's brother started to laugh.

And not a good laugh.

Augustus straightened out of his slouch, and we all turned to the duke as his cold, hard amusement penetrated the fog my announcement had settled over our group.

Wiping tears of mirth away from his eyes, John Ward, the Duke of Kendrick, guffawed. "You expect us to believe that the two of you are going to m-m-marry!?" He made a show of slapping his hand on the table three times. "Do you take me for an imbecile? Although … even marriage to her would be preferable to the military, I suppose."

Even marriage to her … I gasped in outrage.

"Now just a moment," Augie began as my father's eyes hardened.

But it was the dowager who looked to her elder son with a rigid expression. "That's quite enough."

"Seriously, Mother," John slurred. "Augustus is attempting to shirk his responsibilities to his family by—by arranging some scheme with this chit." His hand flung accusingly in my direction and toppled his seventh—no, eighth—glass of wine. Liquid seeped across the table linens and servants sprang into action.

John stood, weaving slightly and finally braced himself on the back of his chair as footmen cleaned up his mess. The dowager stood, muttering apologies before turning to her recalcitrant son in a tone that brooked no argument. "We're leaving. Now."

Shooting a deadly glare at Augustus, the Duke of Kendrick straightened away and quit the room leaving his mother to follow.

If I'd thought the quiet following my engagement announcement profound, then the silence in the wake of their departure was downright hallowed.

Unsure of his reaction, I looked to Augie, but his solemn face was unreadable.

A Bartholomew/Ward Disaster Dinner had never ended quite like that.

"Well," my father said, snapping us from our shock. "Can someone pass the asparagus?"

~

Later that evening, I prepared for bed.

Well, I appeared to prepare for bed.

Gansey bustled around my room as I brushed my riotous blond waves.

"And then what happened?" My lady's maid paused with my wrapper outstretched.

I took the offered garment and met Gansey's green eyes in the mirror before continuing to recount the evening. "And then Augie passed the asparagus and we continued the meal. No one said anything about the duke or the dowager. Mama and Father made polite innocuous conversation. I was quite proud of them."

Eyes wide in disbelief, Gansey bent to retrieve my slippers. Before turning for the wardrobe, she shook her head sadly. "Poor Lord Barrington. That brother of his ..." She trailed off.

Gansey had been with our household since she was very young. Just ten years my senior, she'd witnessed my friendship with Augie firsthand. She'd also borne witness to his brother's mistreatment.

"I know," I lamented agreeably.

Returning from the wardrobe, she took the brush from my hands.

"Did you talk to Augustus following dinner? Sort out the engagement business?"

Wincing as she brushed with far more determination than I'd shown, I replied, "No, Augie took his leave immediately following dinner. I think he needed some space." I would in all likelihood see him later though.

I *needed* to see for myself that he was well after the scene in the dining room. True, we did need to discuss our betrothal. After John's outburst, I was even more determined to prove him wrong and see Augie protected and shielded from his family. But I needed to talk to Augustus. The way I'd announced things had been premature. If he wanted to call things off … he needed to know I would support him.

I would try to talk him out of it, of course, but I wouldn't force his agreement.

Gansey hummed in thought. I winced again as she found a particularly tangled strand.

"Oh hush, you tender-headed thing."

"Well, it hurts!" I whined.

"Fine, then." She smiled at me in the mirror and relinquished the hairbrush with dramatic flourish.

I laughed and scooted over on the bench before my dressing table.

Gansey took the invitation and sat down next to me. "When do you think you'll have the wedding?"

"I don't know, Gansey. I don't know if Augustus will even agree to go through with it." My fingers moved back and forth over the coarse bristles in my hand.

She looked surprised. "Of course he will."

"I mean, I know he would prefer to avoid the clergy or the military, but he has it in his head that he'd be taking advantage of my friendship. Or that he'd be selfish to accept my suit. I don't know. It's preposterous." And it was. I had absolutely no desire to go to London and parade myself among the *ton*, pretending to be someone I was not. I wasn't lying or attempting to appease Augie by telling him he'd be saving me as well. I didn't want that life. I'd never fit in even if I tried.

I loved living in the country. Waking early, riding every day, and living with the freedom to be myself. If I went to town for the season, I would be forced to manage all my time, restrain all my smiles, and forfeit all my freedom. All for what? The chance of meeting a man who would have those same expectations. I'd be sought after as a hostess and a broodmare. Those were not my goals. I had my life here. I had my … goals. And more importantly, I had some self-respect.

I'd seen what an *advantageous* match could do to a woman. My thoughts turned bitter. My elder sister, Patricia, had made a fine match during her first season … to a duke old enough to be her grandfather. Patty had changed. It felt as if I'd lost my sister. She wasn't the same person she'd once been. She'd turned into the perfect hostess, the perfect young wife, and the perfect duchess. But she wasn't happy. I could tell. And now, widowed at six and twenty she was yet again someone unknown and unreachable.

Augie had this ridiculous notion that should we marry, he would be preventing me from finding a love match. Were all men really so naïve? He meant well and I loved him for it. But he just didn't realize how little autonomy women possessed, how little control we had over our own futures.

And a *ton* marriage for a woman like me would be a shackle about the leg.

"Is that what he told you?" Gansey inquired, bringing me back to our conversation. "That he didn't want to be selfish?"

"Yes." I met her gaze in the mirror. "He thinks I'll go to London this autumn and find a lord and fall in love. But if Augie marries me instead, he'll be keeping me from my own happily ever after."

Gansey snorted. "The only way you'd be happy forever is with that boy by your side."

I couldn't argue with that. No one made me as content as Augie. However, he didn't resemble a boy so much anymore. The time and distance separating us these last months seemed to lend Augie a new and mysterious air. I recalled the muscles straining his coat, the sharp line of his jaw. He now had whiskers shading an angular face that used to be soft and rounded by youth.

I could remember the feel of his lips against my hand when I'd quieted his objections before dinner, so firm and well formed. Had Augie's lower lip always been that full and soft-looking?

"I know. Our marriage would be advantageous for us both. I could maintain … my current lifestyle. And Augie could avoid his awful brother and the pressure from his family." I could never continue with my life, the way it was now, as the wife of some bossy noble. A union with Augie would grant us both freedom, but he didn't see it that way. He didn't trust me to know my own mind. After a lifetime of friendship, Augie would always see his role as my protector—the stable one, the dependable one. While my ideas would always be questioned … because of empirical evidence, probably. I'd been irresponsible and reckless too long, and it was coming back to bite me now.

With a confident smile on her lovely face, Gansey whispered into the quiet of my bedchamber, "I've always known you two would suit."

I startled and turned to face her head-on instead of her pleased reflection in the mirror. "You what?" I replied, overly loud.

"Emery, who else were you ever going to marry? Of course it would be Augustus." I could still feel the shock on my face as she continued. "Your friendship is special. You have to realize that. Relationships like yours and Augie's aren't common. Even over time and distance, you've maintained an easiness between you. You pick up right where you left off with every visit."

I supposed I always thought I would remain unwed. I never looked to the future and saw a shadowy husband or family waiting for me. I hadn't considered a marriage to Augie until he mentioned the paths his family was forcing on him. And then it all made sense; fell right into place. At least marriage seemed the obvious solution to me.

"But that's friendship. It isn't romance or attraction, Gansey. It's not the making of a true marriage," I hurried to correct. But truthfully, I couldn't deny that I'd noticed Augie today in a way I never had before—his body, his solemn blue eyes—and found them—found *him*—pleasing. Very pleasing, if I was being honest. And I wasn't. I couldn't admit that to Gansey, much less myself.

"If you are very, very lucky, then a marriage will be founded in friendship. It will be all of those things. The easy way you are with one another, accepting and knowing. You know Augie's mind and his heart. That's marriage in the fantastical. To spend the rest of your life with your very best friend in the world ... that's legend, Emery." Gansey, my maid, my friend looked at me indulgently as if I were an ignorant child. As if we weren't separated by a mere decade of experience. She was indeed notoriously wise and my closest friend besides Augie. Gansey was the older sister I no longer had in Patty.

I thought about what my friend had said. And if Augie and I had this chance, if we could really make this plan work, we should do it. I couldn't let him talk himself out of it.

The summer grass was high and swished agreeably against the simple dress I'd donned for my late-night excursion. I didn't require much light to see by. Having spent the majority of my twenty-two years on this estate, I knew it like the back of my hand. The dips and valleys, the well-worn paths beaten down by horse hooves. It was home, and I marched with confidence toward my destination.

Following my talk with Gansey, I'd waited patiently as she turned in for the evening in her quarters. When the house was quiet and still, I'd changed out of my nightgown and wrapper, pulled on sturdy boots and made my way through the back garden.

Walking by moonlight through our field bordering the Wards' estate—Kensworth Hall—I practiced my speech internally. Usually most of my thoughts formed and evacuated my mouth simultaneously, but this was important. I needed to get it right. It was imperative that Augie come around to the idea of marriage. To me, specifically.

As I drew closer to the tree line, candlelight flickered from a lone candle in the distance and I felt a rush of affection so deep and true, I had to pause in my progress. I hadn't been sure he'd come. Until this moment and the visible proof of his presence, I hadn't been confident our traditions would hold. Augie had been upset and blindsided by my decision to announce our engagement. And then the scene with his brother. My relief that he'd come to our shared and secret place was profound.

Maybe this would work.

The tree house was well hidden by the fullness of the tree containing it. Camouflaged by lush green foliage of the oak in which it rested, we'd discovered the small structure when I was six and Augie was nine. Old and long forgotten, the tree house had been overgrown and covered in leaves and debris. With the help of Anders, one of the Wards' most trusted staff and Augie's companion, we'd acquired a ladder and explored the single-room construction. Augie and I had made improvements over the years. I'd added candles to read by and blankets to ward off the evening chill. And I'd assisted Augie in replacing beams and strengthening the structure as we'd grown. The tree house had transformed from secret hideout for playmates to nostalgic summer hideaway.

As adolescents we'd whiled away the humid, sunny days reading and talking about nothing. We'd utilized the tiny house less and less as we'd grown older though. It was quite small and we could no longer stand comfortably within. I doubted Augie could lie down in either direction now without bumping his head on the walls.

But we'd made use of the tree house when needed. Sometimes occasion called for a meeting after appropriate visiting hours. While our families never questioned the innocence of our friendship over the years, we knew being caught in each other's private rooms wouldn't be tolerated. Augie never wished to compromise my reputation. He allowed the concession of meeting at the tree house because it had never been discovered and seemed unknown to both of our families. Our secret location had remained undisclosed.

It was the backbone of our friendship. Although we'd visited less and less frequently as we'd aged, the tree house was in our shared history. It was the setting of so many Emery and Augie moments … from the mundane joy of reading next to each other to sharing a first kiss because I declared at age eight that I wanted to see what all the fuss was about.

The fact that we both sought each other here, in this place that held so much meaning, on this evening when things were so uncertain made my heart swell and gave me confidence for our future.

Approaching the tall tree standing alone and apart from the tree line behind it, I circled around to find the ladder in place. Climbing carefully, I emerged through the hole in the floorboard. I grasped Augie's gloveless hand as he hauled me up and through the entrance to our secret den muttering a thank-you as I went.

He'd brought a new blanket I'd never seen before and spread it over the wooden floor. We sat side by side in silence, legs outstretched, backs leaning against the far wall.

The moment stretched and I knew I was being cowardly. I could feel Augie's eyes on my profile as I smoothed and straightened my skirts nervously.

I contemplated how best to begin.

And then I coughed delicately.

"Wellll," Augie initiated, drawing out the word for a figurative lifetime.

Attempting to project confidence, I inhaled deeply before replying. But instead of leading with honesty and the speech I'd planned, I spoke foolishness instead. "You should really be thanking me, Augustus."

"Oh, is that how we're doing this?"

I winced at his tone but pressed on. "If anything, the way your brother responded shows how desperate the situation really is. You need me."

"Ah, yes. Every young man hopes to have his marriage described as a *desperate situation.*"

"I would think most young men hope to never describe their marriage at all."

Augie's eyes rolled heavenward but I kept going. "Do you want me to apologize? Fine. I'm sorry! I'm sorry I can't stand the way your brother talks to you or the way your mother agrees with him. And I'm sorry I can't simply sit by and eat my asparagus while they dictate your life. I'm not going to let you be forced into something—"

"*You* are forcing me into something!" Augie exploded, interrupting my apology.

I sat, stunned for a moment before I could absorb anything beyond his anger. A livid Augie was a rarity indeed. I don't know that I could recall the last time he'd raised his voice. We'd quarreled plenty. I was dramatic and loud yet Augie was always calm in the face of my overreactions. That generally only served to ratchet up my fury. No one wanted to be faced with rationality when dealing with heightened emotions. It was counterintuitive. And damning.

Once I could see beyond Augie's shouted reply, I opened my mouth to contradict him. But nothing came out.

Augustus exhaled a shaky breath before looking down at his hands. "You're doing it too, Emery. Forcing my hand. Making my decisions for me. A marriage would affect my life just as much as joining the military or the church. Can't you see that?"

I did. I did see that … now. Emotion heated my cheeks. My nose stung. I sniffed delicately in an effort to stave off threatening shameful tears.

The small sound drew Augie's attention. Looking up sharply, his features softened and his forehead wrinkles cleared. I'd given him irritated forehead lines. Those were reserved for his brother. I don't think Augie even knew he did that when speaking about the duke. But I knew. And I'd caused the same look on my friend's face.

Tears filled my eyes.

Augie sighed. "Em, don't cry. I know you meant well. I know that. You were attempting to help my situation and you acted rashly and without thought."

I huffed a humorless laugh. "You're making excuses for me now." Augie's sapphire eyes moved back and forth between mine. I continued with my former apology but this time without the presumptuousness and impertinence. "I'm sorry I took the choice away from you, Augie. I shouldn't have assumed I knew best. I let my irritation with your brother and my concern for you over-whelm rational thought. You're right. I'm no better than John in attempting to control you and your decisions."

Augustus stared back at me for a long moment. His hair was disheveled as if he'd run his hands through his brown curls in exasperation. I noticed all of a sudden that he was styling it shorter on the sides. Less of an all-over mop and more polished. It suited him, I realized. He looked so grown up now.

What else had changed since I'd last seen Augie over the Christmas holiday six months prior?

Before I could catalog all the alterations to my friend's appearance, Augie spoke. "I forgive you."

"You do?"

"I do." He smiled with just his lips. "I know you thought you were helping." Then Augie's smile grew and reached the small lines beside his eyes I'd never noticed before. "And I don't think I've seen you cry since Beatrice threw you off her back when you were eleven. You must mean it."

I smiled in return, but looked down toward the blue muslin covering my lap. "I miss that horse."

"Me too."

Reining in my instinct to take command, I attempted subtlety and kept my eyes downcast before speaking. "So what would you like to do … about the betrothal? I can tell our families that I misspoke. They'd believe I dragged you along for the ride easily."

Augie touched my elbow and drew my gaze to his. "I would like to tell the truth."

I winced at that.

Augustus continued, "But after John's accusations, I don't know if I could bear proving him right."

"He's not right. You're not letting your family down or avoiding some perceived obligation to do what the second son is supposed to do. That's ridiculous," I rushed to assure him.

Without acknowledging my statement, he replied, "And I spoke to Mother before she went to bed … and she's so damn happy, Em. She seemed relieved that my life was changing course and she was glad it was you I planned to marry."

My eyes widened. Augie's mother, Amelia, and I had always been respectful, formal, and careful with one another. I didn't think she would oppose our union, but neither did I expect her to overtly support it. Perhaps the dowager was less in agreement with John than I thought. I decided not to comment on this.

Hope bloomed slowly in my chest and I hedged carefully, "So, we should … remain engaged and see what happens?"

I was on the receiving end of one of those long, thoughtful Augustus stares as he waged an internal battle and argued both sides of an imagined argument in his head. Finally—bloody finally—he nodded once, slow and deliberate.

I quashed the urge to whoop in triumph. I'd known we were making the best decision, but Augie was right. My methods left something to be desired. Showing any enthusiasm now would prove I'd learned nothing with my careless behavior.

"You're dying to pump your fist in the air, aren't you?" said my friend, the mind reader.

I merely smiled a mischievous grin in return.

Augie snorted a laugh. "Go ahead, then."

I did. I lifted my arm and promptly hit the boarded ceiling of our tiny domicile with my raised fist.

"Ow," I whined as Augie laughed and gathered my ungloved hand in his, applying the perfect amount of pressure to chase away the sting in my knuckles. "When did this place get so small?"

"I think you mean, when did we grow up?" Augie replied with affection in his tone.

He was right. We had grown up. I often viewed Augie through the lens of childhood nostalgia and comfort. But the Augustus before me was no longer a child.

"I'm glad you came here tonight," I said, looking around at the four small walls and one tiny window. My little lace curtains still hung, weathered from the last decade or so.

Augie cleared his throat, drawing my attention before speaking. "I knew I'd find you here as well."

I marveled at my friend. It was like seeing a new side to him. All these little changes in his appearance. I couldn't put a finger to all of them but they were there. I wondered if I looked different to Augie. Had I changed since Christmastime as well, grown and matured in his eyes as he had done in mine? There was something in his countenance that I couldn't place. It made me want to look longer, more than what was appropriate. My face felt very warm all of the sudden.

Before I could ponder too deeply on that, I asked, "A ride in the morning? Beatrice Three is feeling mighty fast these days."

Augustus laughed. "God, you and your system for naming animals. How could I have forgotten?"

"What? It makes perfect sense. When one finds the perfect name, one simply does not abandon it due to unfortunately brief life spans. Daisy Six is doing quite well. She had puppies just last month. And Chickie Fourteen, Eighteen, and Twenty-Two are all in the henhouse if you'd like to pay them a visit."

Augie leaned his head back and his laughter filled the small space just as I had intended. His amusement subsided and he finally answered my original question. "Let's skip the ride tomorrow. Let things settle a bit. As you said … remain engaged and see what happens."

"Alright," I agreed. "Let us see what happens."

Three

AUGUSTUS

The clock on the mantel ticked ominously, a countdown to impending doom. My brother scratched out something in one of the account ledgers, the scraping on parchment joining the rhythmic clacking of the timepiece.

We'd had these pointless meetings for as long as I could remember. Whenever John and I found ourselves in residence together, he required my attendance in order to pass judgement on my latest decision. When I was two and twenty, it was a horse I'd purchased from a famous stable whose stock was well known among the *ton* to be on the decline. When I was one and twenty, the conversations regarding my future had begun. How best I could benefit the family and our reputation. When I was nineteen, it was my unfashionable friendship with Emery. John had encouraged me to fuck my sixteen-year-old friend if I needed to, but to avoid her in public at all costs. My blood boiled at that and nearly every other conversation which ended in mandates from the Duke of Kendrick.

After dinner last night, he had plenty to pass judgement on.

Without lifting his head or his focus, John continued writing and said, "Are you ready to admit to this farce of a betrothal?"

"Why," I began, "would I lie about my engagement to Emery?"

My brother raised his head at my unruffled delivery. "Because you've been wasting your potential for years. And this mediocre match to some—"

"Watch it," I interrupted.

John's smile was unkind as he resumed speaking. "And this *match* frees you from several paths you were reluctant to take."

Fighting for calm I hardly felt, I retained my purposefully slouched position and strove to appear unbothered. "You know, brother, it's not a requirement for every second son to wield a bayonet or a bible."

"Well, that's your own personal rebellion, then. For that is the path I'd chosen for you. The path Father would have chosen for you."

I glared but remained silent. Contradicting John on the subject of our father would get me nowhere. The past was the past. And my long-dead father wasn't here to defend himself, his title, or me.

Things would have been so different if my father had lived. Taken by illness in my early adolescence, the pain of his loss never quite abated. Compounded by John's position and general obstinacy, I felt powerless in this family. My father never would have forced my hand. He would not have dictated my path nor maligned Emery as my choice for wife. If Father were still here, I wouldn't actually need to go through with this ridiculous plan in the first place.

But John didn't need to know that.

I forced myself to relax and cooled my tone. "Regardless, I've chosen my own path. Emery and I will marry and then I'll be one less problem for you to worry about."

"I suppose you'll be happy to know that upon your marriage," John sneered, "you shall gain access to the Barrington estate and neighboring lands—Mother demands it. It is out of sheer benevolence as the leader of this family that I've agreed to allow it."

I'd never bothered establishing a household on the lands bound to my courtesy title. I'd been away at Eton and then Cambridge, and didn't see the point. Despite the failing relationship with my brother, Kensworth Hall was still my home. It held all the memories I had of Father. It was where Emery and I had grown up together. Being so graciously awarded the modest Barrington estate and acreage felt like a final separation. A door slamming shut once and for all.

My brother took one last disappointed look at me before focusing once again on his parchment.

The scratching resumed, joining the ticking clock once more.

I debated internally for several moments before ultimately deciding to speak up, in a futile effort to be sure. John never welcomed my input, often mocking my interest in our family's holdings. But it was painful to watch the lands deteriorate, to witness my father's relationships with his tenants wither and die at my brother's disinterest. I wanted to help, to be involved. Researching agriculture and farming methods appealed to me in a way it never had to John. My interests would benefit our family, if only given a chance.

Despite the obviously wise decision to bite my tongue, I said, "I noticed the plantings and the farmers tending to the growth in the fields on my journey in yesterday. Perhaps we could discuss the benefits of crop rotations following this growing season. I could talk to the farmers, if you'd like." I tried to seem uninterested, as if his response didn't matter. But I knew I'd failed when his pen ceased and cold blue eyes met mine.

"I can talk to my own tenants, Augustus. They serve the dukedom and I am the duke, lest you've forgotten."

I looked away. "Of course not. I was merely mentioning the possibility due to recent studies I've read regarding crop yields and—"

"Oh, do stop. I'm not interested in your advice and I'm growing bored of your constant recommendations. The stewards, estate managers, and I are more than adequately equipped to handle things, little brother." Message delivered, John turned his attention back to the ledger.

I looked at the man before me and thought about how capable he actually was. In his cups every night, skin reddened and puffy from overindulgence. John was overly concerned with appearances and his reputation as duke that he had no idea how to actually be one. Not an effective peer, at least.

The acclaimed stewards and estate managers did nothing more than agree with my brother and regurgitate the edicts spewed from his mouth.

John never attempted to work with the tenant farmers on our land much less talk to them about crop rotation and soil nutrient variation. I don't think he knew any of their names or, in all honesty, what they even grew.

Every conversation I'd attempted over the years regarding the success of our family's estate or the current legislation in Parliament was met with contempt from my brother and promptly discarded, dismissed without thought. I didn't know why I bothered at all.

John made it seem wrong to take such an interest in our livelihood. As if my existence trod along his toes and that of the dukedom. I knew I would never hold the title. My brother was my father's heir. I wasn't confused about my place in this family and in society. But I couldn't help thinking selfishly in the deepest recesses of my mind … that I'd be a better duke than he. A better noble. A better man.

And what a terrible thought to have about one's own brother.

I shoved away my disappointment and my guilt and made to stand.

Assuming our conversation was quite finished, I made it halfway out of my seat before John chimed in again, attention still focused on his work. "I suppose I shall be on the hunt for a wife this season." My brother finally leaned back in his chair. With cool regard, he clarified, "Well, a suitable wife." I ground my teeth at the jab at my own selection of a wife. "I need to start thinking about producing heirs," he continued. "To ensure your succession isn't required. You need to stop playing at duke with all your suggestions and interest in the estate. It's a waste of time."

He was right, of course. I was wasting my time, wasting my breath attempting to reason with him.

Finally straightening to my full height, I met John's gaze thinking all at once how we hadn't been brothers in a very long time, if ever. Unable to understand his resentment and his fears, I allowed myself a superior smile with an edge of meanness. "Well, best of luck in finding a suitable match." For there was no one I'd wish him upon.

~

"Well, my lord. I hear congratulations are in order."

Ah, bollocks.

"Might I offer my most humble felicitations on you upcoming—"

"Alright, that's enough of that," I interrupted the man's *heartfelt* congratulatory remarks. "Anders, I apologize for not telling you about Emery."

Anders entered my sitting room and hissed, "I had to find out from the scullery maid, Augustus." I winced. "The. Scullery. Maid," he emphasized.

"I'm sorry," I said honestly. Despite his dramatics, I knew it had likely hurt Anders's feelings to find out about my betrothal in such a way. He was currently my valet and my oldest friend at the estate. Twelve years my senior, Anders was a valued member of the staff. He always had been. His father, Mr. Weatherby, was our longstanding butler, and before my father's death, one of his most trusted friends. Anders was raised here, at our Hampshire estate, following his mother's death in childbirth. And despite being closer in age to my brother, John, they never got on. John was never interested in befriending the staff, and Anders told me once, in confidence, that he never saw anything in John that warranted his friendship.

So as a child, I'd latched on to Anders as the older-brother figure I lacked through blood and indifference. He'd shown me kindness and encouragement, and I'd learned much from him as a result. Despite the difference in our ages, he indulged me as a companion. My mother often remarked at how responsible I was as a child, and how between my own mature nature and Anders, she'd hardly needed a nurse for my care.

Outside of these walls, I had Emery. But Anders had been my ally within. He'd assumed the role of valet as I'd come of age and the arrangement suited our friendship. He traveled with me to London and abroad. I didn't require much attending, and had frankly never considered him a member of the staff. Anders had always just been my friend. Being well aware of the disparity in our standings, I'd offered several times throughout the years to find him an elevated position or to support him in a trade of his choosing, but he'd always refused. Selfishly, I felt grateful that Anders had chosen to remain. I valued his friendship.

And because I knew him so well, I recognized the hurt in his tone. In general, he hated being bested in gossip by the maids, but my neglect had undoubtedly ruffled his feathers.

"You should be sorry," he groused.

"Did you hear all about the dramatics at dinner, then?" I offered in reparation. I knew the finer details about John's outburst and the true nature of my betrothal had not been circulating amongst the staff. My mother was far too concerned with appearances to ever let that gossip get out.

Anders raised his brows in question before perching on the armchair across from where I was seated at my desk. "No. Only that you returned home a man bound for the altar."

I glanced toward the open doorway behind my friend's head. My spacious quarters were fairly secluded in the family wing. Still, I endeavored to speak quietly to maintain discretion.

I leaned forward and lowered my voice before recounting the events of the evening prior. I was honest about Emery and the fraudulent nature of our engagement. I confessed what had transpired in the dining room and my brother's accusations. "And then he stumbled from the room, Mother following in his wake. I stayed for the awkward remainder of the meal with the Bartholomews."

Anders had gasped theatrically at several points in the story, but now he merely looked at me expectantly, gray eyes intent.

Brows furrowed in confusion, I inquired, "What?"

His eyes widened. "You didn't tell her." Not a question.

I shifted in my chair, not liking where this was headed. "Did I tell who, what?"

"You're going to marry Emery and not tell her you're in love with her." Again, a statement. No question in his tone. Anders looked incredulous.

I stiffened in response. I'd never admitted my feelings for Emery to Anders. Or to anyone. It was a secret I kept locked away. I never intended for anyone to find out.

But I must have taken a moment too long to gather my composure because Anders cut in. "Don't even think about trying that with me. I've known you your entire life, and hers too. Of course I know you love her."

Breathing the sigh of the mortally resigned, I turned my attention back to the maddeningly amused man across from me. "I'm not going to tell her anything. She thinks she's saving me, and I am a selfish bastard to allow this farce to continue."

Pushing away from the desk in frustration, I ran a hand through my hair and began pacing in front of the window. Late morning light streamed in and nothing but a fair summer day met my eyes. It seemed impossible that the weather wasn't all thunder and lightning to match the turmoil within.

Anders smiled. "She has always been able to turn you inside out."

I flashed him a glare, but my friend was unfazed and laughed delightedly.

"I don't know what to do, Anders. You could at least pretend to be helpful instead of enjoying my misery so."

He sobered somewhat, still watching me pace. "Augie, there is no decision to make. She announced your plans to marry and so you shall marry. If either of you break the engagement, her reputation will be in jeopardy and you well know it." I grimaced at the truth in his words, but he continued on. "However, the choice is yours to be honest with Emery. You could tell her about your feelings and perhaps, I don't know," he mused dramatically with a finger tapping his chin, "have a true and happy marriage ... for as long as you both shall live."

I stopped abruptly and rubbed my hands down my face. I couldn't envision his version of the future. There was too much at stake, too many unknowns. What if revealing the truth didn't end happily? What if my love was a truth Emery never wanted to hear?

"Or I could lose her instead," I countered with the fear that kept me up at night.

"Augie." Anders sighed but said no more.

This was an argument I had with myself regularly. I had no interest involving another party.

My gaze returned to the window as a flash of movement stole across the field beyond. It was Emery riding astride, her body folded low over the saddle. She and Beatrice Three, I stifled a snort, streaked across the landscape, the wildflowers parting in their wake. Emery's light blond hair flared out behind her as she moved sinuously with her mount. She exuded freedom and strength and so much damn beauty I couldn't look away.

I could saddle my horse and follow her. Go down to the stables right now and seek her out, chase that independence, that vitality she wielded so well.

But I knew I wouldn't.

Vaguely I heard Anders murmur, "Your Grace." And I startled, looking over my shoulder as my mother entered my study. Turning back to the window, I noticed Emery was gone. Out of my field of vision and out of my reach.

I straightened away from the window pane, not remembering having approached, my fingertips pressed to the glass.

With a hasty retreat, I turned to face my mother. Clearing my throat, I offered a quiet greeting.

She approached with a nod to Anders and kissed my cheek. "Hello, darling."

I noticed my valet's swift departure. *Coward.*

"Augustus, I was eager to discuss the wedding and begin planning. I felt certain you and Emery would want to marry this summer. That doesn't leave us much time."

There was a brightness in my mother's tone. She was excited by the prospect of this wedding. More than surface pleasantries or well-wishes. My mother, Lady Amelia Ward, the Dowager Duchess of Kendrick, was legitimately enthusiastic for my upcoming nuptials.

With the conversation with Anders still festering in the back of my mind, I mustered a smile I didn't quite feel and replied, "Of course, Mother. Where shall we begin?"

As I climbed through the narrow opening in the tree house's floor, I knew Emery was waiting for me. I'd seen the candlelight as I'd walked and felt a rush of … something. Affection, always. But something else. Anticipation, perhaps. Which was foolish to be sure. I told my expectations to settle themselves and maneuvered my width the remaining distance through the entry.

Unsurprisingly, Emery didn't wait until I'd settled beside her on the blanket. She dove right in. "Well, how did it go today with your family? Did they further inquire about us?"

I, on the other hand, waited to speak until I'd successfully seated myself. I couldn't recall ever being so uncomfortable in this tiny structure. But I supposed I had been a gangly adolescent for the most part. People generally didn't realize how much they'd grown until trying to fit themselves within expectations of the past.

Finally settled, I met Emery's inquisitive and eager stare. Her amber eyes fairly glowed by the candlelight. And her golden hair, plaited over one shoulder, shone like a beacon. She was so very lovely. Fearing I'd looked too long with my admiring gaze, I cleared my throat and glanced away. "It was fine, I suppose. John was … John. So, no change on that front. Mother was eager to begin planning the wedding and breakfast and what have you."

"Oh, yes, Mama as well," Emery interjected.

"Mother asked me so many questions about flowers and food." I had been overwhelmed by the sheer number of options presented. I hoped Emery had some opinions and could assist in the decision making. I felt wholly out of my depth.

"Perhaps our mothers can just plan the whole thing, and we'll just show up." Emery smiled at the genius of her plan.

I frowned slightly. "Did you not dream of planning your wedding as a girl?"

Emery's smile dimmed from amused to indulgent. "Honestly I'd assumed I'd be sold off to the highest bidder. The idea of celebrating a *ton* marriage never much appealed. And then Patty made a fine match and the pressure was off of me somewhat. But that notion of reveling over a future I neither wanted nor asked for … well, I suppose it left a bad taste in my mouth. Weddings were not commonly found in my daydreams." She looked away then.

My stomach sank at her words. *A future she neither wanted nor asked for.*

Her head snapped up, as if she knew exactly what I'd heard and was currently fixated on. It was my turn to look away.

"No, Augie. *That* kind of future was one I never wanted. Having a suitor chosen for me. Being married off to a man old enough to be my father. All my freedom stripped from me to merely become some stranger's possession. It would never be that way with you." She tugged on my forearm until I looked her direction once more. "I don't mourn anything about a future as your wife. We'll be happy. I know it."

I felt shamed by my warring desires, to protect her from a marriage she never would have chosen on her own and so desperately wanting her any way I could have her.

Anders was right. I wasn't being honest with her about my feelings. And despite this arrangement being her idea and initiated by Emery herself, I was benefitting the most. The scales were unbalanced. The woman I loved was going to be my wife. And she would gain nothing. Nothing but my secret affections, my longing, my desire.

Perhaps sensing my rising panic, Emery plowed on. "Stop thinking you're tricking me into something, Augie. It's not like that and you know it."

How would I be able to marry my friend? It was hard enough to hide my feelings, but what would happen when we lived together and ate our meals together and traveled together? Oh God, would we consummate the marriage? I'd be the cad getting everything I ever wanted and she'd be my savior simply putting on a good show. A martyr. Or would she want to live separately? Plenty of *ton* marriages were conducted thusly. Perhaps she'd wish to discretely take lovers. I felt sick.

"I can hear you thinking. Now stop it," Emery demanded.

But I was spiraling, envisioning every way this plan was doomed. I needed to get away. I couldn't think with her sitting there in the candlelight, loveliness personified, tempting me to just give in. Only it wasn't right. It wasn't true.

"I feel I need to slap you for whatever thoughts are going through your head. Augie, look at me," Emery fairly commanded. So I did. I met her determined whiskey eyes and took a deep breath to quiet my mind. She'd always been good at this, garnering my attention and helping me return from within. I had memories of her distractions and diversionary tactics. When in her presence, my thoughts sought her anyway. She was merely able to harness them.

Emery searched my face, ensuring she had my attention. "We can do this. We'll figure it out. Together. I promise."

I nodded. She was so earnest and confident, so fierce. But there was so much she didn't know. I feared my feelings would change everything.

"I mean it," she asserted. "I feel like you're doubting me and I'm slightly offended." Emery turned her nose up at me and sniffed delicately.

"Not to contradict," I began but she quickly interrupted.

"Then you should stop right there."

I felt my lips twitch and decided to extend a peace offering for my wild mood and to make up for denying her request the day before. "Shall we take the horses out in the morning?"

My friend abandoned her show of offense immediately. "Yes! A ride will be perfect. Come to our stables. We'll have a glorious ride." She needed to stop saying ride. "Our mothers will plan our wedding. And you and I will be free to live our lives. You'll see, Augie. Never doubt me."

Only, Emery didn't know what she was offering by agreeing to marry me. Because for me, our wedding *would* be a daydream. My daydream. It would be everything. For her, it would be a duty. *A future she neither wanted nor asked for.*

Four

EMERY

I'd just finished saddling Beatrice Three when the sound of hoofbeats caught my ear. I knew it was Augie.

It was early morning. Far too early for any fashionable lord or lady. The sun was up but only just. I'd always been an early riser. Just one more way I didn't fit in with my peers, if one could even call them that. Life in the country started early. By the time aristocrats finished lazing about, half the day was wasted.

I loved this time of day, feeling the chill in the morning air. It made me feel productive. I wasn't necessarily a contributing member of society the same way the hardworking farmers were, but I definitely wasn't a lazy peer of the realm.

Beatrice raised her head as I finished adjusting the length of the stirrups. She nickered warmly to Augie and his mare, a friendly horse by nature.

I sent my friend a grin. "Are you ready to be bested?"

Augie seemed to take me in. If he was surprised by my riding attire, he didn't show it, but … something moved across his face.

His sapphire eyes lingered a bit. Perhaps he *was* scandalized. The thought amused me and heated my cheeks. Augustus was so proper and staid. It was unfortunate for him that his best friend bent the rules whenever possible.

The breeches I wore weren't terribly snug but they weren't loose either. My family and the servants were used to my casual ensemble. The grooms were unbothered by my oddities at this point. But if I went riding to the village I, of course, wore a riding habit and appropriate dress. However, when I was here, at home, I felt comfortable enough to be myself. Had Augie really never seen me in breeches before? Perhaps it had been some time since we'd ridden together. I shifted my weight under a sudden bout of nerves.

Augie cleared his throat and looked down to the reins in his hands. "Bested? Is everything a competition with you?" His smiling eyes finally met mine, and if I wasn't mistaken—I wasn't —his cheeks looked a bit pink. Interesting.

I smiled in response. "I can't help it if I'm a superior rider, Augustus. Besides, I've missed having someone to gallop alongside." I didn't have many opportunities for companionship honestly. I was friendly with the locals in the nearby village but not familiar enough to race across the countryside. The stable hands were used to my constant presence around the horses, but they didn't see me as anything more than their odd mistress. Overhearing many of their conversations had enhanced my vocabulary however. Father would occasionally join me on horseback but at more of a meandering pace. Gansey refused my invitations, never trusting "those wretched beasts." And my younger sister, Genevieve, was often occupied with her own friendships.

I realized just then how much I'd missed Augie. This extended visit for the summer was much needed. His sporadic short-term trips to Hampshire were few and far between. I often had to compete for his attention with visiting guests during house parties. Augie was so well liked, friendly, and sociable.

I was exceedingly glad to have him back home.

"I know what you mean," he replied, tugging absently on his cuffs.

I quickly mounted my horse and we made our way out of the stables as the morning sun shone brightly. Beatrice Three leaned over for an affectionate snuffle for Augie's horse. I gave her a quick pat on her neck.

We let the horses stroll leisurely past the gardens. But once we reached the end of the row of hedges, I looked to Augie. He merely raised a brow. By unspoken agreement, we were off. I gave Beatrice a quick hard squeeze with my thighs and we shot forward, wind on my face. Hoofbeats pounding along were the only sound to my ears, and I let out a whoop at the sheer happiness I felt, the freedom. Reins loose in my hands, I could feel the blood pumping through my veins as I moved with my horse across the flat landscape.

Augie pulled up beside me, his expression mirroring my own. There was something exhilarating about our shared joy in this moment. I couldn't think of anywhere else I'd rather be. In fact, I could do this every day for the rest of my life, and never tire of these feelings. Being known and understood. Seen.

We could be happy, I realized. Our future—our marriage—would feel like this. Exhilarating yet comfortable. Free but content. An endless holiday.

If I went to London for the season, this would all be a dream. Not only would I be forced away from the countryside I cherished, I'd be stuck in London. No matter what Augie thought might happen, I would never meet a suitor I'd feel so comfortable around. There would be no races on horseback. I wouldn't even be able to laugh at full volume, the way I was doing right now as Augie pulled ahead of me and turned back with a fist raised in the air.

I could never have this easiness with anyone else. Somehow, in my heart, I just knew it. Maybe Gansey was right and the most successful marriages were formed around friendship or solidified by it.

I wasn't foolish enough to think a union with Augie was some game. That there wouldn't be strife, illness, mundanity, boredom. But if one could choose, and in this instance we could, shouldn't one choose happiness? I needed Augie to see that we could have this if only we embraced it, claimed it for our own.

I needed him to see this through for both our sakes.

"Stay on for luncheon? I believe Mrs. Pennyworth said something about serving those berry tarts you're so fond of." In truth, knowing they were Augie's favorite, I'd requested them for the disaster dinner days ago but Mother claimed tarts were unfashionable for the evening meal. Our long-time cook and the kindhearted Mrs. Pennyworth promised to whip some up to keep on hand should that "lovely Lord Barrington" come by for tea or a visit.

"Ah, tempting. But Mother has invited the vicar and his wife over for noonday meal and I've been strongly encouraged to join them," Augie replied.

"Next time, then," I offered easily. He'd spent all morning with me. I shouldn't feel proprietary of his time. We had all summer, and hopefully the rest of our lives.

Our early race across the countryside had taken us through the fields and into the woods on both our families' estates. After our spirited ride, we'd watered our horses in the nearby creek on the duke's land. It was wide and shallow and perfect for exploring. We'd done just that as children in the familiar spot. Swimming and splashing, searching for frogs and fish.

The path back to the stables was slow and meandering. We talked of changes in the village since Augie had last been in residence, including the vicar's recent marriage. Augie shared some tales from Cambridge from his final term and his friendships there. He also spoke quite passionately about his family's holdings and new farming methods he was eager to see implemented.

Truthfully, I didn't follow all the details, the acids, the nutrients, and the requirements for successful agricultural endeavors. However, it was impossible to find an impassioned Augie boring. I listened raptly as he spoke, and wondered if he'd ever get the chance to apply this newly acquired knowledge. His brother, John, wasn't terribly reasonable where the ducal responsibilities were concerned. I made a mental note to gently introduce the topic.

We were nearly back to the stables now, the horses picking up speed, eager for hay and the comforts of home. As we neared, my younger sister, Genevieve, and Julian came tearing around the corner, bound for the gardens.

"You'll have to be faster if you except to catch me," my younger sister taunted.

Young Julian was chasing after a laughing Gen who held something aloft as she sprinted for the hedge maze. Julian's answering scowl had me smothering a laugh as he put on a burst of speed and gave chase, and they disappeared from view.

With the sound of their fading delight, Augie cleared his throat pointedly, drawing my attention. "That could be trouble."

I smiled at him questioningly. "What?"

"Genevieve and Jules. You might speak to Gen," he clarified.

"Speak to her about what? They're just friends."

The son of our widowed housekeeper, Julian had been raised and educated alongside Genevieve and myself. The pair were now both fourteen, thick as thieves and just as wild.

"They are just friends," I repeated. "Just like you and me." Except as the words left my mouth, I felt a strange sensation and could no longer meet Augie's eyes. It wasn't shame or embarrassment, but something about the statement didn't sit right and I didn't like the comparison between our relationship and theirs. I couldn't bear the thought of him agreeing with my statement. My confusion intensified as Augie remained silent, and I felt certain he'd be able to read whatever strange emotion was written on my face. I couldn't identify the oddness myself, but Augie very well might. He knew me better than anyone, therefore I kept my eyes averted as we made our way to the row of stalls.

"Speaking of siblings," I began smoothly, proud of my conversational transition. "How are things with John? Have you spoken with him about your ideas for agricultural improvement with the farmers? Your thoughts on the land? The crop rotations you've researched?"

My friend looked down at the reins in his hands. Augie's sigh was resigned and defeated. I hated that sound. And I felt no shame in thinking how much I hated his brother for inspiring it. "We've … spoken on it," Augie said finally, meeting my gaze. "He feels better equipped to manage the properties as he sees fit. Without any input from me."

"I'm sorry, Augie," I uttered, doing my utmost to remain even-tempered. He'd heard me bad-mouth his brother before, but something in the vulnerable hunch of his shoulders told me to manage my tongue in this moment. I wouldn't allow the blasted duke to drive a wedge between us.

Augie dropped his head back, face turned toward the sun while our horses clopped to a stop. When he looked back toward me, one eye squinted in avoidance of the bright light overhead and his lips quirked in amusement, I knew he was about to change the subject. "Thank you for the ride, Em. Perhaps next time you'll win." I made to protest because *What utter bollocks*. I was clearly the superior horseman. "Or perhaps, Beatrice Four will be faster than your current mount."

I reached forward as if to cover my poor horse's ears and spare her from his morbid assertion. "Augustus, that was in poor taste."

He laughed, and I felt relief in my heart at the sound. I wanted all thoughts of his brother fairly vanquished. "You're right." Then turning dramatically to my horse said, "Lady Beatrice the Third, my deepest apologies for referencing your future demise and eventual replacement."

Augie's bright gaze found my own. He was alight with playful-ness, and I was suddenly unable to look away. The amusement from our earlier banter and antics slid away slowly from his expression until all that remained was our eyes fastened tightly on one another.

The moment lingered and leapt until finally, Augie looked away. And then after a seated bow low over his saddle, he straightened and turned his beast toward home. "See you later, Em!"

Fighting for equilibrium after our confusing staring match and attempted brevity, I called, "Goodbye, you menace!"

I was fairly certain I caught the tail end of his laugh returned to me on the warm summer breeze.

Several hours later I found myself back on Beatrice Three at a more sedate pace. We moved steadily through the forest, the ridge just ahead of us.

Intent on finding time for my work, I'd brought with me a small folio of thick paper, a canvas roll filled with brushes of all shapes and sizes, and a small tackle box full of watercolor paint. Not my typical medium, but it was working out quite well for the paintings I'd sold this year.

Beatrice and I made a quick stop after crossing the creek so I could pull a small jug with a stopper out of the saddlebag. Once the container was filled, we traveled another handful of minutes before reaching the ridge.

After looping the reins around a low-hanging branch, I took in a deep breath and simply absorbed my surroundings. The line of trees was mostly behind me and the landscape spread far and wide. Green hills rolled in the distance and with the clouds gathered near the horizon I could tell the sunset would be spectacular.

If my estimation was correct, I'd have just enough time to set up my supplies and get a light wash on the paper.

Plenty of time.

I supposed I could have worked from memory at home or ridden out to simply sketch the countryside. But there was something to be said for capturing the moment. As primarily self-taught, I'd been through much trial and error to arrive and my current process. Working from life suited me best. Identifying the colors and reflecting them back so the passage of time became a true and tangible thing. From the world beyond to the small painting on my board, I strove to reflect the landscape in all its glory. And in order to do that, I preferred working en plein air. I liked the idea of transcribing nature without trying to harness it or control it. It just went on existing independently of myself as an artist.

An artist.

I still had trouble referring to myself as such.

Starting out slowly, I mapped out the terrain in water only. I dragged my brush across the lightly textured surface, noting the slowly darkening hills. These moments when first starting a painting were likely the only time in my life when I was cautious and reserved. Too bad Augie had never seen this side of me. Then he might take me more seriously. He might even trust me to know my own mind regarding our marriage.

No, not even then.

Adding heavily watered-down Prussian blue with the lightest touch, I moved to fill in the darker areas of the sky, those farthest away from the sun making its descent. I would need to work fast from this point on. And then once my rendering was as complete as it could be, I'd pack my supplies and make my way home in the dark. The moon would be full and clear tonight. I wasn't worried.

Tomorrow I could put the finishing touches on the painting in my studio of sorts all while preserving the truth and the beauty I'd captured so faithfully in the evening air. This was one of my favorite locations when painting a sunset. But I had other well-loved and often-visited locations. The forest, the stream, the wild-flower field. These places, taken and translated by my hand, could be seen hanging all across England. In country estates on the coast to the finest drawing room in London.

I felt a little bitter at that. That these strangers got a little piece of my heart. They were able to see the beloved countryside through my eyes without ever having set foot in Hampshire. I had yet to reconcile my bitterness at the wealthy's frivolous acquisitions with my desire to make and sell my art. It was an ongoing strug-gle. Alas.

The colors deepened as the sun slowly worked its way toward the horizon line. I focused on laying in another wash, deeper and more concentrated this time. Mixing the hues to match the transi-tion from orange to pink, using a cloth to remove the moisture from the area where the clouds were still wispy and delicate.

It was a painting of this very setting that put everything in motion, six summers ago. As a gently bred young lady, my governess and my mother insisted on learning the pianoforte, mastering embroi-dery, and educating myself on several artistic endeavors. Well, I was practically tone deaf and bollocks with a needle. But some-thing happened when I picked up a paintbrush: my mind had quieted and my typically brash and bullish actions became soft and muted. I was finally able to have a delicate touch, something that had never come naturally. I'd paint small things in the school-room, a rose cut from the gardens, some fruit in a bowl. I remembered the early praise from my governess and how thrilled Mama had been with my efforts. I was finally ladylike in this one instance—a daughter to be proud of.

One evening I'd been painting the sunset from my window and couldn't seem to get the light correct. It was as if the pane created more than just a clear barrier between myself and my subject. So the next day, I'd gathered my tools in secret and ridden out on Beatrice Two to the ridge I was now admiring and caught the light for myself. Between the fresh air and the landscape that I loved, something moved within me and I'd created a painting I'd been proud of. Not lilies in a vase or a still life with random objects. I'd captured my heart and put it to canvas.

I wasn't able to bring myself to show my mother the landscape I'd painted that day. I hadn't wanted it to be a bargaining chip or proof that I was becoming the daughter she'd always hoped for. But I did show it to my father. He'd been so delighted and supportive. After consulting with a woodworker in the village, a frame had been commissioned and procured. He'd hung it in our formal receiving room because he'd claimed he'd wanted everyone to see it. And true to Father's word, when guests had asked about the artist of the lovely landscape, he'd told them. And they'd dismissed me, or worse, praised my future success on the marriage mart.

Over and over it'd happened. The painting would garner attention, but never in a way that made me feel gratified.

I think Father must have known the attention no longer made me feel special nor proud of my work. He moved the piece to his study, for his enjoyment alone, he'd said. I'd ceased painting for some time. Mama had been disappointed, but she frequently was with me.

And then one day when I was seventeen, a Mr. Jeffries came to discuss some business or other with Father. At the time, Mama turned every conversation to my future marriage and my prospects. I'd lived in fear of being sold off and wed to any stranger she saw fit. So I'd listened from the hallway to ensure that I wasn't to be betrothed to this Mr. Jeffries.

At one point in their dealings, conversation had halted and drinks were poured. I could tell the business conversation was legitimate in regards to investments and not my future hand in marriage. I felt safe enough to turn and leave when I heard Mr. Jeffries inquire about my landscape. "Who's the artist?" he'd said. "It's remarkable."

I'd never forget that word. Someone thought my painting *remark-able*. I wasn't a shy or passive person, even at seventeen. Often more confident and self-assured than I had any right to be, but in this, in my art, I was a foal on wobbly legs. I had no strength of character to support my artistry because I lacked all belief in my abilities. With the added complexity of my natural talent layered upon the expectations of a young woman in my position, the idea of being successful in this endeavor was complicated and fraught. Being talented meant I was more readily marriageable, and that wasn't something I'd ever really wanted.

But this stranger had given strength to the desire that lived within. *Remarkable*. And I'd heard it in his voice. Awed and appreciative at the same time.

I'd held my breath and awaited my father's answer. The inevitable dismissal once Mr. Jeffries learned the painting had been produced by a mere daughter.

"Erm, it's actually a secret," came my father's unexpected reply. "The artist wished to remain cloaked in anonymity and referred to himself only as … M. Barton. Our solicitors handled all the details. The oddest thing, but I was very happy to have acquired such a piece. Remarkable, like you said." I could hear the nervous tone of my father's voice but I was frozen in place in the hallway. Why had he done that? Lied to this man?

Then Mr. Jeffries had attempted to purchase the painting from my father outright, but after multiple refusals, he'd asked if our solicitor could put him in contact with this M. Barton's representatives. Father assured him he could and I nearly hyperventilated on the spot.

And that was how I became a famous painter, shrouded in mystery as the *ton* sought the novelty of my work.

Later that evening, well past respectable calling hours, I heard the creak of the wooden ladder and smiled at the book in my lap.

Moments later, Augie maneuvered his broad shoulders through the opening in the tree house floor. He was dressed simply in trousers and a fine lawn shirt. His brown curls were windswept and endearing.

With no greeting or preamble, he began speaking. "You know, Emery. We've been friends a long time. You might have told me."

I peered over at his hunched form in confusion. "Whatever do you mean?" Had he seen me painting earlier? Did he know my secret? No. It wasn't possible.

Unaware of my internal panic at discovery, Augie continued speaking as he settled himself on the blanket nearby. "The luncheon with the vicar and his wife. You could have at least warned me what I was walking into or advised me to have a snack beforehand."

I burst out laughing as Augie glared in my direction. The vicar's new wife was fanatical about her digestion and constitution. It was widely known and lamented over. She would not share a meal too extravagant and only ate dishes to support a delicate, nervous stomach. No bread, no meat, no cheese of any kind. No alcohol, no dessert ever. Families in and around the village had all learned the hard way at their recent wedding celebration this spring. She and the vicar were rarely guests at local dinner tables due to her insistence on the nature of the meal. I supposed Augie's mother, the dowager duchess, felt it necessary to invite them for luncheon due to our upcoming nuptials.

I was still laughing when Augie cut in, "It's not funny. I had to eat boiled potatoes. No salt or butter or anything with flavor. It was awkward and horrible. Who wants to discuss digestion in the dining room? Why would she find that topic appropriate?"

My laughter continued. He was so delightfully affronted.

"They stayed for hours. I couldn't even escape to the kitchens for sustenance, Emery. You should be ashamed."

"Me?" I exclaimed, attempting to rein in my mirth. "I offered you berry tarts. And you refused me."

"Well, had I known—had you warned me I'd be starving for half the day, I would have swiped a tart from Mrs. Pennyworth prior to that ridiculous meal."

Collapsing in a fit of giggles, I leaned onto Augie's hard shoulder.

He attempted to dislodge me. "No more entertainment for you."

I retreated, but smooshed his cheeks together adorably. "So, you don't want the treat I've brought you, then?" I inquired, all innocence.

Augie raised his brows in question, covering my hands with his own and drawing them off his face. "I didn't say that."

"Perhaps later." I sniffed. "When I feel properly appreciated."

He rolled his eyes but kept my hands in his. Augie was so warm. I felt a little flip in my stomach at his touch. Friends could hold hands, could they not?

Leaving my hands comfortably in Augie's possession, I attempted to determine the reason for the luncheon with the vicar and his gut-obsessed wife. "Did you discuss the wedding? Will it be held in the village church?"

"Yes. Mother shared our news and the vicar enthusiastically agreed to marry us this summer. Seemed genuine in his delight for our future happiness." Augie frowned a little and absentmindedly fiddled with the lace at my sleeves. If I knew him at all, he was likely feeling guilty for deceiving the man as to the circumstances surrounding our arrangement.

I began carefully, lest he retreat even further. "You know, I'm sure vicars have married people for less." He glanced up from my hands still in his lap. "Sometimes marriage contracts don't even allow the bride and bridegroom to meet each other beforehand, much less make the acquaintance of the officiant set to marry them. Our situation isn't like that, Augie. People here know us. They've witnessed our ... relationship firsthand." My mind had stumbled over the word *friendship*, so I'd said *relationship* instead. The substitution still seemed odd. "Let them be happy for us, for our families, for our future. We're not deceiving them. We plan to marry and our reasons are our own. There's no shame in that."

Augie remained quiet, thoughtful, which was the best I could hope for in this instance. His gaze strayed to my hands once more. After a moment, I felt his touch on my arm. "What's this?"

I looked down where he indicated, just above my wrist, and noticed the smudge of pigment. The orange from the evening sky I'd painted earlier had bled onto my sleeve without my notice. I hadn't changed before meeting Augie in the tree house. I still wore my riding breeches and billowy cream shirt.

"Just a bit of something," I attempted to evade. "You know me, always making a mess of things."

He frowned at my word choice as if taking issue with my meaning. In truth, it was a statement that said too much, more than I'd consciously intended.

The oddness of the moment passed as Augie continued rubbing at the fine muslin. The paint wasn't going anywhere however. I felt guilty. I could tell him. I could admit to Augie that the stain was from a painting and I was an artist. But this was a secret I'd kept from him for so long. When I'd first realized my interest and abilities in art, Augie had been away at school. And later when my work became complicated and secret, I didn't know how to broach the subject. I trusted him implicitly, of course. But to tell him now and in this manner, felt wrong. There weren't many occurrences in which I felt weak or susceptible to criticism, but in this … I somehow did. What would Augustus think of me? Was the idea laughable? Would he want a secret painter for a friend? For a wife?

I'd tell him before the wedding, I decided. I couldn't rationalize my reticence. Judgement was a frightening prospect from those closest to you. Support was something valued immeasurably when it was given freely but somehow dreaded when sought openly. My heart would be crushed if Augie was unable to reconcile the elusive M. Barton with the Emery before him.

Moving on, I slowly pulled my hands away. The drag of Augie's skin against mine caused another odd flip in my stomach. Perhaps it was guilt or … or something.

Swallowing against the sudden dryness in my throat, I said, "I spoke to Mama and she wants to leave for London the day after tomorrow."

Augie's gaze narrowed as he waited for me to clarify. "We're to visit the modiste for my wedding trousseau and see Patty while in town. It should be less than a week. Mama is desperate to get back before your mother plans the whole thing."

"Yes, I believe they're meeting for tea tomorrow," he murmured.

I nodded but didn't offer more, already dreading the trip to town.

"Will you be alright? I know London makes you miserable," Augie said suddenly.

I smiled reassuringly at my friend and his worry. "Of course. It's a short trip with a purpose. Not an endless season filled with pointless society engagements. Besides, I'm looking forward to seeing my sister."

"All right."

"All right," I echoed before raising one blond brow. "Now about those tarts."

"God, yes," he moaned. I blinked at his tone, my stomach giving another jolt. "No more holding out on me," Augie demanded.

I moved to the small hamper I'd smuggled out of the kitchens and retrieved two perfect berry tarts, and tried not to think about the secrets I was keeping from my friend.

Five

EMERY

Three days later, I found myself walking down Bond Street with Gansey, my little sister, Genevieve, and my mother. We were due shortly for our appointment with the modiste, a veritable genius with silk and lace. Or so I'd been reminded no less than eleven times.

I'd also been told to smile and watch my manners as many times as well.

My darling Gen walked beside me, arm in arm, blue eyes wide and enchanted. I could tell she wouldn't grow to share my resentment for life in town. She was entranced by the scope and scale, enamored with the fashions and grandeur. Preference for a simple country life was evidentially not catching.

Being blessed with a father who cared little for London, I'd been allowed to spend the vast majority of my twenty-two years at our country seat in Hampshire. He often indulged my mother and would join her for a portion of the season, but Genevieve and I were usually bid to stay tucked away in the country with a nurse-maid, nanny, or governess. Mother escorted my elder sister, Patricia, through her first season nine years past, but I'd had no interest in joining them and Gen had been too young.

Our family no longer kept accommodations in London. On their sporadic visits, Mama and Father let a townhouse in a fashionable area of town and brought a small band of servants with them. In the years since Patty's marriage to the old duke, our family had been welcome at Cawthorn Hall, my sister's extravagant Mayfair home. Patty hadn't returned to the country and preferred living exclusively in town.

It seemed I was the odd duck once again. The only Bartholomew daughter to eschew London life.

As we maneuvered the walkways along the avenue, we were assaulted by droves of people, carriages, and hackneys rolling nearby. The sights and smells of city life were not for the faint of heart. How did people live with so much gray? I missed the green of the countryside, the fresh air, and being able to walk without being rushed, maneuvered, or repeatedly bumped into.

Mama had spent the morning dragging us to look at hats and ribbons and shoes and every other torture device known to womankind. Thankfully our parcels were being delivered to Cawthorn Hall so we didn't have those to contend with as we bustled down the sidewalk.

Mama turned from her place in front of me, Gansey at her side. "Hurry, Emery. We don't want to keep Mademoiselle Russo waiting." Gansey turned and nodded emphatically, brows raised in agreement.

I rolled my eyes but replied politely to my mother. "Yes, Mama."

My mother paused to turn back again as foot traffic streamed around us with put-upon sighs. "And do smile, Emery. You're shopping for your wedding trousseau. No need to look so morose." She resumed her determined gait.

Gansey turned once more to face me. "Listen to your mother, Emery." And smiled like a mad woman, teeth forcefully on display. Gen giggled, and I rolled my eyes once more, but all three of us picked up our pace to catch up to Mama just as she entered the dressmaker's shop.

"Cor," Genevieve breathed, eyes bulging as she absorbed the splendor of the shop. Ready-made gowns decorated the interior along with bolts of silk, lace, patterned muslin, and the finest woven fabric you've ever seen. The colors were bold and expressive and threatened to turn even my unfashionable head.

"Don't let Mama hear you say that," I whispered to my sister. But her youthful wonder made her deaf to my rebuke.

I tried to remember being fourteen, wondered idly if I would have been so captivated by a dress shop. Probably not. Far more likely to be taken with a horse farm.

Besides, my memories as an adolescent weren't lessened by the lack of pretty dresses. I can remember being perfectly content with life in Hampshire at the time, Augie at my side. We were likely fishing or reading the days away. Actually, I believe the summer of my fourteenth year was the one in which I attempted equestrian jumping with Beatrice Two. Augie nearly had an apoplexy when I took a tumble over a particularly high hurdle. I was unharmed, but seventeen-year-old Augustus was a force to be reckoned with. It was one of the few times he tried to dissuade me in earnest from whatever foolish endeavor I had been attempting. He'd threatened to spend the summer with his mother in Devon and leave me to my own devices in Hampshire.

Being young and reckless, I couldn't see it for what it was at the time. But I'd frightened Augie. I had been wild and so sure of myself, never dreaming of falling from a horse or breaking my neck in a riding accident. I had thought myself too good a rider. Still did, in fact. Back then, I'd assumed cautious Augie just wanted to spoil all my fun. But he had seen my foolishness and used his only leverage to control my behavior, threatened to take himself away from me. I'd been good and mad at the time. We'd had a row full of dramatics on my part and chilly eye rolls and rational arguments on his. We'd gotten over it when I declared hurdles to be not nearly challenging enough for a rider of my expertise.

But that fear had been real. And so had Augie's concern. I could see that now.

I shook myself from my thoughts as Gen latched on to my arm and dragged me toward the rear of the shop.

"She's here, Mama!" announced Genevieve. She slid me a private smile before continuing, "Emery was so distracted by the beauty of the shop, no doubt, that she didn't even hear you calling."

In truth, I'd been too focused on thoughts of Augie to notice I was being summoned.

My mother's smile was strained. "Well, do come here, Emery. We mustn't keep Mademoiselle Russo waiting."

Introductions were made, tea was served, and I stood in front of a mirror on a raised platform being poked and prodded for the next three hours.

～

Dinner that evening at Cawthorn Hall was a rather sedate affair after dealing with the bustle of London.

Patty's London home was extravagance in the extreme. My sister's late husband, Lord Albert Henney, the Duke of Cawthorn, was nearing eighty before he passed almost four years ago. If memory served, the house had been decorated by one of Lord Cawthorn's previous three wives. Poor Patty was the most recent in a long line of women who failed to provide an heir. Judging strictly from gossip and the lack of conception over the years, one could assume the issue rested with Lord Cawthorn. But that didn't stop him from trying. In an effort to increase his chances, he'd married my sister at seventeen, but after nearly five years of marriage, Cawthorn had nothing to show for it.

Nothing except a bitter widow and a stranger in the place of my sister.

With no heir, his line had died with Albert Henney. The title and dukedom fell to some distant relation. But the majority of the wealth and the London estate remained with Patricia, Duchess of Cawthorn, until the time of her death, as per the initial marriage agreement.

The very woman who sipped wine at the head of the table.

Mama had kept up a steady stream of conversation throughout all courses. Patty replied politely where appropriate. She was distant and aloof and so unlike my spirited sister that it made my chest ache. Genevieve had retreated within herself, nervous in the setting and honestly unused to being in our sister's presence. She'd been only five when Patty had married the elderly duke.

I remained quiet at the table. Observant for once.

"Are you exhausted from your afternoon with the modiste, then?" Patty inquired, tone flat but gaze scrutinizing.

I replied with false brightness. "Oh, you know me." She didn't, in fact. Not anymore. "I just adore standing for hours on end and shopping for pretty little things."

Patty's smile was amused as she raised her goblet to her lips.

"Well," my mother interjected before Patty could respond, if she even intended to. "Emery complained nearly the entire time. I thought we'd have to get Gansey to hold her down just to get her measurements."

I scoffed, affronted.

Mama continued unfazed. "It was nothing like shopping for your wedding trousseau, Patricia. You were so excited." My elder sister's face blanked of all emotion at the mention of her former self, before she was made a duchess. Our mother continued, unaware of Patty's reaction. "You'd think Emery was being tortured."

Attempting levity, I chimed in, "Well, did you see the size of those pins? I feared for my safety, to be sure."

Genevieve giggled to my left, emerging briefly from her shy little cocoon. I gave her a wink before meeting Patty's gaze. She seemed relieved by my deflection, but the moment passed in the blink of an eye.

I made to continue the conversation, steering it away from my sister and her marriage, but Patricia spoke before I had the chance. "I'd wondered when I'd finally receive word from Mama about your engagement to Augustus."

I frowned in confusion. "What do you mean?"

Patty looked as perplexed as I felt. She glanced to our mother and then back at me. "Well, I just assumed it would happen at some point. I suppose it makes sense that Augie waited until he was finished at university. And he's not the type to sow his oats and then settle down at five and thirty. So of course it would be sooner rather than later. But congratulations to you both, Emery. Dress fittings aside, you must be so happy."

Belatedly I remembered the plan and smoothed out my expression. "Yes. Yes, thank you. I am very pleased."

Our families needed to believe our engagement to be true. They didn't know our intentions in subverting the futures laid out before us.

But … what was Patty talking about? Why did she already seem to think Augie and I were destined for the altar? I'd never spoken to my sister about a relationship or an attraction to Augie or anyone else. Why would she just assume Augie and I would marry? Just because we'd been friends our whole lives?

Come to think of it, I hadn't been forced to play a role—as Augie had put it—at all. No one had questioned our betrothal. There had been no deception required thus far to make anyone believe this engagement was true.

Was Patty saying …?

No, clearly she was confused. Or possibly it was as Gansey had said. Augie and I clearly had a bond. Our friendship was special. Patty obviously misunderstood the connection I shared with Augie and assumed our relationship was something more all these years.

Did everyone see us that way?

I felt a little lightheaded from all the conjecture, and did what any woman overwhelmed by extraneous thoughts was wont to do. I picked up my wine goblet and took a healthy swallow.

Patty's eyes narrowed on me and she looked thoughtful. Best to move this dinner along.

"Mama, tell Patty about the imported lace for my wedding dress."

That was all the encouragement my mother needed.

Forty-five minutes later, Gen was nearly asleep in her blancmange and Mother was still talking. Patty's scrutinizing attention had finally strayed from my general vicinity.

Never let it be said Emery Bartholomew couldn't rescue herself from a sticky situation.

The next morning brought traditional English weather. A steady gray drizzle blanketed the town. We had one full day remaining in London before our scheduled departure the following morning.

Mama had accepted an invitation to a well-attended ladies' luncheon from her friend Lady Hawkesberry. The viscountess warmly received my mother, Patty, and myself. Genevieve wasn't out in society yet and remained at Cawthorn Hall with Gansey while I was forced to endure *ton* gossip and an extremely light repast. This was the part I dreaded and couldn't tolerate about life in London. The interminable chatter was meaningless. No one inquired after anything substantial or true. These women did not wish to know anything about me as a person; it was all so disingenuous. I'd rather have one honest, true friend than a ballroom full of these pretenders.

And the tiny sandwiches didn't help.

I felt like these women were all waiting for me to fail and would relish the circumstances should they ever come to pass. I hated that feeling. Why couldn't women support other women just for being women? Wasn't life difficult enough? It remained a mystery to me. In the same way, I was unable to identify why I became a nervous disaster around other gently bred ladies. Mother's constant reminders and direction made me question my every movement. It wasn't so much the fear of embarrassing her or disappointing her in this setting, but maybe that *was* part of it. Perhaps it was because I knew deep down that I was different. I could never be one of these delicate swans.

I was too loud and brash, overly opinionated. I wore breeches and rode horses. My lady's maid was more like a sister to me than a servant. Rather than enjoying tea in the parlor, I preferred spending my time in the stables with the horses I loved and learning foul language from the grooms. I failed to muster any enthusiasm for fashion, the pianoforte, or embroidery, and was therefore at a disadvantage in nearly every conversation with my peers.

Being among all these women in their fine dresses made me feel ungainly. Perhaps it was my discomfort in my heeled slippers when I favored my sturdy boots. Or the constant fear I would say the wrong thing. But I was perspiring with unease and nervousness.

My countenance must have been worse than I feared because Patty glanced my way, then glanced back quickly once more before taking my arm and muttering, "Let's get you some refreshment."

My sister led me to a table laden with beverages and ladled weak yellow lemonade out of a punchbowl before passing the glass my way. We made our way to a quiet corner of Lady Hawkesberry's parlor before Patty spoke again. "What's the matter? Why do you look like you're about to cast up your accounts?"

Frowning at her assessment, I took a small sip from my glass before speaking. "I don't look like that." Patty merely raised her brows in response.

I glanced around at the ladies assembled. All dainty pastel dresses and well-mannered women, the very picture of what my mother so desired from me. I sighed before turning back to my sister.

"Here," she said and moved to position me so that we were standing near the windows overlooking the garden with my back to the room and her facing those in attendance.

"Then I won't be able to see them approaching," I hissed.

"Don't worry." Patty smirked. "None of these girls have the courage to approach me for conversation." I frowned, but before I could ask what she meant, my sister continued. "Besides, Mama can make the rounds. She lives for these social gatherings. We'll hide in the corner."

That was true. Our mother was taking the opportunity to tell anyone who would listen about my upcoming nuptials.

"Fine by me," I murmured, taking another sip before remembering how terrible the lemonade was.

Patty laughed at whatever sour expression I was making. I realized quite suddenly, I hadn't heard my sister's laugh in some time. Amusement lingered in her expression for a beat before it fell away all at once. But for that moment, Patty looked like herself, from before. Prior to leaving home for her first season, vivacious and full of life. Not the jaded, circumspect woman now standing before me in a dark green striped gown.

"Truthfully, Emery," she inquired earnestly, "why do you look sick with nerves?"

I took a deep breath before stating the obvious. "I don't belong here." Her expression remained shrouded in confusion, so I continued. "You know I prefer life in the country. I just don't fit in here. I'm not like all of them."

"I could understand that making you miserable or bored, but why do you look so troubled and … sweaty?"

"I don't know," I countered in exasperation. And I truly didn't. Inexplicably, being surrounded by high society was one of the only times I felt unsure of myself. My confidence evaporated. "Perhaps I'm afraid of embarrassing Mother or giving them"—I waved my hand in the direction of the dozens of women behind me—"something to judge or find lacking." As my artwork had been so easily diminished time and again before I'd resorted to painting in secret.

This conversation was doubly awful. Here I was, exposing my feelings and highlighting my inadequacy to my sister. Patricia's very existence seemed to contradict my own. Tall and willowy with medium blond hair, Patty was the ideal in London. My sister had played by all of their rules. She'd excelled in etiquette and landed a duke in her first season by doing exactly what was expected of her. She'd changed everything about herself, every-thing I'd loved, to fit the mold of a duchess. Perhaps I'd always disliked the idea of city life but I positively detested it after it stole my sister.

Patty had been so exuberant in our youth. She'd laughed loud and often. I'd been her adoring little sister, so enamored with her lively and playful personality that I'd constantly followed in her wake. Patty used to love to sing, too. I missed hearing her voice in our home. I missed so very much about my sister.

She narrowed her eyes thoughtfully but didn't reply, merely raised her own glass to her lips before wincing. "That is truly awful."

Quite without thinking, I blurted, "Why don't you ever come visit us in Hampshire?"

Patty blinked at my sudden question. Her features remained passive when she replied, "For the same reasons, I imagine, you avoid life in town. I just don't belong there anymore."

How could she say that? We were her family. Laurel Park was her home.

Before I could question her asinine response, she went on. "Besides, I have quite a bit of philanthropic work that keeps me busy here in London."

"You do?" Surprise colored my tone.

My sister blinked again. "I do. Did you suppose I simply attended balls and soirees and filled my days with frippery?"

"I don't know, Patty. You never said." I felt sad and hollow in this strange house, in this city I disliked all while having the longest conversation with my sister in recent memory.

Her gaze became distant and her volume trailed off when she spoke, "I suppose I didn't."

An awkward quiet descended between us, highlighting all the jovial conversation beyond. I turned my attention to the window and the gardens, a riot of color in these summer months. A true bright spot in the miserable gray cityscape.

"You know, Emery," Patty stated quietly. "You don't have to fear these encounters in London. Your path isn't the same as mine." I looked over to her then, full profile on display as she spoke to the pane of glass before her. We'd never spoken of her marriage or how differently her journey had deviated from the goals she'd set for herself many years ago. "You and Augie will be content with one another. You have the opportunity to lead the life you desire without pressures from society or your peers. These visits to town will be few and far between for you as they've always been. But that's no reason to hide yourself away and pretend to be someone you are not while here. You'd be surprised at the people you could meet and even befriend in London. We are not all the empty-headed, gossip-mongering toffs you seem to think we are."

Shame heated my fair cheeks. "I didn't mean to imply—"

Her warm smile cut me off as she finally turned to face me. "You've always been a force, Em. Even when you were a girl. Don't change yourself to suit others. Or one day you'll look in the mirror and barely recognize the woman staring back at you."

With sad blue eyes, Patty kissed my cheek and walked away, exiting the parlor and leaving me behind once more.

My inclination was to chase after my sister and demand she talk to me, explain herself, confide in me. But even I knew that pushing her would do nothing but drive her further from my grasp.

Instead I faced the garden and mulled over her words clearly spoken out of concern and reassurance. At least they felt that way to me. She was right about being with Augie. Second sons weren't expected in town for the season. We could live out our married life in Hampshire on the Barrington estate. We could travel abroad. Augie already knew I was not meant for London's polite society. I wouldn't be forced to follow in Patty's path. Because of my sister and her connections, her advantageous match, I had the freedom to pursue my own happiness. It was due to Patty's sacrifice—and I did view it as such—that I would never be forced to parade myself through a season in hopes of landing a titled and moneyed lord.

Truthfully, I had the funds from painting to support myself. However, with my mother none the wiser regarding my illustrious career, she'd been encouraging me to entertain a season in London for years now. Patty's match had bought me time and leniency, but my mother would not have been deterred forever. And I feared, revealing myself as M. Barton and all my savings would have scandalized her beyond repair. Marriage to Augustus really was the perfect solution—for both of us.

I also considered what my sister had said regarding the potential friendships I could have if I only gave my peers a chance. She was right, of course. I was being judgmental in my assessment of the ladies in this room and beyond. But I didn't think myself superior to them, merely different. Too different perhaps. My own dissimilarities made forming attachments a challenge. Augie was the only one who could overlook my personal deficiencies. He didn't judge me for how I took my tea or my inability to laugh quietly or how I lacked appropriate discussion topics. Well, he did absolutely judge and malign my preference for sweetened tea.

Nevertheless, he was the only person I felt comfortable enough with to be myself. My truest self.

Despite Patty's protestations, I didn't think there was another person in London who I'd ever be able to say the same about.

Gaze unfocused and mind adrift, I abruptly became aware of the reflection in the glass. Beyond my own image was a landscape I recognized. I slowly turned to discreetly glance over my shoulder.

Facing the room at large, I meandered across the room to the familiar painting on the opposite wall.

I'd never seen one of my paintings on display outside of my home, despite knowing all the names of my patrons over the years. Thirty-seven lords and ladies had acquired my work. I'd known Lady Hawkesberry had purchased an M. Barton original, but with the size of the viscount's holdings, there was no way of knowing where the landscape hung or in which estate. I could hardly believe I was standing before it now.

If memory served, Lord and Lady Hawkesberry attended a house party hosted by my mother several summers ago in Hampshire. My mother's friend had taken a liking to my father's landscape and he'd done as he often did, provided the name of our solicitor to handle the commission and resulting transaction.

My paintings were subtle in a way that would be surprising knowing I was the artist. But luckily, no one save myself and my father knew the identity of the painter. One would expect an Emery Bartholomew original to be bold and bright, large and splashy. When, in fact, an M. Barton work was small and contained, understated and elegant. The light moved through the landscape in such a way that it turned the scene ethereal and dreamlike. My goal was to express and convey the peace I felt in the countryside—in *my* countryside.

Seeing this painting again was like visiting an old friend. It was strange yet welcome to see the forest behind my home reimagined for these aristocratic walls.

"Lovely isn't it, Lady Emery?" Having been oblivious to her approach, I started at Lady Hawkesberry's words.

This was awkward.

"Yes, I like it very much," I finally replied, once recovered.

The older woman's eyes moved across the canvas. "Notice how the artist captures the fading afternoon light."

"Fascinating. I can see that." *Painted at sunrise actually.*

"And the spring foliage representing new birth and beginnings," Lady Hawkesberry offered, tone serious.

"Captivating." *Summer really, but no matter.*

"It's an M. Barton original," the woman leaned over to whisper exceptionally loudly, gaze still focused on the muted greens before us.

I had no reply. My brain could hardly comprehend the absurdity of the situation. Bitterness rose swift and spiteful. Lady Hawkesberry had paid a truly obscene amount of money to brag about a painting she knew nothing about. She didn't value the countryside that I so cherished. I hadn't infused my love of the land into the work at all. My painting was a novelty and nothing more. The separation between myself and my peers felt even more vast and cumbersome.

Before I could even worry over my rude lack of reply, I heard someone call out, "Did you say an M. Barton?" And then we were besieged.

I was jostled along as ladies gathered before the painting, each offering speculation surrounding the mysterious artist.

Despite the crowd of women, I felt more alone than ever.

It was definitely time to leave.

Six

AUGUSTUS

I cursed as I wedged myself through the narrow entrance to the tree house. I should bring a saw and widen the blasted thing. Although Emery would probably give me an earful should I change anything about her beloved tree house. She had an odd attachment to this place. But it wasn't getting any more comfortable for a grown adult to position oneself comfortably within.

I didn't even know why I was here. Emery was still in London with her mother and sisters taking care of wedding … things. It was bizarre to consider. Emery and I were getting married.

If I didn't expire of guilt first.

Crouching low, I lit several candles before seating myself on the blanket along the far wall. The book I'd brought with me was in the pocket of my waistcoat. I hesitated a moment before pulling it out, looking at this place and trying to see it as Emery did.

She loved it here, these dusty floorboards, the tattered curtains. I imagined the tree house represented some semblance of freedom. A place that was uniquely hers. Ours, really.

Freedom was what Emery coveted most. It was part of the reason we were set to marry. The only part that felt like repayment on my part. The only thing I could offer her, a life she craved free from the pressures of society and her mother. In that I could make her happy.

I would make her happy. I'd make sure her sacrifice wasn't in vain.

My stomach roiled at the idea. How could that simply be enough? How could I be enough? Was it fair to sacrifice one's freedom for another?

I knew Emery thought she was rescuing me from a terrible future and, in turn, I was saving her from a season in London that could ultimately lead to a marriage and future she'd never wished for. I winced, loosening the grip I had on my book.

I didn't know if I could go through with this.

My eyes caught on some hairpins on the stool in the corner. I can't believe we were ever small enough to sit comfortably on that thing. But I supposed we were. Em and I had spent much of our childhood and adolescence in this tiny structure. I assumed that was also part of what Emery loved about it. For such a straightforward and pragmatic person, she was oddly nostalgic and sentimental. This tree house likely represented a great deal to her: her youth and our shared history. It was a monument to our friendship.

That was probably why I was sitting here right now. Despite Emery's absence, I still wanted to feel close to her. I could have been reading comfortably in my own rooms, but I was wedged inside a tree house feeling sentimental and maudlin instead. If I were being completely honest, I missed her. She'd been in

London less than a week but it had been some time since my last visit to Hampshire. After nearly six months away, I'd been looking forward to spending our summer together. Initially, I supposed—in my bleakest of thoughts—I considered that this would be our last summer together. I'd been putting off the ultimatum from my brother, but I'd realized he wouldn't be held at bay for long. Change had been on the horizon, and I'd wanted what little time I could salvage with Emery before our paths diverged and everything changed. I couldn't have known that the woman herself would turn everything around.

The candles flickered in the warm breeze as I smiled to myself.

I thought about how different Emery looked since my visit at Christmastime. She'd always been beautiful, a wild kind of beauty with long blond hair always trailing behind her, mischievous grins full of knowing, and a laugh that made you feel as if you'd earned it. But when she'd framed herself in that doorway on my very first day back home demanding I propose ... well, she'd looked so grown up. Mysterious and enigmatic. Her thoughts and feelings were no longer hovering there on the surface. She seemed a touch world-weary.

It was growing more difficult to control myself, to not look too long. I wanted to absorb her and learn all these new secrets to someone who had always been so easily known. So very much mine.

And Christ, those breeches she went riding in. It was both miraculous and slightly dangerous that I was able to gallop on horseback with an erection of that magnitude. The fawn-colored fabric had pulled tight across her backside while in the saddle. And with the wind forcing her shirt to billow out behind her, every one of her curves was on display. Even beyond her body, there was nothing more beautiful than a joyful Emery. Her radiance had been tangible, and it was honestly difficult to look away. To only appear friendly in my glances, innocent with my eyes.

How would I control myself for the course of our marriage, our lives?

This was a disaster.

I uncrossed my legs straight out before me as I palmed the front placket of my trousers to readjust myself. My pants were growing increasingly tight at the memory of Emery in hers. Groaning at the contact, I gave my erection another squeeze.

Before I could make the involuntary decision to stroke myself to completion, the ladder rattled and Emery's head emerged through the floor of the structure quite suddenly. "Are you hurt? It sounded like you were in pain."

Oh, if you only knew.

I jumped in startled surprise and quickly placed my book over my lap, forcefully willing my desire away. Clearing my throat, I offered, "No. No, I'm fine."

All the way into the little house now, Emery moved toward me, head bent to avoid the ceiling. "Are you sure?" she eyed me suspiciously. "I could have sworn I heard you moaning up here."

I shrugged my shoulders as if unaffected while trying not to notice the enticing flush of Emery's cheeks or, *Christ* the bodice of her maroon traveling dress as she leaned forward to situate herself on the blanket beside me. "All is well." *Hell. All is hell.*

She continued to scrutinize my features, so I interjected before she had the chance. "What are you doing back?"

Extending her long legs out in front of her and crossing them at the ankles, she smoothed her skirts into place. "We needed to return to prepare for the engagement party your mother decided to announce at the last minute." I winced. My mother had indeed used Lady Northcutt and her daughters' absences to plan and extend invitations to a celebration for our betrothal. Emery rolled her eyes. "We've only just arrived, but I wanted to see if you were here. I slept in the carriage, so I wasn't ready to retire just yet."

"I see." I shifted subtly, nearly back to unaffected dimensions. "Did all go well in London? Were you miserable?"

"Let's just say I'm relieved our future together will not require us in town very often."

I gave Emery a sympathetic glance before she continued. "It was actually quite productive. Patty and I had an interesting conversation." I raised my brows in surprise. I knew how much Emery missed her sister, and how so much of Patricia's experience had colored Emery's own views on marriage and the *ton*. It was likely that resentment that led to this madcap plan to marry her best friend.

"That's good, Em," I spoke sincerely.

Emery fidgeted. "Well, it was something, I suppose. She's still not herself."

I hesitated before responding, knowing how defensive my friend could be regarding the topic of her elder sister. "Maybe this is just who she is now. Maybe you can't keep waiting for her to turn back into who she was. I think—" I paused. When Emery failed to lash out in frustration, I continued. "I think too much has happened for Patty to be the sister you once knew."

Emery's eyes remained averted but she took a deep breath and said quietly, "I think you might be right." She finally met my gaze, solemn and reserved when she was typically spirited on the subject. "I should focus on loving her as she is now instead of wishing for the past." Her brown eyes glowed with intent in the candlelight. "Relationships do change. People change. I suppose I need to allow myself to accept those changes and the feelings that accompany them." Emery didn't look away as she spoke and the moment stretched. I could feel my breath quicken at the intensity in her gaze. Was she … still talking about her sister?

I shook myself internally. I was looking for something where nothing resided. Wishful thinking that Emery was talking about more than just her relationship with her sister. But no, I didn't want that. I didn't wish for anything to change between us. It could mean the end of us.

Like a coward, I looked away, severing the moment. "And the remainder of your time in London? All was well?"

Emery took a moment to answer but said with some of her usual exuberance, "Oh yes. I was assaulted by the modiste." I snorted. "My gown is being prepared as we speak and should be ready in time for the wedding in …" She trailed off, pretending to consult an imaginary timepiece. "Six weeks. Six weeks, Augie!"

"I know. It's mad," I agreed.

Her smile turned sly as she nodded. "Absolutely mad. You know, Mademoiselle Russo," she said, exaggerating the name with a horrible French accent and theatric hand movements, "is preparing quite the assortment of nightgowns for my wedding trousseau."

My eyes widened at Emery's implication. And her abominable

accent, but mostly at the mention of nightgowns. The silence grew and turned incredibly awkward.

It was an odd ability to have opposing views living within oneself. But human bodies were nothing if not a marvel. And I was fighting the image of Emery in a sheer nightgown while simultaneously disregarding the teasing in her tone and feeling like a fucking cad for stealing that imagery for myself. Emery in her undergarments should be reserved for her husband alone. Her husband in truth. And that wasn't me. It couldn't be.

The guilt came swift and hot, like the flush rising to my cheeks.

"Augie," she began on a sigh, reading my response and likely trying to stop my internal debate before it raged out of control.

Well, too bloody late for that.

Perhaps on a night when I hadn't already been thinking about her with heat in my blood. My emotions were simmering on the surface, and my guilt was going to swallow me whole.

"There's still time," I managed to choke out, unable to meet her brown eyes. "We can call it off."

"No, we cannot," Emery replied calmly, wonder of wonders. "Our engagement celebration in your mother's garden is in two days' time. And even if we could back out now, Augie, I wouldn't want to. Would you?"

"I …" I floundered for words. "I don't want to be something you regret. And I want you to be happy in truth."

She smiled then, bright and full, as if I'd somehow cobbled together the correct answer to an impossible question. "Well then, that's easy. All you have to do is marry me."

Two days later, I watched as my mother greeted guests in the ballroom of Kensworth Hall. The chandeliers gleamed with an infinite number of candles. Fresh summer flowers had been brought in to decorate the space in vibrant shades of yellows and oranges, reds and pinks. Refreshments were laid along the wall closest to the patio doors and gardens beyond. Guests were mingling and chatting, drinking lemonade and champagne and strolling along the patio and among the hedgerows.

The scents and sounds would have been fairly overwhelming to me if not for the woman fidgeting by my side. Emery, radiant in a pale rose-colored gown, spoke in a beleaguered tone. "Do we really have to do this?"

Knowing the source of her discomfort stemmed from formalities, I smothered a smile. "Yes."

Extending my elbow, she slipped her warm hand around my arm. "Ugh," she complained. "Can't your mother greet everyone? It is her party."

"It is *our* party," I countered. "She's merely the hostess. Besides, we know most of these guests, Emery. People from the village. Acquaintances of both our families. The only individuals I haven't been previously introduced to are the friends my brother brought down from London."

Noticing my frown, Emery inquired with obvious hostility, "Why is he even here? It's not as though he wishes us well."

I led us slowly toward my mother and spoke quietly, "I imagine Mother strongly encouraged John's attendance to support the family, and inviting his friends was a way to pacify him."

We reached my mother and I greeted her warmly with a brief kiss to her cheek. Her eyes were alight with excitement. Whatever lack of support we'd been shown by my brother was easily neutralized by Mother's enthusiasm for our upcoming nuptials.

Emery, suddenly tense on my arm, pulled away to drop a slight curtsey. "Your Grace," she murmured before my mother laughed and yanked her up in a quick hug. "Don't be silly, Emery. You'll be my daughter soon."

My friend appeared quite shocked that Lady Amelia, the Dowager Duchess of Kendrick, was initiating such informality. Emery's transition from childhood friend to betrothed was instigating many changes. My mother was genuinely happy for our union, perhaps my fiancée would soon accept the reality of that. I smiled at Emery's discomfort before the guilt swooped in and sobered my features.

Somewhat recovered, Emery smiled and said, "Yes, of course. And thank you for this celebration in our honor."

I raised my brows, impressed by the sincerity of her speech before agreeing, "Yes, Mother. Thank you. It's lovely."

My mother, the consummate hostess, beamed, thrilled with her efforts and our appreciation. Several individuals approached, friends and neighbors, and Emery and I spent the next half hour making small talk and receiving felicitations on our upcoming union.

The musicians shifted from pleasing background accompaniment to signal that the dancing was about to begin. Emery noticed the shift and glanced toward the quartet in the corner of the ballroom. Mother turned and said, "Go on and dance. It will encourage others to join in the festivities."

I groaned as Emery latched on to my arm, needing no further encouragement. "Thank you. We'd be delighted."

"You. *You* would be delighted," I groused at the thought of dancing, especially with so few couples joining us on the dance floor.

Emery, never wary of being the center of attention, just pulled me faster as I dragged my feet. "Need I remind you, Augie? This is our party," she emphasized, happily throwing my words from earlier back in my face.

I rolled my eyes but took my place facing Emery as the first strains of the violins began. She smiled and I fought the urge to return it.

We proceeded to move about the dance floor in time with the music as we were joined by other revelers. Part of the torture of dancing with Emery would always and forever be the temptation of touch. The feel of her strong fingers along my shoulder. The delicate curve of her form under my desperate hands. I was tormented by the possibilities. Emery always wanted to dance and I was forever begging off, fearful of my body betraying me. Straying too long, clutching her too tightly, hands dipping indecently low. I dreaded the heat and friction of our movements but was inevitably drawn to the unabashed joy on her face.

These temptations were increased tenfold by the knowledge she'd be my wife soon.

Eventually, after the first set, Emery allowed me a small reprieve to seek refreshment … for her. I escorted her toward the punchbowl noticing the doors to the garden were still open, the early evening air attempting to cool the stifling ballroom. We were stopped several times before we reached our destination. Guests were eager to offer further congratulations or simply remark on how happy they were for us. I'd noticed quite a few individuals had remarked throughout the event on how well Emery and I looked together or how pleased they were to finally hear of our betrothal … as if our match were a foregone conclusion. Emery took these comments in stride, offering warm gratitude in return. Whereas I remained shocked at the implications, often requiring a moment to recover my expression.

Were our acquaintances misreading our lifelong friendship? Were my feelings so easily read all this time?

Befuddled by some of these interactions, I was distracted when we finally reached the refreshment table. My brother held court nearby within a circle of men. I recognized several lords from his association but made no move to interrupt or seek introductions with the rest. John appeared red-faced and loose, something other than weak lemonade in his glass. I knew well enough to avoid interactions in this moment with his preferred audience in attendance. But I feared I'd looked too long in his direction, because John's head rose and marked our proximity nonetheless.

A footman was assisting Emery with her beverage while my attention remained focused on my brother who was closing the distance between us. Em thanked the footman and turned to me, a question in her expression.

"There they are!" John exclaimed, over-loud and clearly inebriated. "The happy couple!" His companions made to raise their glasses as if to toast our happiness, but John's never rose.

I noticed several guests turned in our direction while others discretely moved away. I couldn't blame them. I wanted to avoid this interaction as well.

Emery made to speak but looked around her, likely taking in those assembled. She gave me a quick glance but I shook my head minutely. Better to get this over with than let Emery react to my brother.

"Good evening, Your Grace," I offered stiffly.

"I suppose congratulations are in order. Guess you just couldn't help yourself. Had to ignore my advice regarding our lovely neighbor here." My cheeks heated at his insinuation from years ago, to fuck Emery if I must but to avoid public association with her.

I glanced to my betrothed, taking in her puzzled frown, before quickly turning my attention back to John. This was bound to get worse before it got better.

My brother's expression was haughty and horrible. "But I suppose I should not be surprised. You've ignored all my instructions, haven't you, Augustus? You think yourself above the paths set before you, those of a loyal son honoring his family." He aimed a disgusted sneer in Emery's direction before landing his final blow. "Father would be ashamed."

The musicians and their instruments sounded miles away. I could scarcely hear anything above the blood rushing in my ears as my brother sauntered away, drink in hand, followed by three of his friends. Two remained, looking uneasy at the attention the duke had drawn.

Emery's face flushed with absolute murder, and she moved to follow my brother through the doorway to the garden beyond. Her unwavering support snapped me back to the moment. I stepped forward and grabbed her hand. "Don't," I pleaded.

Her eyes blazed with hatred, promising retribution. And I loved her more in that moment than I could possibly hide. I prayed my expression conveyed gratitude and friendship instead of the depth of emotion clawing its way out of my heart. "Let's go back to dancing."

I surprised her with my words. Hell, I'd surprised myself. But I needed to ground myself. I needed to forget my brother and his painful words. And I needed to revel in Emery and her loyalty. Touch her skin, feel her presence. Dancing was the only way I could get my hands on her in this moment.

Hand still clasped tightly in my own, I led her back to the dance floor where the music continued on as if nothing had happened on the opposite side of the ballroom. Our guests, bless them, averted their gazes and allowed the scene to bleed away into the stifling summer evening. We passed my mother, face shadowed with concern. She'd clearly been on her way to intercede with John, an attempt to smooth things over. I gave her a small, sad smile.

And then I took Emery in my arms and did my best to forget my brother's words.

Our bodies followed in time to the music without thought and I allowed myself to be distracted.

Sometime later, she wordlessly led me from the dance floor. Emery expertly skirted the guests most likely to seek our attention and guided me through the doors to the garden beyond with not a single interruption.

I was reasonably sure this was the longest Emery had ever been silent in my company. She found it nearly impossible to withhold her opinions, so I was sure she had much to say on the subject of my brother. But she was clearly attempting to give me the mental space I so obviously desired. Physically however, I craved her nearness and comfort. One of the benefits of decades of friendship was being able to give what the other needed without even being asked.

The July air was still warm but much cooler than the stuffy ball-room. The slight breeze was welcome. Lit by lanterns and torches along the path, I watched the small hairs loosed from Emery's coiffure stir in the wind.

Guests mingled on the patio and along the pathways in the fading sunlight, but I knew where Emery was leading me. She continued along the hedgerow, deeper into the garden until we approached the large fountain at the center. It was shadowed here, but I could still easily make out her features as the sun set somewhere behind us.

Emery pulled me down to sit next to her, and I prayed the next words out of her mouth were not about my brother. But she didn't speak at all. We sat in silence next to the fountain listening to the water bubble, hands still clasped.

I hoped she wasn't able to read my expression too closely. I felt certain my every emotion lived and breathed on the surface of my skin, straining toward her. The fight with my brother made me too vulnerable to put on my usual Emery armor. Stripped bare before her and defenseless.

My mind was warring again, needing the understanding of my friend and wishing for the comfort of a lover. Trying to reconcile went beyond my capabilities at the moment.

Attempting distraction, I finally spoke, "Just go ahead. I know you are dying to say something."

And as though we had been in the middle of a conversation, Emery offered without hesitation, "Don't you find it odd that so many well-wishers have commented on our upcoming marriage as though it was a rather obvious expectation? I mean, we haven't orchestrated any deception nor have we exaggerated our relation-ship. We haven't needed to convince anyone."

I slid her a sidelong glance. "Yes, it is a bit odd. I was thinking that earlier this evening."

She shifted a bit, her knee pressing warmly into the side of my thigh. "And Patty said something when I was in London about how she wasn't surprised in the slightest and had honestly expected to hear of our betrothal much sooner."

I felt my heart rate speed up in my chest. Perhaps … perhaps I hadn't been as skilled at hiding my feelings for Emery as I'd hoped. "Oh," was all I could manage but it sounded more like a question than an acknowledgement.

Emery looked thoughtful and determined, a poor combination in our history. It usually meant something was about to happen. "Yes. It was odd. And Gansey said something very similar." Now, that didn't surprise me. Gansey knew all.

I felt it necessary to proceed with the utmost caution. "What did Gansey say?"

Gaze intent on my face, Emery replied, "She said what we have … our friendship … is special. That very few people share the bond we have. Through time and distance, we've remained comfortable and content with one another." I swallowed, mouth suddenly dry. "And she said that most marriages aren't lucky enough to have even that."

"I see," I said quietly though in truth I could not see where this discussion was going. Don't get me wrong, I was relieved we were not recounting the scene with my brother. I wasn't ready for that. But something told me I wasn't prepared for the direction of this conversation either.

Emery turned to face me more fully on the concrete wall of the fountain, her knee covered by layers of fabric sliding further up my thigh and into my space. She bit her lip before finally saying, "I can't help thinking about your worries for our situation. Your misguided notion of doing more harm than good. That you're … you're holding me back from a happy marriage with some stranger." I looked away at the reminder, the fear that kept me awake at night. But Emery cupped my cheek and forced me to hear her next words. "Augie, can't you see? I could have no happier union. There is no one who could make me as happy as you do. And perhaps all these people, everyone who believes our betrothal in truth, could see what we didn't. That our marriage, held in the bonds of friendship and respect and affection would be the happiest of all."

She still held my face in her gloved hand, but it was no longer necessary to gain my attention. I was immobile in this moment, stricken by her words. I couldn't look away if I wanted to. Emery was so close and warm. Her brown eyes seemed to catalog my features, alighting briefly all over before finally settling on my lips. They parted under her inspection.

I didn't know what was happening between us but I could feel the shift. Emery had decided on a course of action and I feared my heart wouldn't survive the outcome.

She leaned closer and used that hand on my cheek to draw me in. I came willingly. I feared I always would.

Emery closed her eyes, but I didn't feel safe enough to do the same. I worried this moment would dissolve if I looked away, a figment of my imagination.

My heart pounded in my chest, in both disbelief and wild hope when I felt Emery's breath on my lips. Eyes finally drifting shut, I gave in and gave myself over. Before I could do more than breathe her in, a scream from beyond the hedgerows had us jerking apart and on our feet in the next instance.

"Stay here," I breathed, hopeful that Emery would listen, yet knowing she wouldn't. I dashed in the direction we'd heard the woman cry out, for it could be mistaken for no other sound.

Listening for any further noise to guide me, I slowed as I moved deeper into the garden. Emery stumbled into my back because of course she bloody did. That's when a whimper sounded just ahead, in the darkness of early evening beyond the torchlight and the paths. I turned the corner and the sight before me made my blood run cold.

My brother had a woman pinned to the ground, fumbling with her skirts. The whimpering had stopped but the crying hadn't. I moved without thought and grasped John by the back of his jacket and forcibly hauled him off her. She was a young woman from the village brought in as extra service for the party tonight. Her black and white garments marked her clearly as part of the kitchen staff and my brother was … I couldn't finish the thought.

"What the fuck are you doing, John?" I shouted down to his sprawled form. I couldn't remember ever feeling so unhinged and enslaved by my emotions.

The woman, *Christ*, the girl scurried back on her elbows. Emery gave my brother a wide berth and made to approach the maid, but before Em could even speak or reach out to her, the girl jumped to her feet and ran back toward the light of the gardens and house beyond.

My brother made no move to get up, just rolled onto his back before looking over to me. "Oh, Augustus. Do mind your own business," he slurred.

All my rational arguments and determination to remain cool-headed fled abruptly. I was livid and reckless, thoughts and demands tumbled unrestrained from my lips. "Mind my own business? Are you insane? Forcing yourself on … on … a servant! A girl half your age. On anyone! What the hell is wrong with you?"

"My friends were watching out for anyone to stumble upon us. Although not very well from the looks of it." He pushed up briefly on his hands and gave me a mocking glare. "Don't be such a child, brother."

I moved to stand directly over him, chest heaving with unspent emotion. "You are no brother of mine. You're an utter waste. A drunk. A worthless excuse for a human being. You play at being the duke, lording your authority and position over everyone. But you're a laughingstock. No one takes you seriously. And after seeing you here tonight, I am not the one Father would be ashamed of." I spat my final statement, emotion and rage making my voice shake.

John looked up at me, bleary-eyed but intent. He huffed a humorless laugh before speaking, "Finally saying what you mean, are you?"

Before I could respond, I heard people approaching from behind us, three men advanced from the garden pathway. Moving away from John, I grabbed a fierce-looking Emery by the hand and pulled her behind me before John's friends emerged. They wisely remained quiet and merely lifted their comrade up before supporting him back toward the manor.

I stood there, breathing in the summer air in great gulps, attempting to calm myself. I felt something touch my back a moment before Emery's arms came around me from behind, snaking beneath my own. She clasped her hands across my stomach and pushed her soft cheek between my shoulder blades, hugging me tightly. The weight of her hands brought with it awareness, helping to slow my breathing.

The weight of her presence brought me back to myself. The heat of her body and the strength of her embrace returned me once again to her.

Seven

EMERY

Augie eventually took a shuddering breath and I knew he'd pull away any moment. His sense of propriety had been ingrained since birth and no one was more of a gentleman than Augustus Ward. He knew the risks of being alone with an unmarried woman. Even me, his betrothed. And he would never put my reputation in jeopardy so close to a house party. No matter the situation, no matter how much he needed this. Needed me.

I squeezed his middle one last time before Augie's hands loosened my own and he stepped away. Sighing audibly, I knew he would allow me to comfort him no longer.

Honestly, I was still in shock from the entire evening. The initial encounter with John had been quite enough. Augie refused to let me commit violence at my own engagement party. And wasn't it *my* party after all? I should have been able to throttle the Duke of Kendrick if I so desired. Alas. I had been working up to discussing the scene while Augie and I were by the fountain, but then I'd grown distracted by the fullness of his bottom lip and how very good it felt to lean into his space.

As if almost coming to blows with my future brother-in-law and nearly kissing my best friend weren't enough for the evening, the scene in the garden was positively overwhelming. That poor girl. And Augie's outburst. I was still reeling.

I'd known all along Augie had that frustration and bitterness living inside him, but I assumed it would stay locked within forever. A paragon of restraint, my sainted friend was. I was proud of him for finally speaking his mind. His despicable brother needed to hear it. Not that it would do any good.

Augie was probably imagining all the ways John would make him suffer following this encounter. The hazards of having a best friend who was risk averse and infinitely prepared for any disaster.

But I had a feeling that whatever the duke cooked up this time … Augie wouldn't be able to anticipate.

Turning slowly to face me, Augie took a deep breath before speaking. "We should return to the house. I'm going to have Anders check on the girl."

His mind was already far away, probably trying to figure out how to smuggle her back to her family and away from John and his friends. It was the smart thing to do.

As distracted as I was, I still couldn't put our almost kiss out of my mind. Had that desire been living inside me the same way Augie's pent-up resentment had taken up residence? How long had I secretly wanted to kiss my best friend?

Now was not the time. Augie was preoccupied. We could discuss it later. I needed to think on this some more anyway.

Augie started walking back toward the gardens, determination in his stride. He made it a few more paces before realizing I wasn't following. He pivoted and looked at me expectantly, features murky in the fading light but still discernible.

"Augie, don't you think we should take a moment? You're upset. We can talk about what happened," I offered, already knowing the answer but feeling helpless. I so desperately wanted to make this better for him. I couldn't change his terrible brother or the fact that his father was gone. But I could provide a safe place for him. Or simply help him order his thoughts. Despite my reputation and general need to converse, I could be a good listener. I would be. For Augie.

Frowning, he replied quickly, mind made up. "I need to get back and find Anders and speak to my mother." He broke off abruptly and drew a frustrated hand down his face.

I approached slowly, as if he were a skittish horse. "The party is still happening. Your home is filled with guests. It will hold, Augie."

"It will not hold," he shot back.

He was still angry. So very angry. I couldn't let him return to the house like this. What if he sought out his brother again? What if there was violence? I didn't trust Kendrick. He would hurt his brother if he felt threatened, and he was drunk and unpredictable. With at least three men at his back.

My anxiety and fear were growing. I needed to keep Augie here with me. I'd help him calm down and he would avoid any danger at the hands of his brother. "I think we should take a moment and figure out the best way to—"

"I can't do this right now," he all but shouted, causing me to wince. I wasn't afraid of Augie. He'd never hurt me. That, I could bet my life and my paintings and Beatrice Three on. But as I realized there was nothing I could do to keep him here with me, my fear *for* Augie made my hands shake.

And then again, quieter with his self-control firmly in place, he repeated, "I can't do this right now." With that, he turned and resumed his march toward the manor.

After three steps, he spun on his heel and strode determinedly to me, wrapping me in a fierce hug. Caged in the iron grip of his arms, I frantically clutched his lapels before whispering in his ear, "Please be careful. Don't approach John again. Just … please."

"I won't," Augie promised, voice firm. "I swear it. But please come back to the house. Night is falling. I can't leave you out here alone. Not after … not after that."

Secure in his hold, I nodded. With that, he grasped my hand and led us determinedly back to his family's estate.

When we reached the patio doors in silence, he squeezed my hand once before breaking away in search of Anders. He didn't look back, but I couldn't stop staring after him. My friend, this responsible man, always one to do his duty and solve every problem. What toll must that take?

I swore in that moment that our lives together, our future as husband and wife would never be a problem for Augie to solve, a task to undertake. I would make him happy. We would make each other happy. Our union would be like our friendship, effortless and content. I would do whatever I could to be a true partner to Augie, someone to share his burdens and lighten his load. He deserved so much more than a free-spirited, impetuous wife. It wasn't until that very moment that I understood his fear for our union. What if Augie's love match was out there somewhere? What if I was keeping *him* away from someone perfectly suited to him? I didn't think I could forgive myself if I became one more obligation for Augie. Or worse, another regret.

～

"You're quiet tonight," Gansey remarked from across my bedchamber as she brushed out my dusky pink gown from this evening.

I turned from my spot in front of the vanity and attempted a smile. "Just tired, I suppose. Busy day."

Gansey looked unconvinced but didn't press. Miraculous that. "Some warm milk before bed?"

"No, that won't be necessary. But thank you, Gansey." I started plaiting my long blond hair.

My friend watched me in the mirror with a worried expression, green eyes troubled. "Did something happen at the party?"

I tried to appear reassuring. I didn't think I'd be able to recount the instance with John and the maid. The divide between myself and Gansey seemed wider this evening. While she was a servant in our household, she was also my friend. My family treated our staff with respect and generous salaries. But I knew how common the occurrence in the Kensworth Hall garden this evening really was. Lords took liberties with women in service, abused their power, and wielded their strength. The thought of someone hurting my Gansey made my throat tighten. Why did some men feel compelled to take whatever they wanted? I expect the answer lay in an inflated sense of self-importance and a general misuse of power. And sometimes an evil man was simply that.

Giving Gansey a sad smile, I told a partial truth. "Another run-in with the Duke of Kendrick during the festivities. He maligned our union and made a scene. Augie took it badly. And I wanted to hit Kendrick badly."

She made an affronted sound. "That man. I swear. Make sure to serve salmon after the wedding."

I smiled at my bloodthirsty friend, recalling John's allergy. "Hopefully he returns to London and we never have to see him again."

"One could hope," she replied solemnly.

"One could hope," I agreed.

Perhaps sensing my mood, Gansey departed shortly thereafter. Despite craving time alone and putting distance between myself and my household, I was restless. I wanted—no, I needed—to know what was happening with Augie and John.

Noting the lateness of the hour, I presumed my parents would be abed. I couldn't risk being spotted by either one of them. After returning to the ballroom following the scene in the garden, I'd stayed near my mother for the remainder of the event. It was a dreadfully long hour, smiling and acting as if all was well. If I seemed distracted or agitated, Mama did not comment, but I feared an encounter in my present state, wouldn't go unnoticed. I was a bow strung tight, lacking the wherewithal to hide my internal disquiet.

Placing my ear to the door of my bedroom, I listened for any sounds of movement. Detecting nothing and no one, I secured my white floral wrapper over my dressing gown and slipped on my well-worn leather ankle boots. I creeped quietly through the house and emerged through the kitchen entrance.

Letting out a sigh of relief, I grabbed my skirts and took flight. I ran over the manicured lawn, past the hedges and into the wildflower field. Anxiety fueled my course, and I could feel the nervous energy being expended as my muscles warmed and my breathing quickened.

I didn't know what I would find when I made it to my destination but I knew who I was running to.

It was dark but the moon lit the familiar path to the tree house, through the woods and into the clearing. The structure looked dark and imposing as I approached, a lone tree set apart from all the others. A moment of fear from the frightening events of the evening gave me pause to consider my surroundings, but I refused to let John and his disgusting behavior taint the comfort and safety of this place. I could see no light or movement within, and disappointment enveloped me. I pulled up abruptly, breath ragged realizing Augie wasn't here. He hadn't come.

I tore my frustrated gaze away from the tree house and resumed walking to the base of the trunk. I would wait in case—well, in case he needed me after all.

My attention snagged. There ... a lantern. Augie peeked from behind the tree. He held the lantern aloft before saying my name, low and insistent.

I took off running again, uncaring if I was being dramatic and hysterical. Somehow I knew—I just knew—this tightness in my chest, the fear in my heart would not dissipate until I could close my arms about him.

Lips parted in surprise, Augie set the lantern on the ground and enveloped me as I reached him. I squeezed him tightly and, horror of horrors, began to cry. Not great wracking sobs nor weeping hiccups, just a silent onslaught of tears releasing the tension I'd carried for hours. He was here and he was whole, and I couldn't seem to stop crying. So I tucked my face into his neck and held on.

Augie didn't speak. He simply let me emote all over him. My arms started shaking from the effort of my embrace, and he began rubbing circles on my back, loosening the strain in my muscles.

I felt oddly shy when I finally pulled away. I couldn't pinpoint what, but something felt different.

The lantern cast a small circle of light, illuminating our forms. Augie's concerned frown searched my tear-streaked face. "All right?" he whispered.

I wasn't, but nodding seemed the safest course of action. Augie's frown intensified, eyebrows nearly touching, as if sensing my lie.

"Are you okay? What happened after you left?" I asked before he could fret over the state of my tears.

"I located Anders and asked him to assist me in finding the girl. We escorted her back to her father's house a few miles away. I don't think John would remember her in the light of day after he sleeps off his drink. So I don't believe she's in any danger of retaliation on his part. His friends took him back to the inn they're staying at in the village. Likely for more carousing. You needn't worry, Em. He won't be in the house with me tonight."

I nodded again. "Did you tell your mother what happened?"

Augie's eyes turned hard. "I did. Following the party. She was upset but resigned. I'll speak with her again tomorrow."

Now it was my turn to frown. Stepping closer, I muttered, "What aren't you saying?"

Jaw set and radiating anger, Augie finally answered, "She didn't seem particularly surprised."

Oh. *Oh.*

"Do you think—?" I abandoned the thought, too horrified to finish.

Augie placed his hands on his hips and dropped his head back, speaking to the sky. "I don't know, Emery. I keep trying to think back. There have been maids that have come and gone. Here on one visit home from Cambridge and gone the next. I have no way of knowing why. Anders swore to me he'd never heard of John abusing the staff beyond his typical poor manners and surly attitude. But … I just don't know." His disgust and frustration were obvious.

I stepped closer again, compelled to comfort, and brought my hand to his waist. "You couldn't have known, Augie."

His tortured gaze finally met my own. He gave a jerky nod of acknowledgement. "I'm sorry I yelled at you, back in the garden. I just—" He sighed before continuing. "I just felt like I needed to do something, anything to help the situation. John is so good at making me feel powerless. I couldn't let him or his friends reach that girl and finish what he started. And I honestly hated that you were there to witness everything. That's not how I'd ever want you to see me, Em."

I frowned in confusion. "What do you mean? See you how?"

He took a deep breath before replying. "So out of control."

"Augie, you were …" I trailed off, unable to land on the correct word. Nothing seemed to fit the situation. *Passionate. Unleashed. Uninhibited. A revelation.* "Before today, I was honestly worried that you were going to expire from repressing your feelings and never displaying your emotions. I am horrified by what your brother did. I wish that situation had not been the impetus for you to finally express yourself. But I think you desperately needed to say all of those things. I wish you didn't feel you had to hide part of yourself from me."

He looked stricken. As if I'd unearthed the very heart of him.

I couldn't fathom his expression but needed to do what I could to reassure him. So he'd know. He could always be himself with me. I could handle Augie in all his forms. I might be foolhardy and wild, reckless in my actions. But in this, in acceptance and in friendship, those things weren't a negative. I could love with abandon.

His hands were still on his hips, elbows out to the side, so I snaked my hands around his waist and applied pressure gently on his back bringing us flush together. The hug I initiated lasted several moments before Augie's arms came around me, returning the embrace. He said very quietly, lips beside my ear, "There are some parts better kept hidden, Emery. It's necessary that I stay in control of myself."

Keeping my arms locked about him, I pulled back just enough to look up to Augie. The lantern below us cast odd shadows, and I felt the need to search his features for the familiar. My heart was beating a warning in my chest. I let myself think back to the fountain, to blue, blue eyes and the fullest bottom lip I'd ever seen on a man. I was looking at that lip again right now.

"Funny, that. I've never seen the need." And then I pushed up on my toes and finished what I started in the gardens.

The kiss took him by surprise. I could tell in the way the muscles stiffened across his back. At first, unsure of how to kiss a man, I simply pressed my lips to his, warm and firm. But then I remembered his plump bottom lip and let myself do what I'd imagined, and drew it gently into my mouth, tasting it with my tongue.

Augie made a sound in the back of his throat and then he was hauling me closer, pulling me in tight to his body. He was kissing me back, repeating my movements, drawing my top lip between his own and licking along the seam of my mouth. I opened for him and that was all the encouragement Augie required.

One of his hands traveled up my spine to the base of my neck. He cradled me there under my hair, all warmth and strength and possession. The fear and worry from earlier, were replaced by security and protection. Kissing Augie was as easy as doing everything else with him. I didn't stop to consider the ramifications of our actions. Later I would puzzle out what it all meant. Right now I was content to keep kissing the person I trusted most in the world.

We spent several long moments exploring each other, lips nipping and tongues tasting. Augie's famous control was on full display as we kissed deeply. He was slow and savoring. No wandering hands to be found. I was eager and curious, and he was my counterpoint, content and unhurried. But I felt his attention keenly. I was his sole focus and I reveled in the knowledge. As much as I wanted him to wind his hand around my braid and for his control to slip, I also appreciated the care and devotion he showed me in every one of his movements.

The moment stretched and I lost myself to the feel of his body. The pressure of his hand at my nape, the prickle of whiskers on his chin, and the absolutely maddening softness of his bottom lip.

I didn't let myself think about what we were doing. I didn't want reality to intrude. To remind me that we were best friends who were only betrothed due to deception but who *really* had their tongues in each other's mouths. Because if I considered the lunacy of our situation, I might have had to stop kissing him. And I never wanted to. We should have been kissing all along.

Eight

AUGUSTUS

From the second-floor drawing room I was able to watch the footmen load my brother's trunks into the carriage. It felt necessary to preside over and bear witness to the activity, to ensure he was really leaving. John had returned home very early this morning, disheveled and smelling of drink—unlikely having slept at all. Anders had woken me when he'd learned of my brother's plans. The Duke of Kendrick would return to Kendrick Manor, our family home in Mayfair. I'd yet to determine if he'd return for my wedding in under six weeks' time. With any luck, he would remain in London.

However, that just made my brother London's problem. I didn't know how to protect the staff there or the women in every ballroom, sitting room, or theater in town. My mind conjured so many possibilities, so many ways in which my brother could be a predator. I felt disgusted by his actions and guilty by association.

Hayes, my brother's coachman, ambled out and took his place in the driver's box while I observed discretely from above. Hopefully that meant John was nearly ready to depart and I could take my breakfast in the dining room with Mother alone. We needed to talk.

What a fucking day.

Catching my reflection in the window pane, I saw my fingers pressed to my lips. The unconscious movement brought my thoughts back to last night, back to Emery.

She'd kissed me. I could hardly fathom it.

When you wanted something so acutely, as deeply as I wanted Emery's lips on mine, you didn't even allow yourself to hope for it in your heart of hearts. It felt somehow as if you were more likely to wish it away on the wind than to wish it into being. So you'd take this thing, this unachievable aim, and you'd wrestle it to the back of your mind and the very corner of your heart.

But it had happened. We'd kissed for an age, until my lips were sore and my hands grew restless for more. That was when I'd pulled myself away, reluctantly and soberly. And then I'd escorted Emery back to the field behind Laurel Park. We'd walked in silence. Perhaps she could tell I needed time with my thoughts. Maybe she'd needed time with her own. When in reality, I'd needed to will away my urge to touch her, to ask for more. Watchful and serious, I'd bid her goodnight in the dark. She'd merely slipped her arms around me and pressed a kiss to the line of my jaw before extracting a promise to meet her in the stables this morning for a ride. And then she'd been gone.

I had two hours before I had to face her. Two hours to consider every possible motivation and outcome of our actions. Two hours to argue and debate with myself. Two hours to recall the taste of her.

Two hours was plenty of time to work myself into an anxious lather.

Nothing about Emery felt premeditated last night. We were both raw with emotion. I came to the tree house seeking comfort, I suppose, from a terrible situation. And honestly, I knew Emery would be chomping at the bit to know what had happened upon leaving her earlier in the evening.

What I didn't expect was to find Emery in such a state. I could count on one hand the number of times I'd seen her cry throughout our childhood. Typically such displays of riotous emotion were brought on by anger. But the events of the evening prior had obviously left Emery feeling vulnerable for some reason.

Her relief in finding me in our meeting place was palpable. I'd worn the evidence of her emotions all over the front of my shirt. I'd been so stricken by her despair that when I found myself on the receiving end of her affections, you could have knocked me over with a feather.

I wasn't foolish enough to read more into the kiss or Emery's motivations for initiating it. Oh, I was unwise enough to consider them and fret over them, but to really apply meaning to the actions of my impulsive friend … I'd only be setting myself up for further heartache. Which was, let's face it, inevitable at this point.

I was going to marry my best friend who I was hopelessly in love with. Emery kissing me had done nothing to slow the beating of my heart nor the yearning in my chest. My thoughts were muddled at best and hopeful at worst.

I was too cowardly to consider that the impetuous kiss meant anything more than an overwhelmed Emery being overcome, perhaps confused. The kiss had surely manifested out of some misplaced emotion, hadn't it?

When I saw Emery next, were we going to talk about it? Would she be capable of ignoring what had happened between us? Would I be more or less devastated if she did?

Two fucking hours to figure out how to just *be* around her again.

I scrubbed a hand down my face. *What was I doing?*

Movement by the carriage brought my attention back to the front drive. John, clad in hat, traveling cloak, and accompanied by a walking stick, moved to the conveyance. Moments later, he was away with no fanfare whatsoever, leaving nothing but trouble in his wake.

I made my way down to the family dining room, selecting coddled eggs, bacon, and toast with marmalade from the sideboard. My mother arrived just as I was pouring my tea. She gave me a wary look, undoubtedly sensing my mood, before joining me with her own plate.

I poured tea in a dish and added a splash of cream before placing it before her. "John's gone for London."

She retrieved her tea and took a sip before replying noncommittally, "I see."

If I'd been waiting for further response, it would have been in vain. My mother began eating.

Frustration growing, I attempted, "What are we going to do?"

She met my gaze as her jaw worked slowly. Finally resting her cutlery on her plate, she responded, "What would you like me to do, Augustus? Hide your brother, the Duke of Kendrick, in the cellar? Should I report him to the constable?"

Brows raised in shock at her longsuffering tone, I opened my mouth but no words immediately came out. Once recovered, I managed, "I don't know what to do, Mother. But I feel I must do some—"

"Do you think I have not tried?" she interrupted. "I've spoken to him about these … indiscretions." I made to object to the inaccuracy of her word choice, but she silenced me with a look. "I've a settlement prepared for the girl and her family for their trouble. I'll see that it's delivered."

I made an effort to unclench the linen napkin in my grasp before speaking, unable to hide the revulsion in my tone. "And how many of these contributions have you made over the years?"

Her hand trembled as she raised the teacup to her mouth once more. Without meeting my gaze, my mother answered woodenly, "More than I'd care to say."

Tossing the cloth napkin on my plate in frustration, I blew out a disgusted breath. "There has to be something. Something we could threaten him with. Precautions we could take."

"Threaten him?" Mother questioned. "He's a peer of the realm, Augustus. Your brother lacks the patience to indulge any sort of undermining or questioning on your part."

I frowned. "Only on *my* part?"

Lips pressed in a tight line, her frown answered the question of whether she'd be taking part in a confrontation with her firstborn. "What do you want me to say? He's my son, too."

～

"There you are!" Emery's face appeared over the stall door suddenly.

"Christ." I startled from my place on the other side of the mare I'd been brushing. Her ears flicked back to me in concern. I smoothed my hand over her flank in apology.

"Sorry." Emery grinned, not looking very sorry at all. She looked radiant. Eyes alight with an undercurrent of mischievous enthusiasm. Perhaps things wouldn't be awkward between us. Maybe we were ignoring the whole best friends kissing thing. "I didn't mean to scare you. What are you doing grooming that horse? It's not even your horse."

I had been grooming all the horses. I'd left my mother in the dining room and taken my disappointment and despair to the stables. I'd told the grooms to go ahead and enjoy their midday meal early and leave me to myself. I'd been cleaning tack and brushing horses for almost two hours.

I cleared my throat, slightly rough from disuse. "Just arrived early. Needed some time to think."

Emery's glow dimmed a bit. She looked concerned but didn't comment. Perhaps I should clarify. I didn't want her to think my unease was about her or what had happened between us. Well, I was unsettled about her as well, but in this particular instance I was hiding in the stables because of my family. There would be time to fret over kissing her later. Like now.

Bollocks.

God help me, Emery looked resolved all of a sudden. That was never a good thing. A decision had obviously been made and she was about to execute a plan, however disastrous it may be.

Before I could question the limited space within the stall or voice an objection, Emery opened the door and let herself in. She smiled and cooed at the mare before stroking her sweetly along the column of her neck. Then Emery turned to me with a look I couldn't quite decipher. Part determination, a fair helping of intent, and the barest hint of forced confidence.

I felt suddenly alert, my family the furthest thing from my mind. I had the strangest urge to retreat, but before I could move and with little room to do so anyway, Emery launched herself at me. Her arms twined around my neck as she raised on tiptoes to bring our mouths together. I hit the wooden slats of the stall wall a few inches behind me with a forceful exhalation. Emery giggled into my mouth before her lips parted over mine. The horse nickered in concern but I patted her and took the opportunity to steady myself and stand upright despite the mad woman clinging to me and kissing me. It was my turn to laugh into Emery's mouth. She was ridiculous. I loved it.

I could feel her smile against my lips before she said, "Sorry, I was excited."

I made to pull back but her arms tightened about my neck.

So I guess we weren't ignoring this whole kissing thing.

Moving my hand to cup her cheek, I placed my mouth back on hers. Before long, our smiling lips turned eager and serious, amusement fading to something else entirely. Bringing my free hand to Emery's back, I pressed her close and traced the length of her spine. She sighed into my mouth and I took the opportunity to lick inside before pulling back and grazing her bottom lip with my teeth.

My mind tried to wander. My consciousness made a valiant effort to analyze the situation, to plan ahead for the inevitable fallout.

However, I was determined to be present. To only consider the feel of Emery under my palms, the slide of her tongue against mine, the scent of her—wild and bright—mixing in with the earthy stable surrounding us.

Our kiss deepened, tongues sensuous and teeth tortuous. I wanted to crawl inside her and never leave. My hand on her back drifted lower of its own volition and *God*. These fucking breeches. I cupped her ass and squeezed, indulging in the fantasy of palming her roughly in these trousers that had haunted my dreams.

Emery's groan met my ears and we both froze, lips disconnecting.

"My apologies," I attempted at the same time she demanded, "Do that again."

I wanted to. But I knew I was walking a treacherous path. Nothing was settled between us. Hell, nothing had even been discussed. And I didn't want to push too hard or too fast. If I gave in now, I didn't even want to consider where the morning might lead us. Someone had to be the practical one. And time and temperament proved it would once again be me.

Still paused in our ministrations, I carefully moved my traitorous hand away from Emery's glorious backside. She was breathing deeply and so was I.

With a ragged inhale, she accused, "Why did you stop?"

After putting what little amount of space there was between us, I felt confident enough in my self-control to answer. "I didn't want to force you, Emery."

"Force me?" Her brow wrinkled in confusion. "I practically begged you to continue, Augustus."

"I know. But this is all so new. I didn't want to be too forward and …" I cast about for the right words. "I didn't want you to regret anything."

Emery crossed her arms over her chest, huffing an indignant laugh. "You really do not trust me to know my own mind."

"It's not that," I protested. The mare began to shift restlessly, undoubtedly done with the noisy humans and their ridiculous exchange. The horse pivoted her backside into my space, forcing me closer to Emery and the front of the stall.

I made to exit and nudged Emery in the direction of the gated archway, but she stood her ground. "No, Augie. I'm not ready to leave this stall. Or is my confused feminine brain incapable of deciding where to stand?"

Rolling my eyes, I scooted past her and opened the stall door. "Come on, we can talk out here before this horse tramples you." An aggrieved whinny punctuated my statement.

Emery thankfully acquiesced and joined me in the main hallway of the stable. I shut and secured the stall door before turning to face her, arms still crossed, body alarmingly defensive. "Augie, you need to trust me. I wasn't feeling confused or coerced or pressured by your attentions. It's not like you were holding a … a …" She took in the surroundings before gesturing in annoyance to an implement leaning on the planks beside her. "A pitchfork to my head! If I said I wanted you to grab my ass, I meant it, dammit. I still mean it! Despite how utterly ludicrous you're being right now." I opened my mouth to further defend my position, but she went on. "And furthermore—" Christ, *furthermore* was never good. "This is just another example of you ignoring my wishes and assuming you know best. That I couldn't possibly have any forethought or consideration for the consequences of my actions."

Eyes narrowed, I spoke slowly. "What do you mean?"

"No matter how many times I've told you that I want to marry you, that it is beneficial for me as well, you act as if I'm martyring myself and my future and all possible happiness." Emery took a step toward me and spoke more softly. "Augie, I need you to trust me. I'm a grown woman and I know my own mind. If you respect me and care for me—and I know you do— then I need you to really listen to me. My whole life you've been the only person who has ever really *seen* me. But I need you to *hear* me as well."

I considered her words, remembering the times I'd discounted this fake betrothal, both in my head and out loud. How I'd bemoaned her sacrifice and her rash decisions. I felt shamed by her assessment. I'd behaved like any other highhanded lord, assuming I knew best after failing to consider the validity of Emery's own thoughts and actions.

I looked down at the dirt floor, covered in bits of straw. Worn brown leather riding boots stepped forward into my field of vision before a soft, gentle hand cupped my jaw. Tilting my face up and away from the ground, Emery's caramel gaze was determined but indulgent.

"I'm sorry," I breathed.

She smiled. "I know. And I know you well enough to know that any apology from you is more than words. It's a course correction."

She kissed my cheek, apology accepted.

I kissed hers in return, besotted and grateful.

As we went through the motions of gathering our mounts and preparing for our short ride, I couldn't help replaying her words, the urgency of her demands. And while she'd implored me to consider the truthfulness of her thoughts and to trust that she knew her own mind, she didn't say anything about knowing her own heart.

~

"John left for London," I offered. We'd left the stables and grounds closest to the estate at a far more sedate speed than usual.

"That's good, I suppose." Before I could disagree with her assessment and offer up the multitude of complications his departure had wrought, Emery continued, "Although I suppose now we have to worry about him making trouble in town where we can't see him."

After the painfully illuminating conversation with my mother over breakfast, that *we* was a balm to my troubled soul.

I met her gaze, undoubtedly visibly distressed. "I know."

Emery faced forward again as our horses took a meandering path in the late sunny morning. She pushed some hair behind her ear that had fallen from their pins. "Perhaps we could have him followed. Hire someone menacing to shadow his every move. I'm sure my father's solicitor could recommend someone. He's very well connected in town."

I made to respond, but she threw out another suggestion almost immediately. "Or we could encourage him to take a holiday, the Mediterranean perhaps or India. With a very limited staff. An all-male staff."

I opened my mouth to disagree with the likelihood of John leaving the country right now when Emery spoke again. "No, he's unlikely to leave London with the season looming. He's a worthless duke but he's still a peer with responsibilities in Parliament."

I smiled as my horse approached the tree line. Not so much amused by the topic but by Emery unwittingly reading my mind. And her support and her willingness to take on this impossible task. I hadn't even needed to ask for her help. This was the discourse I'd hoped for this morning with my mother. Even if there was no good answer, I'd needed her to be on my side in this. A united front for decency and accountability. My remembered frustration wiped the smile from my face.

Emery was still talking. "What if we threatened to go to the papers? Out him as a scoundrel and tormentor of women, have him shunned in polite society." She was already shaking her head. "What would those beasts in the aristocracy care about one more ill-mannered, morally reprehensible lord?"

I pulled my horse to a stop, suddenly overwhelmed by my love for this woman. "Em," I called.

She looked back over her shoulder, confusion obvious in her expression, before she steered Beatrice back around and pulled alongside me facing the opposite direction. "What is it? Why did you stop?"

"Thank you," I said rather desperately, hands tightening reflexively on the reins. "Thank you for trying … and for thinking this through with me."

"Well, I was really the one doing all of the thinking," she deadpanned.

I allowed a small grin. "You know what I mean. Thank you for helping me with this … terrible situation. I feel completely out of my depth and incapable of finding a solution."

"Augie, that's what I'm here for. One of us has to be the brains in our duo." She winked before circling around. "Come on, I'll race you to the creek bed."

And before I could answer or respond to her ridiculous assertion, she was off.

I was helpless to do anything but follow.

A short while later, we were returning to the stables. The warm July sun had put some color on Emery's pale English cheeks and down the length of her nose. Her mother would be aghast when she saw her. Hopefully the dusting of pink would be gone by dinnertime, for Emery's sake. But I thought she looked gorgeous, all glowing skin and bright eyes. The weather suited her and helped improve my mood regardless.

The stables were still abandoned when we arrived. The grooms no doubt cataloged my odd request for privacy and extended their luncheon. I was grateful for their renewed absence when after securing Emery's horse in the yard and mine in his stall, I removed my saddle to the tack room and found myself alone with my betrothed.

Emery stalked toward me from the doorway. "I don't want to surprise you this time, so I'll just ask. Will you touch me?"

My mouth felt suddenly dry as I took her in, pink cheeks, wind-roughened hair, and those damn trousers shifting tight across her thighs as she moved closer.

She drifted into my space as comfortable and confident as always. My heart vibrated like hoofbeats at a gallop. Did she lack fear because she'd done this before? Asked a man to touch her. Or was she poised and at ease because she felt she had nothing to lose? That was at the heart of all my fears. Would things change? Could I lose Emery if everything fell apart? And would it cost me this false engagement, this looming marriage?

Her whiskey eyes moved between my own and some of that bravado fell away. "Augie, do you trust me yet?"

Unable to speak for the fear choking me, I nodded, because I did. I respected Emery enough to know her own mind. I could be truthful with her about this. And I was someone who learned from their mistakes.

She brought her middle finger to her teeth and bit down, pulling the fawn-colored kid glove from her hand before letting it drop to the ground. Her newly freed hand pressed warmly to the side of my neck before moving around my nape to play at the short hairs there. "Do you trust me?" she asked again.

This time I found my voice. "Yes." And then I closed the distance between us, wrapping both arms about her waist and pulling her in tight. Our mouths met at last and this time—this time—there was familiarity there. No hesitation. No awkward uncertainty. No surprise attack in a horse stall. We found our rhythm, lips moving in sync and my worries melted into the background.

I felt Emery's honesty in the way she pressed herself to me more fully, breasts warm and soft against my chest. I could hear her asking me to trust her, to believe her, to touch her.

So, I did.

My hold loosened around her waist only to reassert itself lower on her backside, drawing her up and against my erection. She moaned into my mouth but never ceased kissing me.

She felt so fucking good.

I took a moment to pull back and assess my surroundings. Emery made a small sound of protest before I moved us back toward the doorway. While there weren't stable hands and servants about, they could stumble upon us at any time. And while I appreciated my staff and their discretion in most things, this wasn't something I wanted gossiped about. I wanted Emery's pleasure for my own. She was not a spectacle to be had by any passerby.

Closing the door more forcefully than I meant to, I backed her up against it before hoisting her in my arms, the seam of her maddening breeches lined up to my straining manhood. She gasped when I gave an experimental thrust. "Is this still okay? You can tell me to stop, and I will. At any point."

She nodded. "I'm okay …" Emery trailed off, looking uncharacteristically shy for once. "I just don't know what I'm doing. I've never done this before."

I smiled before nuzzling my nose against hers. That question from earlier about the possibility of Emery with another man was answered and I felt dizzy with relief. "We'll figure it out together, yes?"

Finally smiling in return, Emery nodded.

"But clothes stay on, Emery. I'm not making love to you in the stables surrounded by hay and horses and God knows what else." I would worry about my phrasing and how Emery might interpret it later.

She laughed. "Okay, then." And then proceeded to tighten her thighs around my waist and dig her heels into my ass as she rubbed herself against my cock.

My head dropped back and I blinked unseeing eyes at the rafters as I focused on not coming in my pants. She laughed again but it turned into a surprised moan went I bent forward and sucked in the thin skin along her throat. Grinding my hips into hers, I found a rhythm that seemed to work for both of us. A time or two I slowed to lavish her neck with further attention or to move back to her mouth, but Emery quickly dug her heels in to keep me right where she wanted me. I was exceedingly thankful she was such an accomplished rider.

When she suddenly wrenched her mouth from mine and gasped out a ragged, "Augie," I moved just a little bit faster, hips circling, chasing my release as she was poised on the edge of her own. She cried out my name again, tightening her arms around my neck.

I pressed flush to her body then and ground my cock once, twice, three more times to her giving flesh before exhaling in a rush as my orgasm rushed through me.

Several moments later, I came back to myself, one hand grasping Emery's thigh still hooked around my waist, my other arm supporting her bottom. With awareness came the silence of the tack room and a growing wetness between our bodies.

"I'm going to lower you to the ground. Are you good to stand?" I asked, worried that awkwardness would overwhelm what had just happened.

"I'm fine," Emery answered too quickly.

I released her slowly before straightening, but I didn't step back to put space between us. I didn't think I was capable. Instead I asked quietly. "Are you?"

She looked me right in the eyes and said with every ounce of conviction, "I'm better than fine. *Trust me*." Emery cupped my cheek and placed a brief kiss to my lips.

Before I could do more than examine her features for any lingering discomfort or unease, I heard sounds from beyond the door. The grooms had finally returned.

Emery's eyes widened comically, then she whispered, "You on the other hand … I think I yanked on your hair as if it were a mane." She attempted to smooth the curls at the crown of my head before giving up. "And I think you're going to need some new trousers." She giggled quietly.

I mock glared at her before twisting behind me. "I think I have some riding breeches around here somewhere. Probably with my spare boots." After opening a few cabinets, I located the brown trousers. I made to unfasten the moist placket at the front of my pants but glanced up to see Emery staring at me.

"What?"

"What do you mean what? Can you turn?" I requested.

"What?!" An indignant laugh exploded out of her.

"Can you give me some privacy, please?"

"After what we just did, Augustus Ward, I can't watch you change your trousers?"

I glared at her rationale and felt my cheeks heat.

"My, oh my. That is a fierce blush. Fine." She turned to face the still closed door. "I'll do you this favor, Augie. You prude." She laughed quietly again. And I didn't even mind that she was laughing at me and my old-fashioned ways. She could see me naked when we were man and wife which we would be in less than six weeks. Perhaps by then she would be mine, in truth.

I wasn't foolish enough to think that some kisses and stolen moments meant anything to Emery, not the way they meant to me.

This was all new for her, the idea of us being more. I didn't think she was callous or unfeeling. I just didn't know if what we'd done meant *enough*.

Somewhere between remerging from the tack room with Emery at my side to helping her onto her horse and kissing her hand good-bye, I vowed not to read too much into her actions or what we'd done. Perhaps this was exploration for her or simply human nature, base attraction.

I didn't want to overwhelm her with the enormity of my feelings. I'd waited this long. I could keep waiting. We would have a lifetime together. Perhaps someday she could love me in return.

I knew control. I knew consistency. I could wait for the time to be right between us. There was no need to have a big discussion about the new physicality of our relationship. Admitting my feelings following an orgasm would only prove to be a poor decision. I would wait.

I knew Emery. If I pushed too hard or too fast, confronted her or overwhelmed her with feelings she wasn't ready to address ... I could lose her.

I knew I wanted forever with Emery. There was no reason forever had to start right now.

Nine

EMERY

"Well?" Augie asked softly, drawing my attention to his position between my spread thighs. If eyebrows could be smug, his would be. Especially the right one which was cocked arrogantly in my direction. "How was it?"

He damn well knew how it was. My shouts had been nearly impossible to smother. I was sure I'd broken the skin on my bottom lip in the effort. Augie had used that indecent mouth to deliver heated kisses and unrivaled pleasure to my most intimate places. It had been entirely wicked and utterly wonderful.

"I don't know that haughty looks favorable on you," I teased.

Augie laughed, placed a final soft kiss on the inside of my thigh, and sat back on his heels. After smoothing my skirt down from where he'd had it bunched up around my hips, he finally settled at my side, elbow propped and gaze intent as he looked down at me.

I was still immobile. I feared I'd be unable to move ever again. I lived in this tree house now.

Free hand coming to my cheek, he tilted my face gently and kissed me. I could taste myself on his lips, tangy and wild. After a moment, Augie stopped kissing me but stayed very close and whispered, "Did you like it?"

I didn't open my eyes yet but smiled in response. "You know I did."

He pulled back up and propped his hand under his jaw. "Well, I assumed so from all the screaming." I whacked him in the stomach with the back of my hand. "But a little feedback never hurts."

Finally finding the wherewithal to engage my muscles, I rolled to my side on the blanket and mirrored his pose. I noted his smug eyebrow had returned, but there was a hint of vulnerability there as well. Did he really not know how much I'd enjoyed myself this afternoon? "Augie, that was … I don't have words. The feel of your mouth, your tongue *there*. It was the most pleasurable experience of my life. I've enjoyed what we've done so far obviously. But I don't know what could possibly compare to your lips kissing and licking me so intimately." I paused a moment to let him absorb the compliment. And he did, the devil. His smile was a mile wide, blue eyes sparkling like gems. Then I spoke again, "Except for perhaps the feel of your cock. We haven't tried that yet."

Heat flared in his eyes and a warm flush brightened the crests of his perfect cheekbones. Augie was obviously slightly scandalized by the word *cock* on my tongue but, if I wasn't mistaken, he quite liked the obscenity coming from my lips. It was the first time I'd said the word aloud but it felt suitably timed. One couldn't spend the majority of her time in the stable around grooms and staff without picking up some unladylike words. I was grateful for my inappropriate education in this moment.

In the last three weeks, we'd met nearly every night in our secret place. While the tree house had been an innocent refuge in our adolescence, now it was quite defiled. But there was one line Augustus refused to cross. He had explored nearly every inch of my body, leaving pleasure in his wake. We'd touched and teased, but Augie would not make love to me until we were wed. After arguments and debates, I'd finally determined that he would not be swayed. Despite employing my wicked tongue to torment him just now, none of my previous efforts had swayed him either. He was adamant that we wait until our marriage bed became literal.

I could not see the difference. Augie knew the taste of my skin, the shape of my nipples, the sounds I made when I came undone. And yet he patently refused to take this final step with me. I shouldn't be surprised. He'd always been respectable to a fault. I was sure he berated himself nightly for the things he'd done to my body.

And for me, that was the crux of the matter. The things *he* had done to *me*. Augie wouldn't allow me to reciprocate. I knew what he *felt* like, hard and heavy against me, but I'd never seen him, tasted him. I wanted to learn his body the way he'd become a student of mine. The enormity of what was transpiring between us could be explained away through Augie's careful ministrations and experimentation. I didn't want that. I wanted to feel and touch and gasp and … and … scratch my nails down his back.

Augie was becoming an expert at my pleasure while I was learning nothing about his desires. Being the passive wallflower wasn't in my nature. I wasn't about to remain as such in the bedroom, much less in my own marriage. Augie could have his conservative ideals, but he needed to trust that I was in this as well.

I didn't know if this new intimacy between us was just passing attraction or something more for him. The way he went about seducing me with clinical precision made me unsure of his intentions. So much felt like trial and error. Today's experiment had been *How loud will Emery scream if I lick the seam of her sex?*

However, I was having a hard time separating my feelings from the affection we shared. The touches *meant* something to me. The fact that he stopped himself from giving in to the demands of his body made me question the source of his passion.

Was Augie merely passing his time with me, learning and enjoying a woman's body? Had he been with a woman before? A surprising rush of jealousy made my stomach clench. Pushing that thought aside, I considered my other concerns. What did this mean for our future marriage? And could I make our fake betrothal transition to a marriage in reality? Would Augustus even want that?

I didn't have any answers, and it was maddening. Was this how Augie felt all the time? At war with his brain, considering every scenario. It was exhausting.

We needed to talk. I needed answers. I didn't like all this wondering. I'd never had to worry about where I stood with Augie. Now everything was all muddled.

Blowing out a sharp breath, Augie ignored my purposeful baiting and I attempted to focus my attention on him rather than the multitude of questions running rampant through my head. "Shall we find out?" I taunted. "For comparison purposes, of course."

His unruffled stare told me he wasn't amused by my tactics but that lingering warmth on his cheeks told me he was thinking about it, what it would be like to pin me down and erase that final barrier between us and thrust inside.

God, now I was thinking of it.

"Fine. If you aren't going to make an honest woman of me, I need to go." I sat up and gathered my hairpins from the small table in the corner before twisting my hair back into a low chignon. "Mother is making me finalize the menu for the wedding breakfast over tea this afternoon."

Augie grimaced. "Sorry, that sounds awful."

I slid the final pin into place, fairly certain it would hold for the brief ride back. "Yes it does. And since this is also your wedding, I think you should accompany me and lend your valuable opinion on the matter."

He sat up slowly, reaching for the buttons on his shirt. I'd spent some time this afternoon seeing if his nipples were as sensitive as mine. Interesting fact: they were.

"I'm actually meeting with a few of our tenants this afternoon and walking the fields. Apparently John refused a request from them earlier in the summer. Anders brought a few things to my attention. I'm going to try to help."

I smiled. "That's good, Augie."

He nodded and looked away. "So ... see you back here tonight?"

"Yes, please," I replied earnestly, anything to banish that uncertainty in his tone.

He rose, wincing a bit. I noticed his erection still straining the front of his trousers. Augie rarely let me do more than graze his manhood before moving my hands away. Of the handful of times he'd reached completion, it had been like that very first time in the stables, from moving against me while fully clothed. His pleasure seemed only allowed if it was a side effect of my own. In his determination to bring me to climax, he would inadvertently trigger his own release. I hadn't puzzled out why Augie felt like he needed to satisfy me while denying his own desires. I couldn't decide if he was punishing himself purposefully or trying to compensate me in some way. With Augie, the reasons were likely layered and somewhat variable.

We would have a conversation about all of this soon. But not when his unspent longing was staring me in the face and not when he still had my wetness painting his chin. I wanted our discussion to be fully clothed and with no distractions. I needed honesty from Augie, not conciliations and seduction.

Truthfully, he didn't need to seduce me. I wanted him more than anything. I'd spent the majority of my life seeking Augie's friend-ship and company. Now that longing had merely changed shape. I craved his touch and his affection above all else.

However now, I wanted the ultimate prize.

His heart.

Tea and wedding planning that afternoon were relatively painless and uneventful. I simply agreed with all my mother's decisions.

I was currently in my bedchamber sorting through correspon-dence. Father's solicitor had sent two new commission requests for M. Barton and I was planning an outing this evening on horse-back to scout and research potential locations for the upcoming pieces. I would have time to wander the countryside a bit before meeting Augie.

Gansey bustled in with some freshly laundered garments and greeted me warmly. "How did it go this afternoon with your mother? I heard her talking to Mrs. Pennyworth about the options you'd chosen."

I rolled my eyes. "I didn't choose them and you well know it."

My friend laughed. "Everything is nearly settled, then. You'll be a married woman soon."

Gansey was right, but it didn't feel real. In under three weeks' time, Augie and I would begin our lives together. The nearby Barrington estate and accompanying lands were being readied for our arrival. We would have freedom from our families' expectations. We would be free to do other things as well.

"That's quite the blush, Emery," Gansey teased. "Thinking about being a married woman, are you?"

Fidgeting with the envelopes resting in my lap, I attempted to clear my throat. My face had always been too honest, too open. If it wasn't my expression giving me away, it was my mouth. It didn't help that I also lacked the ability to lie or deflect with any success. Keeping this secret from Gansey had already been difficult enough as it was.

Gansey's eyes widened. "Emery!" she whisper hissed.

"Shut the door, then," I conceded in exasperation, matching her volume.

She hurried over in her serviceable gray dress and closed the door to give us some privacy before turning back and sitting in the armchair closest to me. "What's happened?"

"Well," I said, unsure how to begin. "I thought about what you said before. About how my relationship with Augie was special and that most marriages don't have even an ounce of the affection we have for each other."

"Okay," she replied, drawing the word out.

"It just made me really look at Augie, you know? And when I thought of my life without him … well, I panicked a bit. I … kissed him." Gansey's eyes were round as saucers. "And he kissed me back." I fingered the edge of the paper in my hand, unable to meet Gansey's astonished face. "And we've kissed a lot."

Gansey was quiet following my pronouncement, so I looked up from the envelope I'd been stroking absentmindedly as I spoke. Her grin was enormous. "I knew it!"

I frowned, but she continued. "I knew you loved him." She actually clapped her hands together. "This is wonderful news. I mean, I knew you'd eventually figure it out, but I assumed it would be after you two were married and living together and I had front-row seats to the revelation. But this is good. Better even than—"

"Wait," I interrupted. "Gansey, I don't know what's happening."

Her bright smile dimmed a little. "What do you mean?"

"Well, we haven't really discussed it. The kissing. We've just been doing it."

The smile fell away completely now. "You haven't told Augie you love him and want to be his real wife?"

My throat felt dry all of a sudden, and it wasn't shame so much as pride that kept me from swallowing easily. "It hasn't come up."

"Emery, since when do you hide your feelings?"

"I'm not hiding them," I replied, feeling oddly scolded. Gansey could positively land the big-sister role when she applied herself. "I'm waiting for the right time. Augie has been so difficult about this betrothal. Half the time, I'm convinced he'll never go through with it. He has this misplaced sense of guilt and responsibility. I'm taking things slow. The way Augie does things … thoughtfully. He'll appreciate that. I don't want him to think I'm marrying him because I've been ruined and have no other options."

Gansey's eyes bulged. "Have you been ruined?"

"No!" I replied quickly. "Well, not really. Not in the official sense. But if we were discovered, Augie would marry me out of duty if he wasn't already going to marry me. I don't want that either. He's weighed down enough by familial obligation. I won't be one more person he feels compelled to answer to."

"I see." Gansey's skeptical tone made me glance up.

"I'll tell him. I will. I just think I need to take things slowly so I don't scare him off."

"I see."

"You know Augie. He'll think I'm being rash. If I give him time to acclimate to the idea of us, in truth, he'll see that I've really considered this decision and that I really do want to be his wife."

Gansey smoothed her skirts perfunctorily. "I see."

"He won't believe me when it's so new."

"I see."

"Stop saying *I see*!"

Gansey simply looked at me.

Finally setting the envelopes aside, I muttered, "I understand your concern. I know I'm not being myself."

"As long as you're aware."

"I am. And I'll handle it."

Standing gracefully, Gansey clasped her hands in front of herself. "Good. Because I've been waiting for this for a long time. Don't mess it up." With that pronouncement, she swept from the room.

After a moment, I huffed a laugh. She really was exceptionally bossy. I thought about what Patty might say if she were here. But with a sharp ache in my chest, I realized that my overbearing elder sister likely wouldn't know how to respond. It had been a long time since Patty knew me well enough to comment on the poor choices I was making. Gansey might have strong ideas regarding my relationship with Augie, but at least she cared enough to voice them.

With thoughts and feelings sufficiently jumbled, I gathering my sketchbook, charcoals, and smudging stick and made my way down to the stables. I'd work away the remainder of the afternoon, and then talk to Augie tonight.

The ride on horseback would help settle my nerves. The preliminary drawings for my new commissions would help me find control and focus. And the time outdoors would help silence the fears lingering in my mind.

Several hours later with a blanket spread before me, I looked back over the preparatory drawings in my notebook.

After a peaceful ride in the late afternoon heat, I'd found several suitable locations for my next two paintings. Occasionally, a patron wanted something specific for their M. Barton original, and I had to research, plan, and seek out an ideal setting to fulfill the commission requirements.

Of course at this point in my oddly notorious career, I could paint whatever I wanted and sell it in a London gallery. But I preferred working directly through our solicitor and by word of mouth, not through a gallery. The more people who knew my secret and interacted on the business side of the things, the less safe I felt in selling my work. Even when commission requests came in, I could decline. And I often did. But typically lords and ladies who were so desperate to acquire one of my paintings offered exorbitant funds in exchange for the novelty of owning one. Essentially they paid me hundreds of pounds to be able to brag to their aristocratic friends. I didn't begrudge them their boasting, but I did resent it. However, as the person who facilitated it, I couldn't really complain.

I freely admitted to having a complicated relationship with my artistic alter ego.

Nevertheless, I felt excited, as I always did, at the beginning of a project. Despite my impulsive behavior in other aspects of my life, I meticulously planned my artwork. These preliminary drawings would inform my composition and materials. Visiting and sketching at various times of day would help determine light and shadow and optimum color selection for when I began painting.

Satisfied with the progress I'd made today, I packed my supplies into my saddlebag and washed the charcoal dust from my hands in the shallow creek nearby. I mounted Beatrice Three and used the short ride in the waning light to organize my thoughts and considered how best to approach Augie.

When I arrived at the base of the tree house, he was there dismounting his horse. He smiled in greeting before assisting me from my own mount. I slid leisurely down the front of his body and he made no move to release me once my feet met the ground.

"Well, hello, my lord," I said cheekily. I could feel him, already lengthening against me.

"Hello, my lady." He kissed me in welcome.

When Augie finally pulled away, the sun was just sinking below the horizon. He was shadowed before me, the sky full of fading pinks and oranges behind him. What a painting he would make, a masterpiece for my eyes only.

"Did you miss me already?" I asked, amused by his attention and, in truth, feeling nervous for the coming conversation.

"Always," he replied as he straightened, giving me room to step away from Beatrice.

Augie's eyes seemed to snag over my shoulder before narrowing. I followed his line of sight to the saddlebag containing my drawing supplies. They'd shifted a bit on the ride apparently. The flap was askew and the edge of a notebook was sticking out, the blanket having moved below to crowd the other items near the top.

Augie stepped forward to peer at the drawing that had been partially unearthed. "What's this?"

I crossed to him immediately, attempting to right the satchel and hide the sketches from his view but I was too slow. He pulled the notebook out of the bag and spun away from me. "Did you draw this, Em?"

Realistically I knew that I could tell Augie this secret. He would do nothing with the information except support me and likely tease me for keeping it from him. But for some mad, irrational reason my breathing turned shallow and I could feel my heart beating in my throat. The idea of Augie finding out what a fraud and liar I was made my knees weak. I lunged for the notebook in his hands.

He turned to me in surprise but held the papers aloft and out of my grasp, enjoying this game. Either unaware of my distress or too surprised by my reaction to notice, he appeared ridiculously amused. "You did, didn't you? This is your drawing."

I ceased my desperate attempts to retrieve the notebook and stood straight, trying to appear nonplussed. I could be calm and collected, play this off. He'd never know I was a liar and an imposter. I could tell him the truth later, on my own terms. Not backed into a corner and surprised like this. I had plans for this evening, dammit. We had important things to discuss. If the truth behind M. Barton came out now, we'd never figure out our relationship. "Yes, Augustus. That is my drawing. I … dabble a bit. That's all."

He was still smiling. "Dabble?" he scoffed. "This is amazing. I've never seen you so much as lift a paintbrush. I thought you hated all this stuff."

"What?" I asked, genuinely confused.

He started idly thumbing through the other pages and scanning my artwork as if it wasn't a huge invasion of privacy. I didn't have a good answer as to why he could put his mouth between my legs but the thought of him seeing those drawings felt too intimate to contemplate. I made a squeak of alarm or injustice or both, and he finally looked up. "I thought you hated all the embroidery and watercolor painting, singing and playing the pianoforte. You know, all the activities for cultured young ladies. Are you putting forth an effort now to become a perfect society wife?" He laughed, not meanly, but as if in on a secret. A big secret joke. "Your mother will be thrilled, Em. All her efforts to make you more ladylike are finally coming to fruition. But I think the horse has already bolted the barn on that one. You are marrying me to avoid all that nonsense."

He'd resumed looking through the pages distractedly, so he didn't see my eyes welling nor my panicked reaction to the eminent tears. *Oh God.* I took a steadying breath and willed the wetness away. He didn't know. He couldn't possibly see how he'd hurt me.

I continued breathing and the tightness in my throat loosened its grip. The stinging behind my eyes melted away and still he kept turning pages without looking up. I didn't want him to see the pain he'd inflicted. It felt imperative to separate myself from weakness and emotion—those things young women were accused of so often.

"These are really lovely, Emery."

I even managed a cool "thank you" without clearing my throat or exploding in frustration. I should see about a position at the local theater house.

Carefully turning away, I secured my horse and continued to breathe evenly. I didn't even know why I was upset. I'd said those very things to Augie. I'd never applied myself in the feminine arts. Never indulged my mother's attempts to culture me and make me more appealing to potential suitors. Everything Augie had said was true.

I think the source of my pain lay in the mockery in his tone. It felt as if he took something meaningful and precious to me and degraded it, laughed about it. The dismissal I'd faced early in my artistic endeavors had left me bruised and tender where my paintings were concerned. I'd wanted Augie to see my work as something wholly separate from a lady's pastime. I bristled inwardly at the circumstances around his criticism. What would he know about the pressures of young women in society? Lord Augustus Ward, Earl Barrington and the brother to the Duke of Kendrick, required no additional skills to be made marriageable.

Even though I possessed talent with a pen and paintbrush, I had to hide my identity to receive any respect in my field. My artwork was only popular because everyone thought I was a man. Perhaps, in this moment, I resented Augie and his entire sex, for praising my abilities but withholding the credit I was due.

A tiny rational part of me thought … how could Augie possibly know of my interest in art? I'd never told him that my work gave me both stability and freedom. He, and everyone else for that matter, was ignorant of this part of my life. And whose fault was that but my own?

I needed to keep breathing so I wouldn't cry hot, angry tears. And I needed to distract Augie away from this topic.

Walking back to where he was standing, I plucked the sketchbook confidently from his grasp.

Augie frowned. "Wait, I wasn't done looking."

I slid my drawings back in the saddlebag and moved into Augie's space. "Well, I have something more interesting we can do."

Running my hands down his body, I made it to the front if his trousers before he caught my wrists. "Emery." It was a demand and a question and knowing, all rolled into one word.

I stepped back abruptly, hands raised in surrender. "Why do you always stop me from touching you? Do you not want me? Why do you withhold yourself from me, Augustus? Do you have any idea how that makes me feel?"

His eyes narrowed, assessing. "Is this really about touching me?" A pause. "Did I do something …" He glanced over at the satchel containing the sketchbook. A lingering look. And then his determined gaze snapped back to mine. "Emery, talk to me."

Augie was too intuitive for his own good. The disadvantages of knowing someone so thoroughly, I supposed. But I couldn't talk about that anymore. I wanted to move on from the topic of my drawings to the real discussion I'd planned this evening.

But now everything felt muddled. I was too emotional and off-balance to talk rationally over our relationship and intimacy. This was going all wrong.

The honesty I'd planned on sharing tonight had gotten lost somewhere, probably trapped along with the truth inside that saddlebag.

Instead of taking a deep breath and calmly explaining my new and confusing feelings, I opened my mouth and did what I always do … hurled my words with no consideration for where they'd land. "We're going to be married in three weeks. What does it matter if we fuck now or then?"

Augie looked stricken. He raised a hand to his mouth and scrubbed across his chin and along his jaw. "I guess," he started and then cleared his throat. "I guess it matters to me."

I couldn't stand the awful way he was looking at me, as if he regretted the last few weeks. As if he didn't know me at all. All the fire went out of me and I felt cold all over. I needed to salvage this. If I pushed him too far, he might call off the wedding. He'd been reluctant since the beginning.

I was ruining everything.

I was ruining us.

"I'm sorry, that was crass. That wasn't what I meant," I said.

But Augie cut me off. "No, you're right. I'm being hypocritical and setting arbitrary boundaries. That's not fair to you." He was still distraught, taking on all the blame for my outburst.

I stepped closer and reached for him.

And *God* he backed away.

I felt my panic rise like the tide. My bottom lip trembled and I bit down until I could trust it once more. "I'm sorry," I tried again.

Augie was already shaking his head. "You're right, Em. I'm only mad at myself. You're right, and we should take some time, I think."

No.

I didn't realize I'd spoken aloud until Augie countered. "Yes. Things have gotten intense. Confusing. We should take some time apart." He glanced over his shoulder to the tree house. I followed his gaze to the little structure and all it represented. When he looked backed to me again, he clarified, "Some time away from here."

Oh.

"You'll still marry me?" I blurted the question and could have kicked myself for the weakness and desperation in my tone.

Augie looked surprised again. "Of course. Yes, Emery."

I was ashamed to admit I felt relief then. Even angered or disappointed, Augie wouldn't lie to me. If our betrothal was safe, then there was still hope for our marriage. I could fix this mess. I had time. I had the rest of our lives.

In a small quiet voice, I asked, "Then why do we need to be apart?"

He scrubbed his hand across his jaw again, and my hand itched to scrape along his evening stubble there. "I just need you to trust me. I'm doing everything I can to keep our friendship safe."

I waited in the tree house every night for the next week but Augie didn't return.

Ten

AUGUSTUS

My palms were sweating as Mother and I ascended the front stairs of Laurel Park.

My mother slid me an odd look as she reached the landing. "Are you well, Augustus?"

"Yes, of course," I replied, attempting a smile.

Her eyebrows drew lower and she turned to face me more fully, but before she could question my response and my inability to produce a convincing smile, the door opened and Dalton welcomed us to the Bartholomews' foyer. "Lady Northcutt and Lady Emery are in the family room abovestairs. I'll escort you, my lord and Your Grace."

With one final frown in my direction, Mother made her way toward the staircase while I surreptitiously wiped my palms down the length of my trousers.

I needed to pull myself together, but I was anxious over seeing Emery for the first time in a week. We'd parted on such disastrous terms following our argument. I wasn't sure how I'd be received, and truthfully, I was ashamed of my behavior. Emery wasn't one to air dirty bedlinens in public, so I doubted she would be anything less than polite in front of our mothers. But I knew we needed to talk and address what was happening between us.

I should have realized that Emery wasn't going to settle for ambiguity in our changing relationship. Of course I was content to remain as I had been for several weeks past—kissing and touching and pleasuring Emery at every available opportunity. It was only natural that she wanted to discuss the new physicality happening or that she wanted to reciprocate. I didn't really have a plan beyond continuing on until we were wed. And then ... I didn't know. It was short-sighted on my part and entirely selfish. I could see that now. Not to mention a healthy dose of cowardice.

With our wedding still several weeks away, I had been unwilling to confess my feelings for fear of rejection. So I was content to act out my desires. All of them but one.

Just thinking back on Emery's unaffected question made me feel sick.

What does it matter if we fuck now or then?

I'd answered the only way I could at the time. It mattered to me. It still did.

I couldn't fuck Emery without her knowing the truth of my feelings—the breadth and depth of them. The thought of taking that final intimate step, of erasing every barrier between us, as some sort of experiment in attraction made my already anxious stomach roil. What I wanted was to make love in truth, as husband and wife with no more secrets between us. And without turning back.

I was a greedy bastard, desperate to cling to our friendship while fervently hoping that both everything and nothing would change.

That Emery would see me and my love and realize all the ways I could make her happy. I would dedicate my life and our future to keeping our relationship intact. I hadn't been lying about preserving our friendship. I simply wanted to watch it grow in love and change with us.

I never intended to deceive her with my intent. I wouldn't take pleasure for myself and make love to her until she knew of my feelings. It felt dishonest and misleading, and I respected Emery too much to be selfish in that regard.

Dalton cleared his throat and I realized I'd been standing just outside the informal receiving room on the second floor, consumed in my thoughts. I stepped forward and found my mother exchanging greetings with Lady Northcutt and Emery. She embraced my friend warmly and Emery looked surprised yet again by her display of affection. Mother was happy with our upcoming union. I didn't know why Emery couldn't see that.

But then she was looking at me, and *Christ*, she was so beautiful. I'd missed her.

Upon eye contact, her face momentarily betrayed her emotions. She appeared a mixture of eager and hopeful and heartbreakingly unsure. I'd put that uncertainty in her expression. Emery was the most confident person I'd ever known and my words and deeds had stripped her of that where our friendship was concerned.

I needed to make this right. I had to talk to her.

Our relationship was as natural as breathing, involuntary and effortless, completely out of our control. I could get us back there. I would.

Emery and I weren't meant to be apart. That inclination had been wrong following the scene outside the tree house. But I'd needed space. It had been too tempting to be around her. She was so eager and beautiful. All those weeks, touching and tasting. Emery was sensual and responsive. Watching her come undone was everything I'd ever dreamed. When I was with her, I wanted more. And knowing that she wanted that as well … I feared I wasn't strong enough to uphold my honor, my determination to not make love to her until she knew the truth.

I'd lashed out following her callous disregard and punished myself in equal measure. But I would make it right.

"Lady Northcutt, good day," I murmured in greeting.

"Hello, Augustus. Please join us. We have several details to go over before the wedding. Two weeks is not long at all. Emery, will you pour the tea, dear?"

"Of course, Mama," Emery replied before her big brown eyes met mine. "Hello, Augie."

In the face of her open expression, I found a smile within myself, one that I hoped said all the things I couldn't say in a room with our mothers. *I missed you. I'm sorry I was an idiot. You are so beautiful it hurts. Please forgive me. Let me keep you.* "Hi, Em."

Some of my unspoken desires must have translated because she took a relieved breath and gifted me a genuine smile in return. Knowing Emery as I did, hers likely said: *I missed you too. You are an idiot. We need to talk, don't shut me out again.*

Afternoon tea progressed easily as Lady Northcutt and my mother finalized wedding details. They were in matronly form and neither my nor Emery's presence was expressly required. We nodded when appropriate and Emery only nearly fell asleep once during the hour-long discussion.

When my mother made to rise and provide well-wishes for the remainder of the evening, I interjected smoothly. "Actually, Mother, I'd like to speak with Emery a moment. Some last-minute planning on our part as well."

Her worried frown from earlier in the afternoon made to return but Lady Northcutt cut in before it could materialize in full force. "Oh, do stay, Amelia. The children can visit out in the gardens. It's a lovely day. I'm sure there is more we could discuss."

Mother looked back toward Lady Northcutt and accepted her invitation before turning toward me once more, her expression curious. "I'll await you here, then."

"Thank you, Mother." With a quick kiss to her cheek, I made my way to Emery on the settee beside the marchioness. I offered my hand before requesting, "Shall we?"

My betrothed slipped her hand in mine and rose to standing. Her whiskey gaze lingered, and I prayed we could salvage our relationship and our future.

"Our mothers are behaving so oddly. They seemed to have put aside their ridiculous battle of one-upmanship in the interests of our union, but one never knows. I mean, who would have thought I'd consider their rational comradery to be odd behavior. Not that I'm saying I miss the disaster dinners." Emery's words were coming fast, tumbling over one another in an effort to fill the space between us. "Then again there may be a bloodbath to greet us upon our return to the drawing room."

She opened her mouth to continue her frantic, nervous speech but

I placed my hand over hers in the crook of my arm and uttered a quiet, "Em."

"Hmm?" She swallowed, still facing forward as we walked along the graveled path among the hedgerows behind the manor.

I pulled her to a stop ensuring my tone was soft and contrite before continuing. "Emery, I'm sorry."

She watched me struggle through my apology, eyes wide and uncertain. I'd done this to us, created this distance. Instigated it out of fear and weakness. I would never stop punishing myself for the uncertainty I'd put on her face. This face I knew and sought above all others. The face I saw in my dreams.

"I never meant to hurt you with my actions but that doesn't change the fact that I did. I'm sorry for keeping myself from you and for needing space. It was wrong. I missed you and … I never should have punished you that way."

Emery remained quiet. Her atypical lack of response only intensified my unease.

But I could fix this with my honesty. She might not be ready to hear how I loved and adored her but she might recognize the truth in my words if I spoke them. Emery might even understand my position on waiting to consummate the marriage. I never meant for her to feel unwanted or to think I was withholding myself for any other reason beyond my own worries and sense of duty.

I could tell her I loved her. Perhaps our friendship would change, but hadn't it already? We were lovers in a sense. But now the distance between us was expanding. My fears had already been realized. Maybe confessing my feelings could set us back on course. Bring us back to one another and make this marriage a reality.

I didn't claim to imagine that Emery loved me in return. How could she? She was vivacious and spirited, my opposite in every way. But I could love her enough for the both of us. I'd been doing that my whole life.

We could be happily married together. But only if Emery found her way back to me.

"Emery ... I want to tell you something. Just let me get it out and then we can talk about it or ignore it or whatever you think is best. Just ... hear me out."

She straightened and the uncertainty from before melted away as she nodded in earnest. I had her attention now and she was looking at me expectantly.

We'd meandered to the rear of the property near a field of wildflowers, and I turned with her past the last row of hedges. Just as I was gathering my courage to confess the truth, Emery's head twisted in the direction of the lane. A rider was approaching fast, dust trailing in his wake. Tracking the movement, I recognized the livery on the man astride.

Something had happened.

Emery grasped my hand and pulled me along the perimeter of the garden at a fast clip to the front of her home. The rider, George, was dismounting and running toward us. "My lord! My lord! Word arrived from London. It's His Grace. My lord, I'm sorry. But the Duke of Kendrick is dead."

I watched from the second-story window as the footmen loaded the carriage with our trunks. I'd stood in the same spot weeks ago and watched my brother's carriage loaded in a similar manner. At the time, I'd felt a troubling sense of relief at his departure. My emotions now were equally troubling and still quantified by a profound sense of relief. But on the heels of that emotion, I was overwhelmed by guilt.

And so the cycle went. That was how it had been for the last several hours. The sun was beginning to set and I was still in this drawing room with my weeping mother after learning the news of my brother's death.

The Duke of Kendrick had been killed at a gaming hell in London. Murdered over a game of cards. John was accused of cheating and with both nobles well into their cups, cooler heads neither prevailed nor interceded. My brother and his accuser brawled on the floor of the club. The offended viscount produced a blade at some point, and after an unfortunate roll during their wrestling match, John ended up with a knife in his throat.

The viscount was too drunk to know what he'd done and too aristocratic to face any sort of justice. My brother's death was senseless. An absolute waste. I could hardly fathom it.

When my father died a decade ago, I'd felt grief. Sorrow for the man I had loved all my life. It was complete and all-encompassing. Heartache in its most basic form.

No one tells you what it would be like to lose someone with whom you have a complicated relationship. With my father, all the good outweighed his loss. And with John … I was having a hard time remembering anything good. All my hurt was trapped below a lake frozen over with relief and anger and guilt and indifference. There were so many emotions vying for dominance that my brain was unable to settle on one.

My mother's quiet sobs made me simultaneously angry and ashamed. Livid that she could mourn such a monster of a human being, and mortified that I was unable to grieve a brother because it was the right thing to do, the loyal thing to do. My mixed emotions were suffocating every good memory I had of John. We must have had happiness in childhood together but I couldn't find it now, in this room with my crying mother.

Leaning my forehead to the cool glass of the window, I closed my eyes and took a deep breath. After I'd been whisked away from Emery and the gardens of Laurel Park, I'd returned with Mother to our estate to speak with the servants who'd arrived from London. I couldn't even remember saying goodbye to Emery. There was a blank space in my memory where the carriage ride should have been.

To spare her the gruesome details, I'd urged my mother to retire for the time being. However, she'd refused to be excluded from the discussion. She had grown paler during the recitation of events and John's last moments. But she still found the where-withal to mourn her son. Perhaps the bond between parent and child was more substantial than whatever existed between siblings. I couldn't find a thread of connection between John and myself if I tried. Our relationship had always been fraught with power struggles and cruelty and jealousy. What did it say about me that I was unable to remember my brother fondly?

Perhaps John didn't deserve to die, but did he deserve my bitterness after his death? I didn't know.

When I finally raised my head from the glass, the sun was making its very last effort along the horizon, and I was alone in the drawing room with my mother. The servants had vacated at some point and the crying had ceased. The Dowager Duchess sat slumped near the unlit fireplace with a glass of something amber in her hand, expression tired and lined.

She might be ready to talk.

"Mother, what can I do?"

She stared at the drink in her lap. "We'll need to go to London tomorrow to meet with the solicitors and prepare for the funeral."

I moved to sit beside her on the small sofa. "Yes. Our things have already been arranged and the carriage loaded."

"Oh," she said, seeming lost. "Thank you for taking care of that."

I nodded, the guilt swelling once again in my chest. I didn't deserve her thanks. I'd been able to make plans and requests of the staff because I wasn't overwhelmed by grief.

My mother finally raised her gaze to mine. Blue eyes just like my own. Just like John's. "We should move forward with the wedding." I made a sound of protest but she gave her head a swift shake before speaking over my protest. "We shall. It's for the best. You are the duke now, Augustus. You need to put on a strong front. Taking a wife and producing an heir is of the utmost importance. Especially now …"

Swallowing my objection, I felt something rise to swallow the guilt. Something that felt very close to panic. I was so wrapped up in my own complicated emotions following the news of John's death that I failed to consider the ramifications of my succession. My mother's assertion that the wedding must continue shone light on the consequences of my brother's death in an entirely new way.

I was now Augustus Ward, the Duke of Kendrick. And Emery would be my wife.

The wife of a noble and a peer of the realm.

A future she neither wanted nor asked for.

Once again climbing through the narrow opening in the floor of the tree house, I pulled myself up slowly, dreading this conversation. Lamenting the words that I feared wouldn't come. How could I say what needed to be said? How could I let Emery go?

I took in the surroundings before me. Candles glowing softly over a sleeping Emery curled up on the blanket along the far wall.

Crawling closer, I finally settled on the floor near her head. I pushed her hair back behind her lovely ear. Is that what infatuation did? Made you think of ears as lovely?

Christ, I wanted to keep her.

Emery's breaths were slow and even. The hour was late. She'd waited for me. My throat tightened at the implications.

I'd been up talking to the servants, relaying the news of John's death that had already circulated through gossip and rumors. But it needed to be done. I'd spent the remainder of the evening writing letters to the same end.

I couldn't find it within myself to mourn my own brother but my heart was grieving a loss of a different sort, the one right here in this tiny room.

But first I was going to count her eyelashes and stroke her cheek. I was going to commit to memory the shade of her hair in the candlelight and the feel of her small hands in mine. And then I was going to let her go.

Emery looked so young. Her face was relaxed and soft in a way it never was when she was awake. I didn't realize until this moment, but perhaps Emery guarded her countenance more than I knew. Seeing her now, so peaceful, she lacked the confident expression she often wore. The teasing light, the expectant air. I wanted to know what she looked like upon first waking. I longed to see her regard in all its forms. What would Emery look like on her wedding day? After the birth of her first child?

I wouldn't know. I couldn't.

Clenching my jaw in frustration, I smoothed her hair once more over her shoulder and then took her hand in mine. When I felt an answering squeeze, I inhaled sharply. Emery was staring at me. She sat up slowly, positioning herself beside me and gathered my hand to her once more.

"What happened?"

I knew she meant in regards to my brother. I knew what she was asking. So I told her. I relayed the story. She took in the account with a stoic expression, a slight frown that remained unmoved.

When I was quiet once more, Emery finally spoke. "You can tell me."

I frowned in question. "I just told you. That's all I know. All they told us."

"No. You can tell me what you're feeling. What you haven't been able to say all afternoon."

I just looked at her for a long moment before exhaling a long breath and turning away. "I don't know, Emery. I'm feeling every-thing. I feel relieved that he's gone and can never hurt anyone ever again. Then I feel guilty. I think back to my final parting words to my brother—my blood—and I … I … I feel ashamed that I cannot seem to scrounge up some happy memory of John." My words started off full of emotion and frustration, but concluded quietly and disjointed, tumbling over one another, reflecting the tumult within. Pushing a frustrated hand through my hair I continued speaking my truth to the one person who wouldn't judge me for it. "There's just too much. And none of it is appropriate. None of it acceptable."

"Says who?" came her cautious reply. She measured her words carefully as if they were in danger of spilling over. "There is no right or wrong way to feel when you lose someone, Augie. Your relationship with your brother was complicated in life. Why wouldn't it also be complicated in death?"

I squeezed her hand tightly. Emery pulled my body in close before wrapping her arms around me. She offered comfort for myself and not for my loss. I didn't know how I could tell the difference, but I could. Another one of the dangers of knowing someone so thoroughly. She confirmed her loyalty when she whispered in my ear, "I'm sorry you're hurting right now, Augustus. I'm sorry your brother has taken so much from you and that, even now, he's still able to punish you for it."

I considered what John had taken. My devotion and sibling worship as a boy. My relationship with my father, re-cast to belittle and demean. My confidence and my decisions.

But there was something my brother was giving me in return after all: a title. And the consequence of which would take my future from me now.

It was time to do what I came here for. There would be no more garden confessions or stolen moments of intimacy. I needed to remind Emery that I would be duke. And the life she wanted with me, the one I'd promised, was gone. Just like my brother.

Eleven

EMERY

Augie loosened his grip and maneuvered himself out of my embrace—my chokehold really. I didn't know how to comfort my friend in this moment. There were so many layers to the duke's death. So many things I couldn't say. The man had been a menace, a delinquent. A tormentor of women. And a frightful bully who eroded the sensitive heart of my closest friend. John could have had a devoted brother and lifelong supporter in Augustus. Instead he'd acted as a tyrant and made an enemy of me for life. It was undoubtedly a character flaw that allowed my grudges to rule over my heart, but I didn't believe in second chances, and I knew in my very core that the Duke of Kendrick got exactly what he deserved.

While my concern for Augie was true and genuine, there was no love lost between John and myself. Any sympathetic platitudes I could offer were unlikely to read as sincere. I lacked the acting ability to express proper regret for the death of that wastrel, Augie's brother or not. My concerns lay with the man at my side. My only concern.

When Augie's father, the old duke, passed away years ago, mourning had required no forethought. It had been merely a reaction. I hadn't needed to consider ways to comfort my friend, for there was no comfort to be had. We'd simply grieved together, in quiet and contemplation. It was nearness and understanding more than anything else that seemed to ease Augie's pain. He'd needed a witness more than a participant. And that's the truth of comfort, finding it within oneself to be exactly what someone needs.

Now, I was only able to give my friend closeness because I would never understand the varied and complicated emotions plaguing him. And I didn't wish to lie to Augie with false sympathy and pretty words with no meaning behind them. I could offer support because it was Augie's hurt I wished to eradicate, not the loss he experienced.

Finally released from my hold, Augie cleared his throat roughly. "We need to discuss something, Emery."

Something in his tone gave me pause, but I replied nonetheless. "All right."

Augie seemed unable to meet my concerned gaze, his blue eyes alighting briefly around the room before finally settling on his hands, twisted together in his lap. "I'm leaving for London in the morning. Mother and I are meeting with our solicitors and stewards. The funeral will be there as well. And now that … now that I am duke, arrangements need to be made."

I'd known Augie would assume the dukedom. John had no heirs or even bastards as far as anyone knew. Of course I'd known Augie was now the Duke of Kendrick. But it had been an abstract sort of realization. Common knowledge in the back of my mind with little impact at present due to the other thoughts vying for attention.

The ramifications of Augie's new role were floating indeterminately somewhere that I couldn't grasp. But when Augie finally brought his gaze to mine and said slowly, "I'm the Duke," a line snapped taut and tethered the implications to his cautious pronouncement.

I nodded because it seemed to be expected, but I could feel the blood leaving my face. He was Kendrick now. I understood that. Things would change. Why was Augie looking at me like that? Like he was apologizing. As if he'd broken something precious and was presenting me with all the pieces.

"Emery." His exhale was ragged. "We cannot marry. I can no longer give you the life I promised. The kind of future you envisioned when we concocted this scheme." His words were measured and even, rehearsed. Augie had practiced telling me this. Something about that manner of foresight broke my heart a little.

I shook my head reflexively because what he was saying sounded shallow and disloyal. He expected me to accept this new version of events and abandon him. Was that what he was suggesting?

Augie grabbed my hands and squeezed. "Think about it. This is exactly the life you were trying to escape. The London season, the balls, the gossip and backstabbing. Being the perfect hostess. My presence will be required in the House of Lords. My responsibilities just increased infinitely. I will need to live in London at least the majority of the year." I made to protest but Augie pushed on, heedless of the tears welling in my eyes. "Our quiet future in the country, at the Barrington estate, will never be, Emery. Can't you see that?"

"It doesn't have to be—"

But he cut me off with a frustrated sound. "You would be miserable. A future you never wanted nor asked for. That's what you said."

"When did I say that?" I demanded, cheeks wet. "Why are you doing this? Of course I still want to marry you. This changes nothing, Augie." But he was right. John's death had doomed all of our plans. To escape our families' expectations and live our lives in freedom. Augie was now one of the highest-ranking members of the aristocracy and would need a duchess befitting his station. My chin wobbled at the repercussions.

I didn't know if I could be who Augie needed me to be. London and high society made me feel lesser somehow. My confidence abandoned me and revealed my crass demeanor and inappropriate … everything. I didn't fit in. I didn't belong there.

But … perhaps for Augie I could. He was the most important person in the world to me. I couldn't leave him to navigate the treacherous waters of the peerage on his own. He needed a partner, and I could be that for him. Not to mention the love growing and swelling between us. It felt like everything was just beginning. We were lovers. I wasn't ready for this to be over.

Brushing my hand angrily across my cheek, I resented my stubborn tears. Resolving to fight back, I demanded, "You cannot decide arbitrarily what I'm willing to accept. I won't allow you to behave the martyr and fall on your sword to spare me from some hypothetical future. We could still be happy, Augie. You and I. There is so much more happening between us—" I broke off to dash away more angry tears.

Augie looked abruptly alert and panicked. "What do you mean?"

But I wasn't prepared to confess my feelings right then, and beg him to be mine in truth. Too much had happened. He was already overwhelmed dealing with his grief and his guilt. I refused to be one more catastrophe hanging over Augie's head. Dealing with death and change would be too much for anyone. I would not be selfish right now with my intentions nor would I make Augie question my loyalty.

We would marry, dammit. And I would do everything I could to be the duchess Augie needed. I would take bloody comportment lessons if I needed to. We didn't have the kind of friendship where abandonment was an option. And my sense of loyalty would not allow Augie to believe he could be less to me because of a title he'd never let himself want. He would be a wonderful duke, one who actually cared about the bills going through Parliament and who wanted better lives for those under his purview.

Augustus was made for this position. And I would never hold him back. He'd taken such care to provide me a future. I could do the same for him.

Straightening my shoulders, I let determination color my tone and strengthen my voice. "I refuse to let you break this engagement. I'm not giving up on our future together. If it's in London, so be it. I'll work on improving my waltz. And I'll support you every step of the way."

"No. You don't know what you're saying, what you're agreeing to. I refuse to make you unhappy in this. Our agreement no longer benefits you."

"Hang the agreement, Augustus. I'm a grown woman and I know what I want. I know it's not what we discussed or agreed upon at the beginning of the summer. But things change. So much has changed." Breath catching, I continued, "I want to be there for all of it."

He looked startled and confused, hair a riot of curls from exasperated fingers. Augie thrived on planning and expectations. He'd clearly entered this tree house with the express purpose of breaking our engagement and sacrificing himself for the greater good … for me.

He should have known better than to dictate to me.

I was nothing if not unexpected. With a great propensity to ruin the most carefully laid plans.

I startled awake when I heard voices. Augie was whispering frantically to an animated Anders. Why was Anders in our tree house?

My foggy brain roused all at once as I sat up in alarm. The last thing I remembered was being wrapped up in the blanket and the warmth of Augie's embrace. Once he'd realized I wasn't going to stand for being turned aside, he'd reluctantly admitted that his mother wished to proceed with the wedding celebration although as a more subdued affair with only family and very close friends. I agreed with the plan and assured Augie that we'd have time to discuss everything upon his return from London but that I would not be changing my mind. He was stuck with me.

After that, we'd snuggled together on the blanket. Augie seeking comfort as I sought reassurance. I needed to know we were still in this, and feeling the stubble on his weary jaw and the firm shoulder beneath my head, went a long way in giving me faith in our future. Augie talked and I'd listened. Everything from his boyhood with John to the most recent quarrels they'd had this summer. It turned out that Augie *could* recall happier times from his youth. The guilt and anguish in his tone was heartbreaking.

But I'd remained quiet, simply being present for his thoughts to work themselves out aloud. We must have fallen asleep as the night wore on.

At my movement, Augie became aware of my attention and turned from Anders. "We have to go. Anders and Gansey came to retrieve us lest we are discovered absent from our bedchambers."

"Gansey is here?" I questioned, looking around the small space but I could only spy a beleaguered Anders.

"I'm out here," came a disembodied voice from outside. "Now hurry up. We need to get you back."

I stood up as much as the space allowed and greeted Anders warmly. He'd always been a good friend to Augie. "My lady," he replied, looking everywhere but at me.

I tugged my wrapper tighter about my dressing gown before the three of us descended the tree house ladder, blowing candles out in our wake.

Gansey waited with a lantern and put-upon expression. I suppressed my laughter because now was definitely not the time.

"Your Grace," she muttered in Augie's direction, and his step hitched noticeably before finding his footing again.

"Good evening, Gansey." His reply was choked and uneven. Was this the first time someone had addressed him using the honorific since learning of his brother's death? Surely not. Perhaps it was merely the first time it had registered.

I reached down and grasped his warm hand in mine, offering a tight squeeze palm to palm before lacing our fingers together.

"What time is it?" I inquired as our little band walked purposely through the wildflower field.

"Just after four. The maids will be about shortly," said Gansey, censure obvious in her tone.

"What are you doing here together?" I eyed Anders and Gansey suspiciously. "And how did you know we were missing? How did you even know where we were or that we were together?" My steps slowed as I thought through the curious turn of events this very early in the morning.

Anders and Gansey shared a look. I glanced at Augie to see if he'd noticed as well. His eyebrows were high on his forehead. I made a face somewhere at the intersection between horror and hilarity. I feared it would manifest itself into a rather unladylike snort.

"Well? Aren't you going to tell us?" Augie asked.

Anders sighed mightily but finally responded. "I've always known. I remembered this tree house from when you were children. It's not as if you escaped your respective homes with any covert stealth. You've been sneaking out for weeks. But you always returned. Tonight we were concerned and combined forces to bring our lost lambs home."

Gansey snorted. "You just need to accept that we know all."

Augie nodded sagely in the light from the lamp. "I've always thought you were overwhelmingly astute, suspiciously so."

My maid returned his nod and gifted him a small smile, softening slightly under his appraisal. It was my turn to snort. Gansey's head snapped in my direction. "I'll deal with you later."

Augustus, the traitor, huffed a surprised laugh and then tried to cover it with a cough just as we reached the border to our neighboring properties.

I used our linked hands to pull Augie to a stop a few feet from our interloping friends. "Be careful in London. I hope things go smoothly with the transition."

He sobered before nodding. "Thank you. We'll talk when I return, yes?"

"Yes," I agreed. I hugged him tight, my arms around his middle. "But you're still marrying me. There's no getting out of that."

Augie's arms clutched me in return. "You're a menace."

"You better believe it," I teased.

He pulled back to meet my gaze, serious once more. "Thank you for today."

I nodded, unsure of actually having done anything helpful. But I would accept his gratitude even though it wasn't required. Augie was such a singular creature. To be his partner would be a joy and a feat. "When do you think you'll return?"

"I don't know. No more than a week, I would imagine." He looked unsure again, like the Augie of my youth.

I didn't want him to look so worried and uncertain, especially not when attempting to formulate a suitable farewell. So I reached on tiptoe and brought my lips to his. A breath shy of making contact, I said, "I'll miss you." I felt my mouth graze his as the softly spoken admission landed warm across his lips.

Augie closed his eyes then. I felt his free hand cradle my jaw, warm and comforting. And then he was kissing me, crossing that barely there distance to give me the goodbye I deserved.

"Genevieve, what's the matter?" I asked my sister as she sat moodily at the breakfast table.

"Nothing," she replied in that aggrieved manner that only young adolescents could manage.

To be honest I was feeling similarly sulky. Augie was still in London following his brother's funeral. It had been eight days already. He'd written to say that he would return soon. But his duties and his new position felt bigger and more time consuming than he realized. I was concerned. Our wedding was, after all, in less than a week. And I was also nervous. If even Augie felt ill prepared for the peerage, then I had no hope of managing. Anxiety gripped my stomach painfully and I pushed away my plate.

Gen sighed from her position across from me. I quirked a brow but said nothing.

It was Sunday, and the majority of the staff had the day off. I imagined I knew what ailed my sister on this particular morning.

"Are you perhaps feeling lonely, dear little sister?"

She scowled, either at my singsong tone or my reference to her being the baby of the family.

"Come. Spend the day with me. We can go riding. There are lots of places to explore. Or we can retreat to the library and read away the day." In truth, I needed to make some progress on my commissions. The composition didn't feel quite right just yet. But I sensed that my sister needed me. It had been a while since we'd spent time together, just the two of us. She was always with Julian, and didn't seem to need me as much anymore.

With another long-suffering sigh, Genevieve finally relented.

"Fine. We can go for a ride. But pack some of those little orange cakes I like while Mrs. Pennyworth is away at church."

A few hours later, my sister and I were situated under the shade of a large oak tree on the far side of Laurel Park. We'd ridden and raced for a time, then walked and talked for even longer. The soft quilt allowed us to spread out with our books and our orange cakes as the warmth from the August sun made for an exceedingly pleasing morning.

I'd just turned the page, book propped on my knees when Gen said apropos of nothing, "She doesn't want me spending time with him."

I looked over to my sister in confusion but her gaze was still firmly on her novel.

Pushing up onto an elbow, I gave her my full attention. "Who?"

"Mrs. Moore. She doesn't like that Jules and I are friends. He's never allowed to see me on Sundays. His mother says they must attend church and visit her family in the village. But I know it's because she doesn't like me." Gen looked so young and vulnerable. I'd come to think of my baby sister as a lady. At fourteen, she was beautiful in the way women were who rarely care for such things. Her lovely light brown hair gleamed and fell pleasantly with very little effort on her part. Genevieve got her blue eyes from our mother and she had the longest eyelashes you'd ever seen. I used to tease her when she was seven or eight and call her my little doll, so fine was her porcelain skin and wide gaze.

But her confession stripped away some of that maturity and the young woman staring down at her lap resembled a shy girl more than anything.

Closing my book, I sat up fully. "You don't know that, Gen." I sought to comfort her, but I tended to agree with her assessment. I'd seen Mrs. Moore with her son. She was strict and exacting. She often warned him to mind his manners and his place. It was quite obvious she did not approve of the friendship between Julian and Genevieve.

I'd always considered Jules one of the family, and treated him as such. He'd been on the receiving end of my pranks and teasing over the years, and even my sisterly advice a time or two. One could hardly interact with Genevieve without Julian in attendance. They were joined at the hip.

Genevieve didn't often seek me out, as she had a friend so readily available in Jules. But we'd been very close growing up. I could remember being completely enchanted when Gen was born. I'd been seven at the time and called her *my* baby. I'd wanted to rock her to sleep every night and had likely driven the nurse mad with my interfering every time my baby sister cried.

Genevieve was very much on the verge of tears now. She sniffed delicately before replying, finally looking in my direction. "I do know that, Emery. I've heard her talking to Jules. She doesn't think our friendship is appropriate. That Julian should be with children in the village and I should keep away from him."

"Mrs. Moore is a hard woman, you know. She's had a difficult life being widowed so young, raising a son on her own while working to support them both. She's likely just cautious and doesn't want Julian to get hurt." Augie's words from weeks ago floated back to me, questioning the friendship between them, seeing something more to be concerned over. I didn't think my sister harbored romantic feelings for Jules. But what did I know?

Clearly very little because Genevieve asked suddenly, "When did you know you wanted to marry Augie?"

"Um … well—" I attempted.

But she cut me off before I could formulate a response. "Because I know I'm going to marry Julian. I love him. I can't imagine marrying anyone else. Not some old lord or some dandy from London. Jules is who I want. Who I'll always want." Her tone was defensive, needlessly so. I was not ever going to be the person to tell Gen what she could or couldn't do. Nor who she could or couldn't love.

"And does he love you as well?" I didn't soften my tone. I didn't want her to think I was building up to a rebuttal. My voice was direct and even.

Her gaze dropped at my question. "I don't know. We haven't discussed it. All he cares about are horses anyway."

I smiled at her disgruntled yet age-appropriate reply. "That's okay. You have plenty of time. There's no need to rush." I hesitated a moment, unsure if I should voice my thoughts and draw the comparison to myself and Augie. I didn't want to give my sister false hope. Because there was a world of difference between me marrying Augie and Genevieve marrying the housekeeper's son. But I pushed on anyway. "Your friendship with Julian is very special, Gen. That connection will grow and evolve if you take care of it. And who knows what will happen in the future."

And who knew? With two sisters holding high-ranking positions in society, perhaps my sister would be free to pursue her heart.

She looked pensive and I knew she was considering how my relationship with Augie had developed over time. My sister wanted to look in my direction and see her own future reflected back at her.

I didn't know the path Gen and Jules would take. But I prayed, for my sister's sake, that it wouldn't end in heartbreak.

Only time would tell.

Finally nodding, she settled back again on the blanket with her book. "Would you please pass me an orange cake?"

"I can't," I replied solemnly.

"What?" came her indignant question.

"We ate them all."

"You mean *you* ate them all. Honestly, Emery. You have to fit into a wedding gown next week."

I squawked in mock outrage. "Just for that I'm going to eat this very last orange cake that I was saving for you."

Genevieve lunged for my arm in an attempt to steal the treat I held aloft, laughing all the while. She managed to pin my skirts to the blanket and draw my hand containing the cake close to her face. In our frantic scrambling and hoarse laughter, I smashed the orange frosting onto her nose and mouth. My sister collapsed in a fit of giggles licking the sugary icing from her lips.

I finally handed over the remaining bits of cake from my palm. "Here. It already has your face all over it." She laughed again and then shoved the whole thing in her mouth in a most unladylike fashion.

I smiled at her ridiculousness. She reminded me of me at that age. Wild and unconcerned with societal conventions or ladylike demands. Genevieve had always been a bright spot in my life. After Patty was married off, it had just been the two Bartholomew sisters. I thought back to that little baby in my arms, and then the toddler chasing after me, and the little girl often begging for my attention.

I'd never really considered having children of my own someday. Before this madcap plan with Augie, I'd never expected to wed of my own volition. But perhaps a family was in our future. That might be nice. I wondered if Augie would want children with me. We would be married after all.

Abruptly my thoughts shifted. Of course Augie and I would have children. He was the Duke. He would need an heir.

My stomach twisted as I considered once again the demands of a duchess. Bearing sons was just one of the things expected of me now. It had felt a lot simpler when I was thinking about a hypothetical baby with my blond hair and Augie's curls. A tiny face with his impossibly blue eyes.

I looked over to find Genevieve's expression still open and happy from our antics and the joy of smuggled cakes. I thought of her friendship with Julian and what the future had in store for them. And I prayed their path wouldn't be as complicated and muddled as the one Augie and I were currently on.

Twelve

AUGUSTUS

"Augustus, did you hear me?"

I looked up, finally noticing Anders from his position near the wardrobe.

"The patterned waistcoat or the solid cream velvet?" He spoke slowly as if concerned, and it became obvious this was not the first time he'd inquired after my preference.

I blinked and replied, "The solid, please." Best to go with traditional. Since I *was* getting married today.

Anders's worried frown followed me as I moved to the mirror. My hair was a disaster. Too much anxious tunneling from restless fingers. I attempted to tame the longer chestnut curls on top. Anders was still looking after my reflection. "I'm fine," I asserted.

With lips in a tight line and eyebrows raised, he turned back toward the wardrobe.

I *was* fine.

I was *fine.*

I was just nervous. And worried. Also a little concerned that Emery was making the biggest mistake of her life.

Shaking my head, I could not believe I'd let her talk me out of calling off the wedding following John's death. But she'd dug in her slippered heels. And if I knew Emery at all, when she set her mind to something, she would not be swayed. I'd unknowingly triggered the very heart of her with the idea that ending the betrothal would be disloyal. Emery never backed down from a challenge, and I should have foreseen her reluctance to award London and the *ton* victory over her. Alas.

We were getting married. Today. Shortly. I glanced at my pocket watch. In ninety-six minutes.

If I could manage to wrangle my worries, I might be astounded that Emery and I had pulled this off.

I was marrying the love of my life today who was unfortunately none the wiser.

Everything had gotten so turned around. I'd wanted to tell Emery of my feelings, but then circumstances had spiraled out of control. From our interruption in the gardens to the days following John's death … it was all changing so fast. I had truly intended to call off the wedding and release her from the obligation of marrying me. But then she'd remained unmoved, and I'd been away for too long tending to business and duties in London. Having only returned two days prior, everything felt so rushed and stressful. The wedding was already in motion. Yet, I'd still hoped to continue our conversation and talk her out of this madness. But there was no time and she wouldn't hear of it. All we'd done was quarrel since my return, until Emery stubbornly refused to see me until we met at the altar.

She'd forced my hand. But as conflicted as I remained, there was a tiny flame of hope that lived within. I was still marrying my best friend, and part of me reveled in that fact. Her willingness to support me through the trials that lay ahead, made me simultaneously relieved, grateful, and morose.

I didn't want to need Emery, but when had I ever not? She had always been first and foremost in my mind. Now she would bear my name and share a home with me. It was every fantasy realized.

All but one.

But how could I tell her I loved her now?

She was so convinced that she needed to support me, and as a result, doomed to lead a life she never wanted. I refused to tie her to me further. What if admitting the truth of my heart gave her one more reason to stay? Another life she didn't ask for but felt too loyal to abandon? What if she tried to force herself to love me in return? I couldn't tolerate her pity or worse, her understanding. I'd rather carry on as we had been, friendship with an added layer of physicality.

I didn't want to pressure Emery. If she wanted to take pleasure for herself and that's all she ever wanted, it would be enough.

I couldn't confess my love and earn her sympathy as a result. I feared it would destroy everything good and true between us.

True to her threat, I met Emery at the altar.

Since arriving at the little country church, I was oddly calm. Resigned was not the right word, for I was neither disappointed nor stoic in the face of the day. I felt conflicted, but my heart beat steadily in my chest. My breaths were even and my hands neither shook nor fidgeted.

I had imagined I'd be an anxious mess and perhaps that path was still before me. But when Emery floated down the aisle wearing the brightest, knowing smile in existence, well, any nerves that were threatening just sort of evaporated.

She looked so beautiful. But more than the elegant cut of her blush-pink gown or the graceful curls adorning her head, Emery radiated confidence and sheer happiness. She looked as if she had a secret—which, fair, she actually did—and we were the only two people who knew it. It was being solidified by association, unified in mystery, and everyone else in the world was excluded. I felt powerful and connected, and so very alive.

The ceremony progressed as they often do. I hardly recalled anything beyond Emery's eyes and her lips, and in one instance the vicar had to clear his throat to gain my attention.

We were surrounded by a small gathering of family members and a few friends of our mothers, but I was unaware of it all. Emery had my attention and my heart.

Following the marriage proceedings, our families gathered at Laurel Park for the wedding breakfast. Nearing midday, I found myself surrounded by Bartholomews. Silas had returned from the continent to attend our nuptials and was encircled by his siblings, all eager for his company. Patricia was also in attendance which I knew Emery would have mixed feelings about. Her cautious hopefulness was difficult to watch. But Silas's presence was a wonderful distraction. I'd known him my whole life. Just a few years older than myself, Emery's brother was charismatic and inclusive. He was popular in London and nearly every marriage-minded mama sought him for a match.

Silas wasn't ready to find a wife however. He openly avoided his own mother's attempts to marry him off and traveled abroad regularly during the season, but the Marchioness Northcutt likely would not be thwarted for long. Luckily the only non-relation unwed ladies in the room were my mother and Gansey. I'm sure Silas felt a sense of relief at that.

As I watched from the sideboard where I was retrieving bacon for my new bride, he was currently telling a story with large hand movements about some misunderstanding in France that had Genevieve and Emery in stiches and had even pulled a reluctant laugh from Patty. I approached slowly to give the siblings time to themselves. But Silas glanced up and motioned me over. "Get over here, brother. You'll love this part. And I fear Emery may become feral if she waits any longer for that bacon."

Emery whacked him on the shoulder but her smile never retreated. I, however, mentally stumbled over the *brother* that fell so easily from Silas's lips. It was true that I'd been welcomed within the Bartholomew family since birth. I was familiar and comfortable with all of Emery's siblings. But that relaxed endearment gave me pause. When had my own brother ever referred to me so? Had I only ever been called brother with disdain and derision, a reminder I was the inconsequential second-born? I felt guilty for comparing the two. Silas wasn't my blood. And John … well, he was gone.

On the brink of spiraling out of this moment, I felt a soft hand in mine, and a squeeze firm enough to distract. I looked gratefully to the owner of that hand. Emery gave me a sincere smile before saying, "Yes, husband. Join us."

And that word, that identifier, uttered for the first time from those lips made my chest tighten and warmth flood my veins. I didn't think of my brother again.

"I feel I must thank you, Augie," Silas said, interrupting my undignified, heartfelt new-husband feelings. For which, Emery would have surely noticed and mocked me good-naturedly. "I'm so relieved that you offered to marry my sister. Someone needed to take this mad woman off our hands. And while I wouldn't necessarily wish her on you—you're capital, you are—you are the best man to manage our dear Emery. You've been doing it for years."

Emery scowled at the affable teasing. "Listen here, brother dearest—"

But I cut her off before she could do violence with her words or her fists. "My lord, I assure you I am the fortunate one in this arrangement."

Genevieve looked ready to swoon. Patty eyed me with indulgent appreciation, as if I were a particularly well-behaved puppy. Silas smiled broadly in response. "Yes, of course." He winked in exaggeration and Emery delivered another whack to his shoulder that had him laughing.

My wife—Christ, my *wife*—finally looked in my direction. "I think our union was a foregone conclusion actually." My heart rate picked up. "I can't remember whose brilliant idea it was at the time." I smiled at her cheek. "But perhaps we are both the lucky ones."

~

We'd spent the remainder of the afternoon with our families and following well-wishes we'd journeyed to the cottage. The carriage ride had been quiet. Emery had been unusually subdued.

The hunting cottage two miles from Kensworth Hall had been aired out and made ready for our arrival. It was relatively small with an open living area, adjacent kitchen, and attached garden filled to bursting with wildflowers at this time of year. The small cabin was sparsely but very comfortably furnished. It was completely isolated, off the lane and deep within Kendrick lands.

With total privacy, only one bedchamber and one rather good-sized bed, it was the logical choice for the newly married. I was unnerved by the implications, and I'd perhaps been remiss in not discussing the plan for our stay here with Emery. For the next three days, the cottage would contain no servants for utmost privacy. The kitchen had been stocked for our short visit and our trunks had been delivered ahead of time.

Upon arrival, I lit several lamps. The sun was a few hours from setting but the cabin was surrounded by thick forest and the rooms within were already darkening. Emery fidgeted inside, near the open door.

I removed my jacket and placed it over an armchair. I glanced in her direction, unsure how to quell whatever thoughts made her so hesitant. "Would you like some tea?" I offered.

"Yes, thank you," she replied woodenly.

I smiled. "Would you also like to come in?"

She turned back toward the open entryway as if noticing the door for the first time. "Oh, of course." Moving quickly, she closed the door and resumed standing just in front of it.

I filled the kettle but set it aside before lighting the stove. Walking over to Emery, I extended my hand. She took it and allowed me to pull her toward the bedroom. "There's something I want to show you."

Her brows rose high on her forehead.

I laughed. "Not that."

With her gloved hand in mine, we turned the corner and entered the master's suite and approached the great bay window overlooking the forest. Emery had always been enamored with the countryside. She could never abide the gray and stone of London. I felt a swift stab of grief that I would be taking her away from this, the land that she loved. But for now, for this moment, I could give her this to ease the tension in her muscles. Alleviate the nervousness in her wide gaze.

"Oh," she murmured, approaching the glass. Emery pressed her fingertips to the windowpane and stared beyond. The sun lowering toward the horizon painted the light all orange and fire behind the line of trees silhouetted so lovingly by the landscape.

I stayed back, quiet and still, giving her this moment to center herself. After several minutes, Emery loosed a deep breath and began peeling the long ivory gloves from her arms. "I'm scared, Augie."

My middle clenched painfully. "Don't be. There are no expectations. We don't have to—"

She shook her head but still faced the window. "No. I mean, I don't know how to be your duchess. I'm loud and wild. I've never fit in in London. I'm scared I'm going to say or do the wrong thing and embarrass you." I stepped forward then, eager to comfort and reassure, but she kept talking to the horizon. "I would never let anyone hurt you, Augie. But what if *I* am the one ruining everything?" She turned to me then, eyes lined red and lashes sparkling. "I don't want you to regret me."

I gathered her to my chest, arms coming around to hold her tight. My lips brushed her golden hair, and while I couldn't give her the truth of my love, I would give her honesty in this. "I could never regret you. *Never*. I don't care about London or the *ton*. None of that is real. And you are truth, Emery. You are the most beautiful person I know, so full of life you're brimming over with it. If they can't acknowledge that or appreciate it, then that will be their loss entirely. You're like the sun, and I feel unable to do anything but bask in your brilliance." She was clutching me ruthlessly, little breaths hitching and releasing.

Emery was so rarely without confidence that it was hard to imagine her needing reassurance. But it was my failing that I'd never told her how fervently I admired her. Praise should be given freely and often, not a favor won under the threat of tears.

Her hands grasped my ivory waistcoat, desperate and fraught. I rubbed slow circles on her back in an effort to soothe, to quiet her mind so my words could sink in.

After another moment, her grip loosened and she pulled back enough to stare up at me. Her amber eyes were bright but determined. "I could never regret you either." I tried to look away as feelings of guilt threatened, but she cupped my jaw, drawing my attention back to her face. "I know you think you're forcing me into something with this marriage, but all I've ever really wanted was a future with happiness and hope. And, Augie, that *is* the path we're on because it's you by my side. I will never regret that."

I swallowed against the tightness in my throat but acknowledged the truth in her words. I could have argued, claimed she didn't know what she was saying. I could have expressed my fears for her future resentment, but I was unable to protest her lovely speech. Because she pushed up on her toes and brought her mouth to mine. Her lips were warm with earnestness and eager in their movements. There was no question or teasing in this kiss. It was one of intention and purpose. And I felt helpless to resist.

This was my wife, and she was kissing me like she was my future.

I smoothed my hand up the row of buttons along her back, both resentful and thankful for their presence. Finding purchase at the base of her skull, I slipped my fingers through her mass of curls. My hand loosened pins and her flaxen hair fell freely down her back. The pins didn't make a sound as they landed on the thick carpets under our feet.

We maintained our positions near the window. Emery moaned into my mouth and sought the skin beneath my shirt. Realizing my waistcoat limited her access, she brought both hands to the buttons there and began her work. Never breaking our kiss, she deftly slid the buttons through the ivory fabric and loosened my waistcoat before sliding it from my shoulders entirely.

Still licking into her mouth with unhurried movements, I jolted suddenly when her hands came to the front of my trousers and palmed my erection. Shuddering at her eager exploration, pleasure threatened to swallow the apprehension I felt in this moment. Her lips stayed close but she whispered urgently, "Please. Let me. Don't stop me this time. We are man and wife and I want to touch you, to know you. The way a partner knows her husband."

I swallowed painfully against her pleading tone. I hadn't intended to consummate the marriage yet. That wasn't why I'd brought her here. I didn't want Emery to feel pressured by our union nor give her one more duty as my wife. But something about her request shamed me. I *had* withheld myself from her before. I'd wanted to wait to lie with her in truth, with my feelings on full display. I'd told myself I could bring her pleasure because *that* was honest, that indulging her growing desire was in service to her. But I'd punished her by ignoring her requests for more. In my effort to remain honorable and noble, I'd once again discounted her feelings and asserted my dominion. I'd abused my power by demeaning her own.

Voice shaky and desperate, I finally asked, "Are you certain?"

Her smile was quick and devastating. "Yes, husband. I am."

Husband.

Emery was close enough to see my reaction. The absolute ruin in her wake.

"Say it again," I begged.

That smile turned calculating and possessive. She leaned close to my ear before leaving my will in shambles. "Husband. Take me to bed."

With a staying hand on her shoulder, I circled behind and took in my target. Pushing Emery's hair over one shoulder, I worked my way down the long row of pale buttons starting at her graceful neck. For every inch of warm skin I revealed, I placed a lingering kiss until I rested on my knees behind her. The dress fell in a delicate pool of fabrics around us before I loosened Emery's corset and slowly lowered her drawers. They had tiny pink bows sewn along the hem and I couldn't help but smile at the frivolity, sure she'd had nothing to do with their design.

"Don't laugh at my underthings, Augustus," came her demand, still facing forward.

"I'm not," I said, but there was laughter in my voice and she could hear it. She laughed too.

I placed a hot wet kiss to the skin of her lower back and trailed my eager fingers over her stockings and up the inside of her creamy thigh. Emery hissed a breath and raised her hands to press against the glass of the window we'd yet to stray from.

I gave a playful bite to the top of her full, round bottom and she gasped before bending slightly forward at the waist. Her position had her top half leaning more fully against the glass and her ass pushed out toward me.

My hands continued their ascent and found her center. Emery widened her stance and I rewarded her foresight by sliding two fingertips through her silken folds. She was so wet and soft, and she was all mine.

Despite the conflict I felt over our weeks of playful touching in the tree house, I now knew what she liked. The time I'd used to learn Emery's body and know her pleasure for my own made this moment less virginal fumbling and more muscle memory. I knew she liked to be teased, to circle her apex before applying pressure. So I did that now. And I'd discovered she enjoyed another teasing finger at her entrance, sliding slowly in and out of her womanhood until I could work myself deeper and surer.

Now she was panting against the windowpane, face pressed against and fogging the glass as she murmured in the wake of my touches. *Yes* and *please*, then *more* and *God.*

I gave another wet kiss to the skin of her back all the while circling her clit, finally reducing those maddening circles to direct pressure. Emery's back arched as her chants pleaded for release, and with those erotic sounds vibrating off the glass, her crisis hit.

She tightened rhythmically around my finger and moved her hips in time to the waves of pleasure.

Emery slumped bodily against the window and I rose quickly, sliding my arms around her waist, supporting her boneless state. After a quick moment, she turned in my arms, still clad only in her stockings. She moved to embrace me, arms gripping my shoulders as her eager lips moved over mine.

Lifting her easily, I yielded to her previous demand and placed her gently on the bed.

Before I could follow her down, Emery popped up onto her knees above the coverlet. "Wait! I want to help." Then she began to expertly divest me of my cravat and shirt. I placed my hands on her nude waist and tried to hold very still. I could tell this—her active participation—was important to her, especially after being denied it for so long. I marveled at her speed and efficiency. Perhaps it was for the best that my wife was undressing me. I doubted my fingers would have been nearly as steady.

Emery's hands paused briefly on the placket of my trousers as she made eye contact for the first time since she began disrobing me. I hated that I'd put that uncertainty there—in her expression and her hesitation—as if she was waiting for me to grab her hands and still her movements. So I squeezed her waist in encouragement, and she went back to unfastening.

When the last stitch of clothing had been removed, Emery looked up and asked quietly, "May I?"

I nodded in answer and she took me carefully in hand.

I groaned as her tentative hold and delicate exploration teased more than anything. But I ignored how painfully hard I was so she could touch how she liked. I'd denied her this before. I wouldn't do that again.

"You're so warm and smooth. The skin softer than I ever imagined," Emery wondered aloud. "Are you quite sure it's going to fit?"

I smiled and met her gaze. "I imagine it will. I hope so."

Her brows drew low for a moment before surprise overtook her features. "You mean … you don't know?"

I could feel my cheeks heating. Looking away, I muttered, "Not from experience, but I think we'll figure it out."

"Augie." Her tone demanded eye contact. It was surprise and a question and command all at once.

So I took a deep breath and willed my embarrassment away. I hadn't done this before and, of course, that made me nervous. But I couldn't regret my decision to abstain. A tumble at university or a night carousing with friends at a brothel could never compare. Why would I seek companionship that shallow and meaningless? I'd always thought it would do a disservice to my love for Emery. So I'd remained thus. And now, with my wife and our future before me, I was glad I was here—full of love and inexperience.

I met Emery's warm gaze as her smile bloomed with wonder and something close to relief. But before I could think on it too long, she surged forward and kissed me, hands rising to cup my jaw. And then she pulled me down on top of her.

In a tumble of limbs and laughter, I smoothed my palms along her velvet skin. Her legs widened, hips cradling me in a way that disintegrated all amusement.

Emery reached between us and grasped my erection firmly, no hesitation this time. She positioned me at her opening. Instinctually, I wanted to push and plunge and make Emery my wife in every sense of the word. But I remembered myself and paused. "I'm sorry, Em. This first time … it's going to—"

"Hurt," she finished for me. "I know, Augie. But you'll make it up to me." Her cheeky smile made me lean forward and steal a kiss.

Bracing on my hands, I slowly inched my way inside her body. Jaw clenched in restraint, I watched Emery's features, searching for signs of pain as I moved. Feeling resistance after a moment and pinch of her brows in response, I pressed kisses all over her face uttering *I'm sorry* and *almost there*, then sighing and groaning low in my throat.

Emery's face was flushed but she said with conviction, "It's okay. I'm okay. Please don't stop."

So I didn't. I thrust deliberately in and out, feeling a wet heat and a slow glide. Emery's legs wrapped around my own and her stockinged heels dug into my calves as my thrusts intensified. Her murmured encouragement facilitated my movements. I didn't think anything had ever felt so good in my entire life.

And just when I thought I wouldn't survive the pleasure snaking its way through my limbs, that feeling centered itself at the base of my spine and burst along my veins as I found my release.

I slumped forward and took my weight onto my elbows, resting my sweaty forehead on Emery's shoulder. She was raining kisses upon my hair and scratching her nails lightly across my scalp in a way that spoke of comfort and familiarity.

I didn't raise my head. I feared I couldn't just yet. If I saw pain or disappointment or unhappiness on Emery's face …

"Augie." Her voice sounded bright and curious.

"Hmm?"

"Did you like it?" she asked, tone casual but amused. And I remembered when I'd asked the very same question after I'd tasted her for the first time and she'd climaxed on my tongue. I'd been fairly confident in her enjoyment, so my question was likely smug and unnecessary. The parallel was not lost on me.

Her intention was confirmed when my head snapped up to meet her self-satisfied expression. I didn't have the energy to roll my eyes at her, so I just kissed her instead.

When I was halfway to hard, still inside her, Emery pulled back. "Can we have a bath … and do that again?" Her expression was coy but earnest. This wasn't a request for my benefit.

I responded without thought. "I've been waiting for this my whole life, I think I can manage another attempt." I didn't consider the honesty of my words or the way Emery might interpret them. I just followed her out of bed and began planning all the ways I'd make this—us—worth it.

All of it.

Thirteen

EMERY

The plan was to spend three days at the cottage on Kendrick lands. And if I had my way, we'd do little more than make love, eat sweets, and ride horses. Maybe not ride horses. If it required clothing, I wasn't interested.

The morning following our wedding, I woke to Augie tracing delicate shapes on my shoulder. I was splayed across his firm chest, one leg cast across both of his. The bedding was a tangle around my hips. When I finally opened one eye, I gazed down the length of my husband's—my husband's!—ivory-covered body to see one very masculine foot sticking out from beyond the covers. Augie had hair on his big toe. A peculiar thing to note, for sure. But I couldn't ever remember seeing adult Augie's bare feet before. What other oddities and secrets would marriage reveal? Would I gain access to every facet of my new husband? I was giddy with the prospect.

I'd already learned that I very much enjoyed lovemaking. Beyond the pinch and pressure of our initial joining, I was able to find pleasure the second and third time we'd consummated our marriage.

Last night had been a dream. Admittedly, someone else's dream. For I'd never known to wish for it. I couldn't have imagined how it would feel to connect with someone so viscerally. The closeness I felt with Augustus was raw and primal but also sensual and otherworldly.

I'd thought I'd known everything there was to know about my very best friend. But seeing him lost in his pleasure was something else entirely. And the tender expression he'd turned on me before we'd finally settled to sleep in the early morning hours … I couldn't put a name to what it was to know that part of him. I only knew I felt privileged to experience it. Something so private between lovers.

"Are you awake?" Augie finally asked, voice rough from sleep.

In answer, I lifted my head and turned to prop my chin upon his chest. Gazing up, I noticed one arm bent behind his head. Augie had coarse-looking dark hair in the pit of his arm. It was so male and unexpected. Another secret marriage discovery.

My gaze moved higher. The hair atop his head was a tragedy, curls detonated across his white pillow. I smiled. I'd done that. I'd tugged on those chestnut locks when I'd been unmoored, seeking purchase so I hadn't floated away in my pleasure while Augie had licked and sucked and bitten me to completion.

His lazy smile returned my appraisal. "What's that look for?"

I ignored his question. "I am your wife." His grin grew, eyes crinkling. "Your *wife*, Augustus."

"It's madness, I know," he agreed, still tracing designs only he could see on my bare shoulder.

I brought my hands up so I could stack them under my chin. "I feel like I did something bad and broke every rule. But I got away with it. And then ate an entire cake to celebrate." This exuberance couldn't be contained. I wanted to shout, jump on the bed, ride my horse entirely too fast, and kiss my husband until the world caught fire.

"I know," Augie admitted, eyes warm. "I feel it, too."

I carefully moved my leg between his. "How did we get so lucky?"

"Well." Augie's hand snaked from behind his head down under the sheet to grasp my thigh. "I came up with a stellar plan that we should marry … earlier in the summer. You might remember it?"

"Is that right?" I deadpanned.

"Indeed," he answered while hooking his hand behind my knee and pulling me across his lap.

I sat up now, straddling him as he brought both hands behind his head, watching and waiting for me to refute his claim. Waiting for me to pounce. He'd thrown the gauntlet and I rarely backed down from a challenge.

The white sheet was still tucked around my hips and legs but from the waist up I was completely bare. Augie's eyes seemed undecided on their destination because they shifted restlessly between my face and my breasts, stopping occasionally on my stomach and lower to where I was seated across his hips.

"Really? Because I could have sworn, and correct me if I'm wrong, but I was fairly certain that I proposed to you, husband." The hardness that had been growing and lengthening hotly beneath me gave an urgent twitch. My smile was predatory.

"I don't recall that, wife." Augie's hands extended to grip my waist.

I gave a helpful wriggle before rolling my hips and giving in to the warm, wet slide of flesh on flesh. His member was hot and impossibly firm against my core and that secret place that seemed to take my pleasure and ignite it throughout my body.

"Yes," he hissed. "Take whatever you need, Emery."

I was lost to this—the feelings and desire heating my blood. It felt like it would never be enough, like I would forever be wanting him, craving this intimacy between us.

I abandoned the little game we were playing with the origins of the proposal. I didn't want to consider that line of questioning right now, whether in playful jest or feigned argument. It was a reminder that our relationship, or marriage, hadn't occurred naturally. It had been a plan set into motion. And while I didn't regret the results, me here and now in this bed with Augie, I felt conflicted about how we'd arrived, and more importantly, where we were headed. I wanted to be more than friends who found a way to thwart their families' expectations. Something beyond lovers exploring each other's bodies.

I wanted to be Augie's wife. I wanted a family. And I wanted his heart.

I lifted my arms and braced myself on his chest, seeking friction and pressure and *there, there, there*. Feeling so close to coming, I released a desperate "now" hoping Augie would know what I needed.

He did. Of course he did.

Augie lifted my hips enough to slide me back down on his cock as he thrust up and inside. Groaning at the contact, he moved his thumb just north of where we were joined and found his mark as my body tightened with release. He continued to thrust underneath as I squeezed around his hard flesh, my hands still braced on his chest. With a low shout, Augie folded himself up, arms coming around me as our hips pressed tightly together. I could feel him warm and wet and twitching inside me.

His cheek rested against my sternum, arms locking us together. His wild curls tickled my chin as my breath came in harsh pants.

Augie resumed tracing shapes on my shoulder, and I thought greeting the day as man and wife might be the finest way to wake up there ever was.

We spent the entirety of our second day together. We read. We picnicked. We walked the forest. We made love. I was still picking the bark and moss from my hair after a particularly spontaneous bout of lovemaking against a tree. I was sore in the best possible way.

As I gazed at Augie asleep next to me in our bed that evening, I didn't feel small or quiet or any other thing I'd assumed a woman would feel upon her marriage. I felt so very alive.

And yet I knew our days like this would not last. Augie had responsibilities. He was due to leave for London the day after tomorrow. It would not always be midday lovemaking outdoors. It was however, one more added benefit of life in the country.

Yet I knew we could not maintain this simultaneous sense of peace and urgency. The feeling of languishing a day away together. And of reaching desperate hands in the night. Our lives would eventually settle into routines and the mundane. Even then, I couldn't wait for that sort of life with Augie, for it would never be without joy and contentment and partnership. Our long friendship was testament to our compatibility. I didn't have to worry about getting on with my husband. Because he was my best friend, and I couldn't fathom tiring of his company or his conversation or his smile.

I didn't know how Augie felt, but this thing growing between us over the summer had culminated into a victorious realization. I loved Augie. Beyond friendship. Beyond rational thought.

I felt untethered. Like I was one strong summer breeze away from being lifted off the earth. It was having a wondrous secret and being so deeply in it, you were consumed. Love was knowing only the joyous musings whispered in your heart. And if you were very lucky, the heartbeats of your beloved whispering back.

I smiled softly and traced his long lashes with my eyes, sooty half-moons that graced his lovely cheeks. Lips barely moving, Augie murmured something in his sleep before rolling more firmly toward me, seeking my warmth. Blowing out the candle, I gently cradled his hand that lay between us and settled onto my pillow.

Despite the knowledge in my heart, I felt fear just out of sight. Like the unknown on the other side of a locked door, I couldn't know Augie's mind. In so many ways I was headstrong and, quite frankly, a force to be reckoned with; however, in this, I could feel myself placing caution above all else. My heart, I could be sure of, but what did I know of the mystery that was Augie's. And what damage would I do if I forged ahead with no subtlety whatsoever. So while I knew I wasn't being myself, I couldn't seem to make myself buck up and tell Augie I loved him and that I wanted to be his wife. His real wife. The stakes felt too high for me to be my usual self and throw caution to the wind.

There were times when I looked at Augie and saw his tenderness and care, and thought he felt the same. But what if I was wrong? What if I was reading nothing more than my own love and happiness reflected back to me?

Our new marriage felt slightly tenuous. And where I was bold, Augie was cautious. Where I was rash, Augie was thoughtful. Where I was impatient, Augie was slow and steady. If I broached our marriage and my feelings before he was ready … the possibilities frightened me. And that fear of losing this—Augie breathing deeply on my pillow—of losing everything, made me hesitate.

When I was six years old, my sister taught me how to ride a horse. This new facet of my relationship with Augie was a lot like those early lessons. With a horse prone to spooking, Patty said I needed to remain calm and composed. He would feel the tension in my seat and my uncertainty through the reins. I couldn't push Augie to give me more before he was ready, before he trusted this new version of me in his life. I needed him to have faith in me and rushing would be a mistake.

I must have fallen asleep with my thoughts because when I awoke on the final morning of our stay at the cottage, I was alone.

Blinking sleepy, confused eyes, I took in the morning sun and stretched languidly before throwing on my wrapper and going in search of my husband. Next to the kettle in the kitchen I found a note informing me that Augie had gone to fetch our horses and would return shortly. He'd woken early and thought we might enjoy a ride today before returning to the main house this evening.

The cabin was two miles away by road, but not so far through the forest as the crow flies. Augie's journey would not be difficult, but it was an exceedingly thoughtful gesture likely done solely for my benefit.

The carriage that had conveyed us to the cottage following the wedding had departed immediately. The Wards' driver was supposed to return today to bring us back to Kensworth Hall so that Augie could prepare for his trip to London in the early morning. The thought of his return to town so soon after our nuptials made me irrationally disappointed.

Neither the trip nor Augie's new responsibilities were surprising. Yet I still didn't want things to change. I liked this time together, secluded as we were in this house in the woods. Despite our closeness and knowledge of each other over the years, here we were learning each other in entirely new ways. I coveted Augie's time and attention. I loved learning his body and sharing this new intimacy in our relationship.

But our time here would not last forever, I knew this. Our responsibilities placed us in town for the season starting in October. Augie's upcoming trip would keep him for no more than a fortnight before he rejoined me here for the remainder of the summer. We'd have a month to ourselves in the country split between the main estate and here in our little cottage hideaway.

The selfish part of me wished we never had to set foot in London again. But Augie's duties in town and with the House of Lords were very important to him. I needed to be supportive of that.

I felt an anxious tug in my stomach at the thought of the city and moved to heat water for tea. Resolved as I was to be a proper duchess, I could not help the nervousness and worry that consumed me.

What if I wasn't good enough?

I vowed to be perfect in every ballroom and drawing room. I would mind my manners, make polite conversation, and be the consummate duchess. I could do this for Augie.

Adding a sugar cube and giving a quick stir, I placed my tea on the table before turning to the bedroom to retrieve my sketchbook from my trunk. I needed a moment to center myself, and my artwork always helped me focus.

I sat down with a bit of fine charcoal and started sketching quickly in between sips of tea. Drawing from memory, I thought of Augie falling asleep beside me last night, his head on my pillow. Those inky black eyelashes fanning out. My hand moved across the page as I mapped out the edges of his square jaw and the boundaries of his dark curls. Not details yet, just a vague suggestion of shape and form.

The tea gone cold now, I shaded in areas of light and dark with the edge of my charcoal, transitioning to create the illusion of dimension on the page, the way the candlelight had lovingly caressed his features. Augie's soft mouth took shape as I smudged the area under his generous bottom lip with my charcoal-covered index finger.

I wanted to remember that moment forever, looking upon my husband with such love in my heart. Now I had a record I could come back to and visit any time I wished. My tender heart scratched out across the page.

When I felt satisfied with this version of Augie, I set down my charcoal on the table. Looking up, I nearly fell out of my chair when I saw Augie—real Augie—seated directly across from me, elbow on the table, chin resting in his palm. He had been silently watching me draw. *How long had he been there?*

In an effort to appear unruffled, I laughed, a strangled nervous thing that caught in my throat. Slowly closing my notebook, I remarked, "Goodness, you startled me. I didn't hear you return."

Augie was looking at me curiously, as if I were someone new. Or some new version of myself. Newer even than the Emery who shared his bed and married him in a church. "You were working so earnestly. You didn't hear me approach with our horses nor when I entered the house. I poured myself a cup of tea and just waited."

"Oh."

"Emery," he began, but seemed unsure how to finish. I'm sure he was remembering the time he found my sketchbook in my saddlebag and our subsequent argument. I had been wrong then, to react so badly. He was likely trying to figure out what he could say now to avoid my ire.

I wasn't angry precisely, but I was embarrassed. I'd drawn Augie's likeness as a memento to keep for myself. It seemed a strange thing to do without his permission, and yet irrationally, this felt like an invasion of my own privacy. I felt slightly juvenile and foolish, as if he'd caught me scribbling our names together to see how they looked in union.

I could just tell him the truth of my odd profession. I wanted to. But our previous conversation regarding my drawing left a bitter taste in my mouth, and my current embarrassment made it impossible to approach that sort of revelation with the confidence I'd require. If Augie was this befuddled from simply watching me draw for fifteen minutes, I couldn't imagine his reaction to finding out I was a wealthy artist.

What a mess.

Finally finding his voice, Augie spoke again. "That was amazing, Em. Watching you lose yourself like that. I had no idea you were so talented." He rubbed his palm across his chin and the layer of scruff that had accumulated during our time here. "Is that—" He pointed to my notebook. "Is that how you see me?"

Feeling panic rise, I followed his gaze to the innocuous-looking pages bound together before me. *What did he see in my drawing? Could he interpret my feelings? See my love splashed across the parchment?*

I toyed with the edge of the cover, unable to meet the intensity of his questioning stare. "I suppose it is." And then thought better of the emotions leaking through in my quietly uttered reply. Transitioning brightly, I continued. "Or at least, that's how you looked last night asleep on my pillow after a trying day with your new wife."

He smiled at my jest … or my deflection. I couldn't say for sure.

Without giving him a chance to respond, I rose and walked to the washbasin to scrub the black dust from my fingertips and the side of my hand. "Thank you for bringing the horses. If you give me a moment to dress, I'll be ready to go."

Quiet for a moment, I could hear Augie deciding to let my evasion go. He finally offered, "I'll pack us a hamper for breakfast and we can picnic on the ridge."

I dried my slightly shaking hands, attention still focused on my task and not on my too observant husband. "That sounds wonderful."

Walking by the table, I made for the bedroom when Augie's hand snaked out and tugged on my wrist. I turned toward him in question. "Emery, tell me you packed your riding breeches."

"Which ones?" I asked, already picturing the fawn-colored fabric folded neatly in my trunk.

"You know which ones," he insisted. "Tell me you brought them."

"Perhaps I did, husband." My smile returned and slow heat began to unfurl in my belly. The morning and my awkward drawing forgotten.

Augie groaned in reply as he relinquished his hold. I skipped down the hallway, laughing as I went.

I turned back at the last moment to meet my husband's heated gaze. "And perhaps I'll let you take them off me."

Augie and I eventually made our way back to the cottage around midday. We'd ridden out to the edge of the Kendrick property where the trees on the far side of the estate melted away into farmland. Augie showed me tidy rows of various plantings full of summer produce and greenery. He'd mentioned farmers and their families by name. I could tell from his attention and the look of pride on his face that he was ready to take on his new role. Augie wanted to help these farmers and work alongside them to yield the heartiest crops. He'd always wanted to be involved in the estate, but John had belittled him and withheld so much out of pointless pride and jealousy.

Augie's excitement and energy were nearly palpable. I was happy for him. Even though we'd discussed his guilt and mixed feelings regarding his brother's death, he wouldn't let that affect his drive and determination to see the Kendrick holdings succeed.

After walking the land on horseback, we'd retreated to a secluded ridge for our midmorning meal. I may have tempted and teased my husband to the breaking point because he did, in fact, strip me out of my breeches and make love to me on a blanket in the sun.

Resplendent and easy on our way back to the cottage, the arrival of the carriage and driver that would take us back to Kensworth Hall dimmed those earlier emotions.

"We'll take the horses back and send our trunks ahead in the carriage," Augie suggested.

I felt so disappointed that our time here was over, but I attempted a cheerful nod. "Of course."

Drawing his horse to a stop, Augie said, "Wait, Em."

I looked back questioningly, but circled Beatrice Three to pull alongside him in the opposite direction. "What is it?"

Augie was fretting with the reins. His horse, sensing his unease, shifted on his hooves. I remembered suddenly those riding lessons from my sister.

"What's wrong?" I questioned again, voice soothing and unhurried.

Augie's gaze searched my face. "I just want to ask you something but I don't want you to feel pressured." Now I was the one fidgeting in the saddle. "I wish we could have stayed here longer. Hell, for the rest of the summer. But with John's death and all the business I need to see to in London … I'm sorry that isn't possible right now. And I know you hate it there, but I don't feel right leaving you after our time here together. Would you—" He hesitated. "Would you come with me to London? I'm not sure how long the trip will take. I hope to return to Hampshire in under a fortnight, but it's hard to plan as invitations will arrive as soon as I reach town. It's weak of me to ask, but I can't help it. After everything, I can't imagine leaving you here and spending my days and nights without—"

"Yes, Augie." I cut off his adorable rambling. "I'll come. I didn't want to be separated either. I'll come to London with you."

His smile was cautious and tinged with remorse. I wanted to ease his regret and banish that restraint entirely. I wanted his joy without bounds.

Leaning over to grasp his shirtfront, I hauled my husband closer and claimed his lips in hopes of conveying my eagerness and willingness to join him. I wanted to be with Augie whether that be in a ballroom in London or naked in the woods.

Obviously I had a preference there, but for this man—for my husband—I could do this.

Pulling away reluctantly, I said, "Come on, let's head back. I need to pack. Gansey is going to kill me."

Augie's smile was less fraught this time, and not to sound boastful, but a touch dazzled after that kiss. "Okay. Let's go, then."

When I came rushing into my bedchamber that afternoon to see about the items for the trip, Gansey wasn't angry at all. In fact she'd already packed our things in preparation for the journey to London on the morrow.

Augie was right. Gansey did know everything.

Fourteen

EMERY

Kendrick Manor was in the fashionable area of London, surrounded by other aristocratic Mayfair homes.

Augie and I had just arrived fresh from our travels and the butler, Malvern, and the housekeeper, Mrs. Fathom, insisted on introductions for the staff. I saw nothing wrong with this demand phrased as a request until I realized *I* was the one being introduced.

"Why would they even care to meet me," I hissed toward Augie.

He directed his baffled eyebrows toward me before replying slowly, "Because you're the lady of the house."

Oh.

Oh.

"But your mother—"

"Isn't in residence. And you're my wife. My duchess." Augie emphasized the title and the odd nervousness in my belly returned.

"Well." I pasted a smile on my face that strove for genuine but likely landed somewhere east of pained. Brushing my hands nervously down my favorite maroon traveling dress, I stepped forward to do my duty.

Mrs. Fathom lined up the many servants of Augie's London home and I made my way down the line, my smiles growing more sincere as I greeted each individual. They obviously found the whole spectacle as awkward as I did. But I could easily read their warmth and welcome for Augustus as their new lord and master. A vast improvement over his predecessor who used to spill and throw things and never had a kind word for anyone, much less servants. Even I could read the relief in their expressions that a known predator would be troubling them no more.

Once Augie and I had been welcomed by the maids, footmen, groundskeepers, the stable hands, and the cook, we retired for the evening. I was tired from traveling and could still feel that ball of tension rattling around inside me. Just being in London did that to me not to mention the added anxiety of being *the lady of the house*.

I'd only ever been myself around our servants in Hampshire. I wore breeches and charmed footmen. My lady's maid regularly rolled her eyes at me. To say our household was rather informal would be an understatement.

But now I felt like I'd be expected to assume the role of duchess in my own home. That was odd. I didn't know how to think of the stately manor as my home. The hunting cottage in the woods felt more comforting and preferable. Hell, the tree house was more my home than any residence in Mayfair. Especially Kendrick Manor with its marble floors, plush carpets, and grand staircase. Its gilt everything. Perhaps I just needed to make some memories here. The more time Augie and I spent in residence, the more comfortable I'd become, I'd wager.

After a bit of confusion and secondhand embarrassment, Augie successfully instructed the footmen to deliver my items to the duke's quarters. Everything seemed to plague me with uncertainty, and I felt the need to apologize constantly. But Augie's quietly uttered "of course you'll sleep in my bed … in *our* bed" went a long way in settling my nerves.

Anders and Gansey had accompanied us to London and were busy unpacking our belongings when we arrived in the duke's rooms—in *our* rooms.

Gansey took one look at my face and announced that she and Anders could finish up in the morning. They fled to their respective bedchambers abovestairs.

"Well, I suppose you're attending me this evening," Augie surmised.

"Apparently." I moved to inspect the furniture and décor in the room. It all seemed minimal and much less garish than the rest of the house. It reminded me of Augie, so simple and discerning in his tastes. I wondered absently as I maneuvered around the room if Augie had moved John's belongings to another suite. "Gansey seemed fairly frightened of whatever expression I wore."

Augie smiled as he removed his gloves and cufflinks. "Your features conveyed those of a feral animal about to reach her breaking point."

Stopping near the headboard, I huffed a laugh. "Are you comparing me to a wild animal?"

Augie shrugged off his jacket before approaching me slowly, as if I really was in danger of attacking. "Less wild animal. More domesticated pet unsure of her new surroundings. Nevertheless, still unwise to be trapped in an enclosed space with you."

"Ah, but you're confined to this room with me." I closed the distance between us and wrapped my arms around Augie's waist. "Are you not afraid?"

My husband carefully removed the hat from my head and smoothed back the fine hairs near my temple before replying, "I'm not frightened." His touch was gentle and his tone calm, ever the tamer of the wildness inside me. "It's going to be okay." Still stroking my hairline, he delivered a chaste kiss to my forehead.

Inexplicably near tears, I marveled at Augie's ability to see through all my insecurities to the heart of the matter. He was attempting to calm my London nerves. It was shocking that he couldn't also look in my eyes and see my love for him spilling forth. Augie knew me so very well, but apparently *that* was the one truth that eluded him. I felt a laugh threatening at the absurdity of it all. I loved Augie and we were wed, but I was too scared to admit my feelings because I didn't think he would believe me.

That was all right. I'd take things slow and steady—the Augustus way—until he could no longer doubt my devotion. Using actions and deeds, I would solidify my place in his heart until he was unable to deny my sincerity. Consistency and thoughtfulness. I would approach my duties here in London in the same manner. Calmly and carefully work my way into society. No sudden movements. All things in moderation. And do my best to acclimate without standing out.

Plan settled, I endeavored to cast all my worries aside and enjoy this new setting with my new husband. I brought my lips to the underside of his stubbled jaw and murmured in between kisses,

"Are you ready for bed or do you have to check on anything this evening?"

Augie's hands moved from my hair to cradle my jaw. "It will hold until tomorrow. The only place I wish to be is here with you."

And I believed him. Augie's attention was singular. I didn't feel the pressure to be the perfect duchess as he removed the pins from my hair. My throat tightened with emotion from the tenderness in my husband's gaze, not from the uncertainty I felt in this town. When Augie loved my body with his hands and lips, I forgot all about my reservations and paranoia. My fears paused their forward progress and retreated deep within as Augie worshiped me.

I didn't feel the dull ache of self-consciousness when I was so very well loved by my husband in our bed in our new home together.

But I didn't know how to harness the sense of peace I found in Augie's embrace.

And when I awoke the following morning to dozens of invitations for the new Duke and Duchess of Kendrick, those fears washed up tangled and twisted like very persistent seaweed on the shore.

Augie assured me that we need not accept very many. We could simply ease into life in town. Most members of the *ton* retreated to their country estates in the summer months anyway. And while in mourning for the late duke, our presence in society would be minimal. But there were still people in London who desired our company. Well, they desired Augie's company. Friends from university, associates of the former Duke of Kendrick, and a handful of family friends and acquaintances all vied for attention. I was merely an amendment to his invitations. A novelty, shiny and new. Someone suddenly entering their orbit. My express purpose and worth had yet to be determined, but these early showings would supply the gossips for the season to come. I'd never before been so consumed with making a good first impression.

"Don't worry," Augie assured me over breakfast on our first morning in London. "We'll spend the day here. You can get used to the house. I have several meetings with solicitors and stewards and John's former financial advisors. But we can dine together this evening, just you and I."

Stirring sugar into my tea, I managed an agreeable nod.

"And then perhaps tomorrow we could take tea with the Marquess Daly? I've been acquainted with Andrew for ages. He's a decent sort, and someone I looked forward to seeing at Cambridge." Augie seemed cautious in his suggestion. I didn't know if he was waiting for me to pitch a fit regarding tea with his friend or if he assumed I'd take offense to Augie merely having other friends besides myself.

No matter. I was his *best* friend. Obviously.

Trying on my new confident ducal persona, I made my features even and was the very picture of courtesy when I replied, "That sounds lovely, Augie. I would be delighted."

His thoughtful demeanor didn't change. If anything, he appeared more careful when he continued. "And then the following day, we've been invited to Lady Thisby's soiree." A pause. "She and the Earl are friendly with my mother. I should probably accept." Another pause. "I think you'd quite like her. She's always been very kind to me. And she has an amazing art gallery. You might enjoy seeing their collection. She and Lord Thisby are quite the collectors."

Oh, I knew. She'd attempted to commission an M. Barton landscape no less than four times. The first two requests had been denied simply because I'd been too busy with other paintings at the time. And the latter requests … well, I hadn't appreciated her tone.

However, I directed my new genteel smile in Augie's direction. "I would be pleased to attend her event."

He started at me curiously. "What is that … smile? I think it's a smile. Well, you're baring your teeth anyway. What's happening there?" His finger circled in the general direction of my mouth.

I narrowed my gaze. "What? That's my polite society smile."

"That's what you think your face is doing right now?"

"Well, not right now. But before. Here, I'll do it again." I raised my chin purposely and offered my well-mannered-lady smile.

Augie actually cringed. "Please don't."

"What?" I cried, indignant. "I am beauty and grace and all things duchessly with that smile."

"Perhaps," he said and I nodded. But then he continued, "Perhaps it's because I've seen your actual smile that I find this one so unnatural."

I gasped. "Unnatural?!"

Ignoring me, Augie looked about the room. "We need to find someone to test this theory on. Someone unfamiliar with your genuine smile." His attention zeroed in on a liveried footman near the sideboard. The young man's eyes widened. "Gregory, might we trouble you for a moment?"

Gregory approached uncertainly.

"Try it on him," Augie advised.

I shot my husband a glare before straightening in my chair and turning my aristocratic smile on Gregory.

He startled backward quite suddenly.

Augie dissolved into fits of laughter.

"Wait," I protested. "Let me try again!"

Gregory continued to back away slowly, hands now raised in surrender.

In an effort to compose himself, Augie choked out, "Thank you, Gregory. Feel free to escape the dining room."

I frowned after the footman's retreating back, thinking I should practice my smile some more in the mirror while also plotting how to murder my husband.

Having finally wrangled his mirth back under control, Augie turned to me and said very gently, "Smile your own smile, Emery. Be yourself, and I promise they will be helpless to do anything but love you."

He looked so earnest that I wanted to believe him. Perhaps things wouldn't be as bad as I feared.

Two days later, I found myself in Earl and Lady Thisby's ballroom. The tea with Marquess Daly the previous day had gone rather well. Perhaps I'd gained a misplaced sense of confidence as a result. But as Augie had indicated, Lord Daly was indeed a good sort. We'd spent the afternoon comparing embarrassing Augustus stories. Naturally I'd won for sheer quantity but it was quite interesting to hear about a new side to my long-time friend and new husband. My version of Augie existed only in Hampshire. The university man described by Lord Daly had been fascinating.

Our visit had been very relaxed and casual, and I felt confident that I had been well received by Augie's friend. I was grateful to my husband for offering himself up as a sacrifice for our teasing and enjoyment. I knew the tea with Daly had been a purposeful introduction, a way to dip my toe in the chilly waters of London high society. Augie was doing his utmost to put me at ease, and I was so very appreciative.

Tonight's event seemed more formal but markedly sedate. Likely not overly crowded due to the time of year, but most attendees seemed well into their later years. A conservative crowd to be sure. I felt more easily able to charm the older set than to convince peers my own age that I belonged among them. Again, I could detect Augie's hand in curating the invitation. My breaths came easier and my smiles less brittle than if I was surrounded by young lords and ladies.

"Ah, there you are, Lord Kendrick. So lovely to see you." Lady Thisby smiled warmly at Augustus.

"My lady. It's wonderful to see you as well. Thank you for the invitation. Apologies for the short notice but we've just recently arrived to town."

"No trouble at all. Please accept our condolences on the death of your brother, Your Grace. We are, however, delighted you and your new wife could attend this evening. Congratulations to you both." Our hostess offered me a kind smile which I returned.

I cleared my throat delicately. "I'm so happy to make your acquaintance, madam."

"And you as well, Your Grace." The honorific slipped easily from her tongue, but I still had trouble stomaching it.

Augie smoothly cut in. "Emery and I were discussing your amazing art collection. Is the gallery available this evening for viewing?"

Lady Thisby's eyes shone brightly. "Yes, of course. Feel free to make your way there. It's so wonderful to have other art lovers in attendance."

"Thank you, my lady." My smile was genuine. I was grateful to have something to do this evening besides be introduced to people.

We left our hostess and made our way to the gallery on the upper floor. Several formally attired gentlemen meandered along the hallway, stopping occasionally to inspect Lady Thisby's collection.

Augie stiffened as a man approached. He looked to be a few years older than us, dark hair and eyes. He cut a striking figure with his black evening jacket expertly tailored to his form contrasting with the snowy cravat at his throat. The expression on his fairly attractive face was one of despair however.

Leaning down to whisper in my ear, Augie said quietly, "He was friends with my brother. I'll speak to him. You go ahead and view the paintings."

"Are you certain?" I whispered back, unwilling to abandon Augie to this awkward conversation but also unsure if my facial expressions could manage any sort of sympathy for someone who could actually miss John Ward.

"Yes, go." Augie gave a little nudge to the small of my back.

And off I went, passing the mystery gentleman. Turning back as I reached the first painting, I saw the man was fairly emotional and clung to Augie's arm following a hearty handshake. Poor Augie. Always cleaning up other people's messes. Hopefully this wouldn't take long and he could extract himself.

The hallway was lined on either side with paintings. It was quite the collection. A central viewing wall had been constructed down the middle of the hall creating two lanes. I meandered down one side, and when I turned the corner, I nearly collided with a young woman about my age in a pale lavender dress. "I'm so sorry!"

She laughed quietly. "No trouble at all. I'm afraid I was distracted by the painting of Lady Thisby's hounds."

I stepped closer to the wall to see her meaning. "Oh. That's … a lot of hounds."

The stranger's blue eyes twinkled as she laughed again. Voice lowered conspiratorially, she said, "There must be forty dogs in that painting."

I laughed as well. "Quite a collection," I agreed.

Turning toward me, the lovely young woman introduced herself, "I'm Victoria Gratton."

"I'm Emery Bartholomew." I smiled in return, happy to have made an acquaintance on my own. No ducal husband required. Husband. *Oh bollocks*. "I mean Ward. I'm Emery Ward." Miss Gratton frowned in confusion. I rushed to explain. "We've just married recently. I'm unused to introductions and my new name."

Her face cleared and she nodded. "You're the Duchess of Kendrick."

It wasn't a question but I felt the need to confirm. "Yes, that's me. It's lovely to meet you," I rushed to add.

Miss Gratton's smile seemed kind. "You as well, Your Grace. Well, I'll let you get back to the artwork. I should return to my sponsor."

"Yes, of course. And don't worry, there are not so many hounds that direction." I indicated the path I'd already perused.

She smiled brightly before strolling away.

Well, that went relatively well. She seemed kind despite my awkward forgetfulness. Perhaps I was being too harsh on my peers. I remembered my sister Patty's admonishment several weeks past. Maybe if I gave these women half a chance, I could find some worthy friendships.

After a glance further down the hallway, I could see Augie still trapped by John's friend. I picked up my pace and made my way toward them. The gentleman was speaking rapidly and Augie was nodding, his face kind and sympathetic. Perhaps I could rescue him.

My husband's eyes widened as he realized my intention to interrupt.

The gentleman straightened and made an admirable effort to collect himself at my approach. Greetings were exchanged and thankfully our new acquaintance excused himself a handful of moments later to allow us to return to our evening.

"How was the art?" Augie inquired, sounding slightly strained from the encounter.

"Oh, fine. Lady Thisby has some lovely pieces." Hoping to

distract him from the awkward run-in, I offered, "Do you want take a look?"

"Not unless you're eager to avoid the ballroom. I only mentioned the gallery because I hoped you'd enjoy it."

I smiled at Augie's thoughtfulness and made to turn us back toward the gathering. I shouldn't keep him away from the other guests just because I was reluctant to engage with all the lords and ladies in attendance.

Upon reentering the ballroom, I noticed Miss Gratton among a small grouping of ladies. I'd missed their youthful presence upon earlier examination. These young women were all well dressed, their pastel frocks indicative of their unmarried state. Their fans were fluttering and they appeared deep in conversation, but Miss Gratton's eyes met mine and she beamed a smile in my direction.

I could feel Augie's attention as my own strayed. He paused briefly in his steps but followed my gaze to the young women forming a half circle off to the side of the dance floor. "Everything all right?"

Gratefully, I returned Miss Gratton's smile before turning to Augie and tugging him toward the dance floor. "Yes. I met one of those ladies earlier. She was very sweet."

"That's wonderful, Em." And he must have meant it because he made no objection as I led him to join the next dance.

After several turns about the floor, Augie offered to retrieve some refreshment for me. Rather than stand awkwardly alone awaiting my husband's return, I bucked up the courage to approach Miss Gratton and her acquaintances.

Feeling somewhat nervous, I located the young ladies near the open balcony doors attempting to gain some fresh air in the stifling ballroom. Taking a bracing breath and preparing my greeting and introduction in my head, I made my way toward Miss Gratton. But before I could make my presence known, I heard my name on their lips and quickly maneuvered behind a nearby column.

"Did you get a look at her gown?" one girl spoke.

"Gorgeous to be sure. But she's no match for Kendrick," came Miss Gratton's scoff. "I met her upstairs in the gallery and she might as well be a country bumpkin."

"Truly?" another girl spoke.

"Indeed," confirmed Miss Gratton.

The original lady who questioned my gown spoke once more. "And her face is quite plain. Poor Kendrick. Surely he could have found a more beautiful and suitable duchess."

"I heard she never even had a season. That they are family friends. He probably married her out of pity."

I couldn't breathe. This was exactly what I'd feared. Miss Gratton had seemed kind, and I'd stupidly thought I'd made a friend this evening. Or perhaps the potential for one. Why bother pretending kinship at all? I couldn't understand the meaningless deception. This was the reason I found London so confusing and myself so off-balance here. The layered deceit and subtle malevolence. It all seemed so pointless to me, an utter waste of energy.

Whatever else those girls said about me or my dress or my plain face was drowned out by the sound of blood rushing in my ears. I needed to pull myself together. I didn't want to alarm Augustus when he returned. And more importantly, I didn't wish to make a scene.

"Why are you holding up this column?" came a low voice to my left.

I started before taking in the worried face of my sister Patty. From behind her appeared the curious face of another woman, one of whom I didn't recognize.

"I …" I had no idea how I was going to finish that statement.

Patty frowned before turning me by my shoulder and nudging me in the direction of the hallway. She pulled in front of me and began leading, her odd friend following at my back. I was so distracted I hardly noticed Augie's approach.

My sister intercepted him before I even had the chance to greet him. I felt absurdly grateful. Augie would have known right away that something was amiss. Patty spoke quickly, "Good evening, brother. I'm going to introduce Emery to a few friends. You just mingle and I'll deliver her back to you shortly." Patty reached back and grabbed my hand to pull me along.

I paused, feeling conflicted about fleeing the ballroom, but the strange woman at my back placed her hands on my shoulders and directed me forward before calling over her shoulder, "Don't worry, Duke. We'll take good care of her."

Patricia's grip didn't loosen even up two flights of stairs. I had no idea where we were going but this looked suspiciously like the family wing. The stranger behind me squeezed past and opened a door, indicating Patty should enter. Left with nothing but mounting confusion, I followed as well.

I took in a large, well-appointed sitting room filled with candles and seating for at least eight. An open doorway beyond showed an equally lavish bedchamber. My sister's mysterious friend walked over to the balcony doors and pushed them wide, allowing a cool evening breeze to permeate the space.

"Come. Sit," advised my sister. Patty had arranged herself on the patterned settee. She patted the cushion next to her.

I sat slowly. "What is going on?"

"I don't know. You tell us," Patty said. "I saw you in the ballroom, hiding behind a column looking nearly catatonic."

I remembered why I was hiding and what I'd overheard. I didn't want to admit any of that to my sister.

The woman by the balcony lit a cheroot and smiled at me. "Don't worry, my dear. I won't bite."

I looked questioningly at Patty.

"Oh, this is Mary Lovelace. The daughter of Earl and Countess Thisby—our hosts this evening—and my good friend. I was bringing her over to introduce you, but I felt a rescue was more in order. Why do I keep finding you looking brittle and uncomfortable at London events?"

"Because I *am* brittle and uncomfortable at London events," I snapped. I fidgeted in my seat and found it painful to admit even that shortcoming.

Patty glanced at her friend with a look I couldn't decipher. A look that was somehow all about me while also excluding me entirely. I bristled inwardly and made to stand.

Reaching up, my sister grabbed my hand and yanked me back onto the settee. "What happened?"

I heaved a sigh inherent to middle siblings before crossing my arms over my chest.

"Em?" Patty tried again.

So I told her. I told my sister and this peculiar stranger about meeting Miss Gratton and then overhearing her and her gossipy friends. It wasn't difficult to recount. I didn't care that they'd called me plain or countrified. It was admitting that I agreed with some of their criticisms that made the retelling challenging. Augie *could* have found a better duchess, someone suited to this life-style. But instead, he was stuck with me. Someone unfit, lesser.

I stared down at my lap with its rose-hued silk organza skirt shifting and catching the light. It truly was a gorgeous dress. Much too fine for me. Those gossipy chits didn't have an ounce of sincerity but they did have good taste in formalwear.

My attention snapped up to Mary when she exhaled smoke loudly and said, "Well. Fuck. Them."

It was an odd feeling to realize that I was perhaps not the most brash and outspoken person in the room. For that hadn't been the case nearly all my life.

"What Mary means is," my sister started, drawing my attention away from the balcony doors and the profanity therein. "What does it matter what those unmarried girls think? They are bored and full of gossip and hate and snide remarks. They do not matter."

I opened my mouth to respond but Mary followed on the heels of my sister's pronouncement. "No, what I meant was fuck them. But to your point, Patty, I would agree. Who are those infants anyway? They were wallflowers in a ballroom. Jealous and angry that you were on the arm of a handsome duke. They weren't criticizing you specifically, Emery. It was everything you represent. Everything you have that they have been denied thus far. But not to worry. With youth and connections on their side, I'm sure they'll find some decrepit lord three times their age to marry them." Mary winced before shooting my sister an apologetic look.

Patricia waved her off and I wondered at the friendship before me. Who was this woman who had leave to so casually reference my sister's painful marriage? I took in the tall figure still smoking by the open archway. Her dress was well-made and lovely on her fine-boned form. Mary was tall and very lean with little curves to speak of. Her face was long and not … traditionally beautiful. But she was striking. Her features were all strong: straight, Roman nose, angular jaw, and deep-set dark eyes. Mary's flame-red hair was barely contained, curls wild. They were one strong gust of wind away from exploding outwardly and cascading in all directions. She blew an escaped tendril that fell across her brow, smoke wafting with her forceful exhalation.

I narrowed my eyes, feeling irrationally indignant and replaceable and one thousand other things, before facing Patty once more. My upset with Miss Gratton and her friends felt trivial all of a sudden. Yes, those girls were young and what they said didn't really matter. But they did echo all the worries and insecurities I had within myself.

But I couldn't feel comforted in this room, with Mary and my sister. The chasm between us felt wide and deep. Why was Mary good enough to confide in, to find worthy of friendship? And how could those ladies belowstairs read all my deficiencies so easily from across a ballroom? Could my sister and her friend do that now?

I wanted to leave. Find Augie and go to Hampshire and live in peace.

But I knew I couldn't do that. I needed to find a way to accept this new version of my life where I was a duchess and I couldn't trust anyone's kindness. And where my sister had a best friend who wasn't me.

"Em, don't let those girls get to you. I'm sorry they hurt your feelings, but Mary is right. They're young and jealous. They're not the right friends for you. There *are* people in this town worthy of your time and your fierce loyalty, but those girls … it's not them." Patty smiled then, cautious and close-lipped. "I know you're upset, but I'm so glad you're here. I've missed you."

I'm sure my expression was caught somewhere between hurt and confusion. But Patty continued, clasping my hand in hers. "I meant it when I said I didn't feel like I could go back to Hampshire, but I never meant to leave you behind. I'm sorry that it felt that way. I can see that now. I'm so grateful you and Augie will be in London. We can see each other so much more now. I can help you get settled and introduce you to more people. People you can trust with yourself. I've wanted you to meet Mary for such a long time." My sister's eyes were bright and liquid. "She reminds me so much of you. I knew you'd get on."

Patty's words cut me in so many different ways and I didn't have a ready response beyond a broken nod. This was the apology I sought in my imaginings and my daydreams. I was desperate for her to miss me and to be affected by my absence. And here was my proof. Her friendship with Mary felt like a spike through the heart, especially with that comparison. But if Patty felt she couldn't come home, I was glad she'd found friendship with someone who reminded her of me, a sister in her heart.

It sounded as if she wanted my new life in London to encompass her as well. I wanted that, too. I wanted my sister back. Perhaps our relationship wasn't a battle to be won. And maybe Mary wasn't an adversary but someone who could have my back in a ballroom as well.

I felt raw and exposed after so much needless drama this evening. But meeting Mary and seeing her friendship with my sister made me see, made me believe that there could be genuine relationships in this town. It wasn't all fluttering fans and malicious gossip. It could be ballroom rescues with no questions asked and a soft place to land. It could include my sister ... back in my orbit once more.

Mary stubbed out her cheroot and made her way to join us. Sitting on the armchair closest to me, she smiled warmly. "I'm so happy to finally meet you, Emery. Your sister has talked my ear off about you. And I look forward to formally meeting your handsome duke. I know you don't know me yet, but as a woman in London who is often mocked and gossiped about, my advice is to simply surround yourself with people you can trust and ignore everyone else. Pay no mind to their whispers. Disregard their looks. For the only people who matter are the ones who matter to you."

I could read her sincerity. This extension of friendship because she cared for my sister. Only a fool would hold on to jealousy and resentment in this moment. And I was no fool.

Feeling more like myself, I raised my chin. "Fuck them, right?"

Mary winked at me, her grin wide with mischievous comradery. "That's right, love."

Fifteen

AUGUSTUS

I heard a swish of skirts and footsteps but continued moving my quill across the parchment. The sound stopped. I glanced up momentarily but there was no one in the doorway to my study. I'd been sequestered for several hours this morning returning correspondence. I needed to get this done before I rode out to the fields in the afternoon. The late summer harvest was in full swing and I was eager to pitch in where I could. I didn't wish to be in the way, but I had a vested interest in supporting the tenants and their farms. Building trust went both ways, and repairing the damage done by my brother was a top priority for me. So to the fields I would descend this afternoon.

The sound of footsteps resumed. I paused once again and returned my gaze to the empty doorway but no one emerged. No skirts came into view. No blond hair or curious amber eyes.

I placed my quill down very quietly and rose from the desk. If Emery wanted to play games, I would happily oblige. In the weeks since we'd returned from London, there had been many happy instances. Emery was in good spirits following our visit to town which both surprised me and gave me hope. Perhaps our season in London would not be misery for my wife.

My wife. Christ, I would never get used to that.

I knew Emery was anxious for my attention. Hence the spectral hovering in the hallway. She seemed apprehensive about interrupting me, but I never minded her kind of disruptions. I felt compelled to take regular breaks and we'd found a great number of uses for the desk in my study.

I moved on silent feet across the plush carpets and approached the hallway carefully. The shuffling of footsteps had stopped once more, but I knew she was there. With a controlled leap, I sprung into the corridor … and found Molly the abovestairs maid dusting the portraits. She jumped back with a squeak that she quickly attempted to muffle. Wide startled eyes met mine, and before I could apologize profusely for having scared her, Emery pounced from behind me with a victorious shout.

It was my turn to squeak rather indelicately before my menace of a wife dissolved into giggles. "You should have heard the sound you made," she wheezed.

"I did hear it. I was right here," I groused, turning back to Molly. "I am terribly sorry. I assumed Emery was in the hallway being devious and I was correct. Molly, I'm sorry for frightening you."

"Of course, Your Grace. It's no trouble. If I had known Her Grace was about on this floor, I would have taken my duties elsewhere." Molly blushed furiously before dropping a quick curtsey and scurrying down the passageway toward the stairs.

"Sorry, Molly!" Emery called belatedly. "I think we've scandalized that poor girl."

I turned a beleaguered expression on my wife. "Well, you were terribly loud the last time." Emery looked confused. "Against the bookcase," I clarified.

With a thoughtful expression she nodded. "Oh that's right." Undeterred, she continued, "Well you should make sure those shelves are more secure."

I smiled indulgently and she returned it with a wicked one of her own.

Strolling closer, Emery mused, "Hmm, since you're here and I'm here … perhaps I can practice being quieter."

I thought about it. About tugging Emery into the study and locking the door, peeling her stockings down and bending her over the desk. But I also thought about the work that awaited me on that very same desk. I considered how busy I'd been recently and how often we'd been forced to settle for a brief interlude in my office. While enjoyable, I hadn't been able to spend the time with Emery that I wanted—that I needed. I didn't want another quick fuck. She needed to know I craved her time and attention, not just her body.

Sensing my hesitation, Emery aborted her prowl. "Or I can let you get back to work." Her words were measured and even, but I could feel her retreating, the playful light in her eyes receding.

Reaching forward, I grabbed her hand and pulled her to me. I kissed her deep and slow, fighting to reassure her. Insistent with my lips and tongue. Giving her my full attention in a way I couldn't with everything else.

When I eventually pulled back, I pressed our foreheads together. "As much as I would enjoy lifting your lovely skirts and bending you over that desk, how about I take the next hour to finish what I need to? And then you and I can take the horses out. I'll be able to spend more time with you once these tasks are finished and before I need to meet the farmers this afternoon. What do you think?"

Emery's hands grasped the lapels of my coat as she tugged me closer. Lifting up onto her toes, she pressed a quick kiss to my lips. "Yes, let's do that." Another peck. "I'll make sure the horses are ready." Once more, smiling as she brushed her lips with mine. "Now get back to work."

It was my turn to nip her lips playfully before I darted back toward the study, fighting the impulse to wrangle her inside and do more than kiss. I felt a swat to my rear as Emery dashed away laughing.

This would be an incredibly long hour until I could escape.

Exactly fifty-eight minutes later, I was walking in the direction of the stables after having pilfered the kitchens for a few items to bring on my ride with Emery. We should have plenty of time to stop for a quick luncheon.

With a small hamper in one hand and a blanket tucked under my arm, I hastened my steps. I was eager to see my bride. After two weeks of hurried lovemaking and brief conversations over informal meals and before falling asleep each night, I was impatient to have a few uninterrupted hours with Emery.

I felt quite guilty that my new duties required so much time and attention, especially considering our newly married state. With our upcoming trip to London imminent, I had hoped to make our final weeks in the country a sort of honeymoon or, at the very least, time that Emery could enjoy Hampshire before pulling her back to the gray cobblestones of London. To the gossipy misses and eager ears of the *ton*. Perhaps there was another solution, one that wouldn't make Emery miserable.

I knew that these fields and this land was her home. She seemed happy at Kensworth Hall with me. Mother had absconded to the dowager's residence on the estate a few miles away. Several days following our return from London, she'd declared that we needed our own space and wished to spend the rest of the summer on her own before traveling to Devon in the autumn. She planned to rejoin us for the holidays back in Hampshire. Emery and I had both assured her of a place with us, that of course she was welcome to stay. But Mother had been fairly resolute, and as much as I hated to admit it, she still seemed to be mourning the loss of John. Subdued in her manner, she claimed the solitude would do her well, and she was looking forward to spending time with my aunt on the Devon coast as she routinely did at least once per year.

Following the evening of the engagement ball, the full extent of John's nature and his crimes had been realized. At the same time, I'd also been faced with my mother's failings. I'd likely never see her the same way again. She'd protected and enabled my brother through a variety of heinous offenses, and even in death, her devotion felt absolute. I couldn't reconcile these truths with our future relationship. I'd honor and respect my mother, but knowing the depth of her loyalty to John, I now saw her through dull and discolored lenses. I wasn't happy she'd departed but I couldn't help but acknowledge the strain looming in our future encounters. But for now, I felt relief at the time and distance between us, as shameful as that was to admit.

I'd been enjoying my time alone with Emery, settling into our new life and these roles we'd claimed as our own. But I didn't know if that would translate to London for months on end. I didn't wish to make my wife unhappy. Perhaps she could stay in Hampshire for part of the season, especially while the weather was fine. She could visit her family and go riding whenever she felt like it. And then she could join me in London after the season was underway and the most immediate demands on my time had passed. It would be difficult to leave her, but if it made her happier in our arrangement—in our marriage—then I would respect that.

Frowning at the mere hypothetical thought of our separation, I rounded the corner to the stable and found Emery walking toward me, holding two horses by the reins. Her smile was like a blow.

How could I be without her now?

"Good, you brought food." She'd changed into her breeches— those breeches—and I fought a groan. Emery only ever wore trousers when riding. She'd eschewed the casual garments she'd typically worn before our marriage for more traditional day dresses here at Kensworth Hall. I hadn't commented on the change in her. I honestly didn't care what she wore, as long as she was happy. I definitely wasn't going to question or dictate to her.

Loading the items for our meal in the saddlebags, I replied, "I figured we had time."

I helped Emery mount Beatrice Three and then swung up onto my own horse. We moved to the rear of the property before Emery moved into a trot, calling out to me, "Where to?"

"Wherever you want. I'll be right behind you."

That was all the encouragement she needed. Emery was off like a shot, and I found myself in the same position I'd always been in … unable to do anything but follow in her wake.

After a spirited chase over the open fields, the September sun warmed my skin and I dismounted near a bend in the shallow creek bed.

With the horses drinking nearby, we spread out our blanket and settled in the shade. I turned to offer Emery some of the bread I'd retrieved from the kitchens, but was tackled instead. She settled her warm weight atop me and my startled confusion turned rather quickly to the most basic of thoughts … teeth and tongues, need and desire.

Emery pushed her eager hand down the front of my trousers and took me firmly in hand. Each stroke ratcheted up my desire, my sensitive flesh hardening for her touch alone. I gasped into her mouth as her pace increased.

"I want you," she whispered, the words landing hot and demanding against my open mouth.

With considerable effort I pulled her hand away before turning us and lowering Emery onto her back. She was already undoing her breeches and pushing the fawn-colored fabric down her thighs. I pulled her boots off one by one and then found her enterprising hand back in my trousers. I laughed brokenly as I began tugging the fabric down my own legs.

"Now, now, now," Emery chanted her demand.

I lowered myself into her waiting embrace and kissed her deeply as my first thrust inside had her digging her nails into my backside. I set a punishing pace as Emery spurred me on. *Yes* and *please* and *don't ever stop.*

This was supposed to be time well spent, not like our quick tumbles in my office. I'd planned to take my time. I'd wanted us to talk and just *be* together. And instead here we were, rushing ourselves and hastening our pleasure.

I deliberately slowed my thrusts as Emery made a small sound of protest but I silenced her with another deep and drugging kiss. Tongues battled because this woman was nothing if not maddening.

My hips kept up their unhurried movements, pushing forward until I bottomed out inside her. Emery's hands on my backside continued to urge me on, and every time I thrust in, I ground against that perfect spot, the one that made her squirm, breath gusting out. I made it my mission to target that tiny bundle of nerves with every forward movement until Emery was shouting her release for the countryside to hear. I was close behind. My crisis struck as her intimate muscles tightened and fluttered around me.

Movements jerky and broken, I pressed my face into the warm skin of Emery's neck. Her breaths were ragged, and her heart a beating drum beneath my own.

After a moment, I wrestled my trousers back into place and flopped down onto the blanket. Emery did the same and finally settled next to my side, head resting on my shoulder as she draped her arm across my chest.

As much as I coveted her body and lost myself to her touch, I treasured these moments of intimacy just as deeply. It was the tangible proof that our friendship could survive whatever we were doing to each other. We'd always been comfortable in each other's lives but now we were comfortable in each other's arms as well. This safety, visible and quantifiable, gave me hope that our relationship could survive being lovers. Even if Emery never knew of my love … this could be enough.

"Are you hungry? We could eat now that your other hunger has been sated," I teased.

She laughed, the sound loose and open. "I'm not ready to move. How glorious is this day? I want to make love outside every day." Emery laughed again, shorter this time but just as freely.

Her comment sobered me. I was stealing that freedom away. There wouldn't be lovemaking outdoors for us soon. We'd be trapped in London by my own hand. The guilt swelled within and I squeezed my arms tighter around her.

"Emery, do you think you'd be happier here?"

A pause. "What do you mean?"

I could feel her head turning against me, trying to catch my eye. But if I was going to do this—suggest leaving my heart behind— then I couldn't look at her. "I mean, you could stay. Here in Hampshire for part of the season, and then join me later in London. I would hate to take you away if it would make you happier to stay on without me."

Emery sat up quickly, her hair a ruin. Evidence of our lovemaking falling down around her shoulders. "You don't want me to come to London with you?" It was an accusation with a healthy dose of hurt to help it along.

I sat up too. "Of course I want you with me, but I also know how much you dislike it there. I don't want you to be miserable just because I want you with me. And I'll be so busy there at the start of the season. I would hate for you to suffer because of who I am now."

It was as if my words didn't register. She spoke without acknowledging them. "But I've been trying so hard. I thought I was doing well … not like my normal self at all."

Frowning, I demanded, "What do you mean? Not like your normal self?"

Her features were heartbreaking. Because while she was visibly frustrated and overwhelmed by the turn the conversation had taken, she was also wilted and unsure of herself. It made me reach for her quite desperately.

But she pulled away. "I was trying so hard to be the perfect duchess for you, Augie. I want to fit in in London. I'll do better." Her eyes were wild and unfocused, hardly seeing me and the confusion I was surely wearing. "I'll work on my society smile. I'll try harder. I want to be where you are even if that's London."

Was she … did she truly think she wasn't good enough? I'd assumed she'd put these reservations to rest. Had I allowed this? Made doubts creep in and turned my best friend into this frantic creature before me? I thought back to that morning in the dining room when I'd teased her and she'd smiled for the footman. She'd been serious. She'd thought … she needed to be someone else, someone different.

I was going to be sick. "Emery," I attempted to quiet her agitated rambling. Grabbing for her hands again, I tried to bring her attention back to me. "Emery, stop this. I married *you*. I want *you*. I don't want some perfect duchess, some ideal. I only want you to be yourself. You needn't practice a smile or a curtsey or any other thing. You're my wife. I'm not worried about you embarrassing me or anything else."

"But I am, Augie. Those ladies at Lady Thisby's ball. I heard them."

I kept Emery's hands in mine but she still refused to meet my gaze. "What ladies? What happened?"

She made a reluctant sound before sighing. "I overheard some women talking about me. About how simple and plain and countrified I was. And how you could do better for yourself and for the dukedom."

I considered her words for a moment and thought back to that evening. "Emery, you did nothing for them to criticize. They were just being mean and spiteful." A new thought arose. "That's why your sister whisked you away. She knew?"

"She found me after I'd heard them, embarrassed and shaking in the ballroom." I could tell it pained Emery to admit her reaction. "Don't you see, Augie? I don't know how to behave because they don't want someone like me in London. I can never be myself because it would hurt you. The *ton* doesn't want a woman like me, someone wild or loud or a successful artist or any of that."

"An artist? What? And how could you ever hurt me?"

Emery ignored my questions and my confusion before pressing on. "I don't know how to be what they want because even when I try … it's not good enough."

Squeezing her hands, I said with all the feeling I could muster, "I don't want you to change who you are, Em."

Finally—fucking finally—her gaze rose to mine, but what I saw there broke my heart. "Well, what if who I am isn't right for you?"

❧

What felt like a lifetime later, I made my way to the tree house. We hadn't used it since we'd married, but I knew without a doubt that I'd find Emery there. She wouldn't be waiting for me in Kensworth Hall.

Upon returning from my busy afternoon, I'd dropped my mare off at the stables and made my way on foot through the wildflower field, needing a moment to collect myself.

I'd worked in the fields and consulted with the farmers until night had fallen. The men had used all the daylight to harvest and I'd done my best despite being distracted and anxious to seek out Emery.

After our midday lovemaking and that confounding conversation that had not gone the way I'd intended, Emery had needed space. She'd essentially suggested we weren't right for each other and then fled on horseback knowing I couldn't follow her. Letting her gallop away had felt wrong on a visceral level, but I knew this woman. I'd hurt her with my well-meaning intentions and she needed time. I didn't wish to hurt her even more.

I knew how to make this right. I just needed to see her, to apologize. I never should have asked her to stay behind. Unknowingly, I'd played on her fears and insecurities. Admittedly, I hadn't known the depths of those worries. I needed to reassure her that I wanted her with me, just as she was. She needn't assume some role or change herself for me or her title or anyone in London.

I would fix this. I would tell her every day if necessary.

The night had grown chilly, but it was clear and bright. With the moon hovering overhead, I followed a path from memory and longing. When I saw the light from the tree house shining in the distance, I let loose a relieved breath that I felt like I'd been holding in all afternoon.

Picking up my pace, I closed the remaining distance. Eager to drive away the distance that my actions and thoughtlessness had put between us.

Pulling myself through the narrow entrance, I started speaking before I even laid eyes on Emery. "I'm so sorry. I never should have asked you to remain in Hampshire. It was foolish and above all, a lie. Of course I want you with me. I'll always want you by my side."

Emery was seated on the blanket, watching me ramble and force out all the things I wanted to say. Everything except how much I loved her. I couldn't use those feelings to convince her of how much I wanted her with me. I refused to manipulate her that way.

I didn't provide an opening for her to respond, but kept speaking. "Everything changed when John died." *Truth.* "I just felt so damn guilty." *Truth.* "I never wanted to change the terms of our arrangement." *Lie.* I wanted to make her mine in every way that mattered. In every way that was honest. "This marriage was supposed to be for us both, but I've always known I would be the one who would benefit the most. And here is the proof. You being forced to leave the country you so love."

"Augie, stop. I don't care about all of that. I've never kept score between us in our friendship or in … our marriage now. That's not how a partnership works."

Finally settling myself before her, I admitted, "I feel like all I ever do is disappoint everyone around me."

Emery made a wounded sound before cupping my cheeks. "Shhh, Augie. No."

But I interrupted her attempt to console me. "No, I should have told you all along. You are perfect and I don't want you to change yourself for me. I'm so proud you are my wife, though I have no ownership in you. You are entirely your own person and exactly who I want by my side."

Eyes brimming with emotion, Emery nodded jerkily before pressing her lips to mine. "Promise me you'll stop keeping score in this marriage. Let us lead and follow when the situation requires it."

Pulling her hands away from my jaw and cradling them in my own, I responded in earnest. "I will try." Still maintaining her gaze, I issued a request of my own. "Promise me you'll stop belittling yourself by trying to be someone you are not."

She smiled then, a small lift to the corners of her lips that seemed to say *touché*. "I will try," Emery echoed.

I didn't deserve her. This beautiful creature. She should always be free and happy, not confined in a corset and bound by society's demands.

Remembering something she'd said in her panic earlier in the day, I thought back to her sketchbook I'd confiscated from her saddlebag. And the drawing session I'd trespassed on during our stay at the hunting cottage. "Are you ready to tell me about being a secret artist now?"

Emery sighed and then huffed out a laugh. "I don't know why I kept it from you. Why I ever kept it from you. I suppose I thought you'd think me a coward—"

"I could never."

Her gaze warmed at my assertion or perhaps the vehemence in my tone, before she finally admitted, "I'm M. Barton."

Shocked, I opened my mouth but couldn't seem to form words. Eventually I managed a strangled, "How?" as I took in the surprising woman before me.

"Well, I discovered a decade or so ago that I enjoyed painting and drawing. You were away at school, and later … I just didn't know how to tell you. Father hung one at Laurel Park and it was often admired but quickly discounted when it was found out that I, Emery Bartholomew, was the artist. Until one day when someone asked after the landscape, my father lied. He made up a mysterious painter who only worked via commission through a solicitor. And that's how my legend was born."

She seemed nervous to admit this bit of history to me. I couldn't fathom it … Emery being nervous about anything. But then I thought back to her working intensely at the table in the cottage— drawing me. She'd gone somewhere inside herself, and had created something deeply personal. I'd regretted my intrusion immediately but I'd been too consumed by her and witnessing a different side of Emery I'd never before seen.

"Who else knows?" I wondered.

"Just Father," she admitted. "And now you as well."

"You're so talented, Emery. That's amazing. I'm sorry it's become this secret that you have to hide yourself away. I understand why. And I wish that wasn't the case. You deserve fame and accolades as yourself, not some mysterious male counterpart."

Emery nodded but said nothing.

Gentling my voice, I said, "I'd love to see more of your work … if you'd ever like to show me."

"I'd like that." She laughed lightly. "I'm relieved that you know, honestly."

"I'm honored to know, and I'll keep your secret for as long as you'd like me to." I had an idea and spoke it aloud at once. "We could turn one of the guest suites into a studio for you. You wouldn't have to hide away in our home."

"Thank you, Augie." Emery's smile was wide and grateful, and I felt such relief in that moment. Truthfully I also felt shamed that such a small show of support had gone such a long way in assuring Emery of her place.

"I know it's strange, but it's your home too. I want you to feel comfortable there. To be happy. Even when you're upset and need space, you don't have to run away to the woods."

"That's not why I came here. It wasn't to escape you or our new home together."

I frowned. "Then why? Is it the nostalgia of the tree house? I know it contains our history and our friendship within its walls. That's how I see it, too, I suppose."

Emery tilted her head slightly, looked at me with a curious expression before she seemed to steel herself. "While all of that is true, we did grow up here together. Our friendship grew here as well. That's not why I came here though, and that's not really how I see it anymore. I came here because this place ... it's where I fell in love with you, Augie. All those weeks becoming *more*, learning and exploring each other. *Here* is where everything changed."

I said nothing. I couldn't. I was hardly able to breathe through her casual delivery of such an unapologetic claim.

She looked completely unruffled. "Stop shaking your head, Augustus." I wasn't aware I had been. "How are you this shocked?"

Covering my mouth with my hand, I scrubbed the whiskers along my jaw in frustration. "What?" I managed.

Emery's eyes widened. "Of course I love you. I've loved you my whole life. Now it's just different. It feels different here." She reached for my hand then and pressed it to her chest—to her heart.

I pulled back as if burned. Why was she saying this? It was utter cruelty. Emery didn't love me. She couldn't. I wasn't good enough for her. I never would be. We were too different and she didn't know what she was saying. The prospect of her love did nothing but tear me in two.

I wanted to stand and pace away from her but this damn tree house was closing in around me. It was made for children. We should have left it in our youth and never returned. I needed to escape the possibility of this—of something I never let myself hope for because it was as vast and unwieldy as the ocean. Emery was everything good and brave and so very alive. I was the overly practical force at her back, the quiet voice discouraging her wildness. And the titled lord taking away all her freedom. She couldn't possibly love me. I was a future she'd neither wanted nor asked for.

I made for the ladder, attempting to put space between us. Without turning back, I said, "You don't know what you're saying."

For once, Emery was composed and rational in the face of battle. I was the one unhinged and unmoored, feeling out of my skin and on the verge of shouting.

Her words floated to me, even and calm. "I've tried to take this slow. I've been patient. For you, Augustus. For you. Showing you every day that I meant it. In my actions and my words and in our life together. I love you," she said again, causing me to wince as I paused by the hatch in the floorboards. "It's been true for a while now. I wanted to take my time, do things your way. Steady and safe." A shaky exhale. "You've been my best friend, my person, for my whole life. I've shared my body with you. I want our future to be real, Augie. A marriage in truth. Where we are husband and wife and we have a family and we are happy. No arrangement. Nothing fake about it."

Bracing my hand against the wall, I snapped my gaze to Emery at last. While her voice was measured and her words were delivered softly, her whiskey eyes blazed with fire. I had a moment to appreciate that her confidence had returned after our earlier conversation. Her poise and ferocity hadn't abandoned her in the end. And for what? To confuse us both. To break my fucking heart.

After a deep breath, I tried again. "You don't mean all that. It's not possible."

That amber flame licked higher. "Well, I just bloody told you I loved you. So, yes. I do mean it."

I shook my head, attempting to dispel the hope warring in my soul. "It's easy to get confused, Emery. You got caught up in all of the new intimacy between us—"

"Oh!" She cut me off, all fire now. "You think I can't tell the difference between feeling good in bed or against a bookcase or bent over a desk and what I know in my heart when I look at you? When I simply think of you?"

Hand still pressed to the wooden slats, I ground my teeth before finding my voice one last time. "Our marriage is an illusion, Emery."

I made it halfway down the ladder before she shouted her reply. It was a dagger, flying end over end before landing true, right between my ribs. "Well, it felt pretty damn real to me."

EMERY

"Of all the ridiculous, asinine, pigheaded, idiotic ..." My muttered complaints devolved into grunts punctuated by intermittent curse words.

After my imbecile of a husband had fled into the night, I'd blown out the candles—wouldn't want to burn down the physical embodiment of our friendship—and ridden Beatrice Three back home. Well, back to my family's home. I wasn't going to Kensworth Hall tonight. I'd likely murder Augie or worse, burst into angry tears.

I was determined to hang on to my anger, clutch my righteous indignation to my breast, and make him suffer for being so insufferable.

After finding an empty stall, I relinquished my horse. I removed her tack and provided water and a bucket of grain in an attempt to soothe. Beatrice, ever sensitive to my moods, had absorbed my rotten attitude during the short ride to Laurel Park. I couldn't blame her for being cross with me. I was cross with myself.

What had I been thinking to admit my feelings to Augie? But also how could he have possibly been unprepared for my admission?

The past few weeks had been busy but blissful. I knew Augie was distracted by his ducal duties but I'd attempted to make our time together, however brief, fun and eventful. I wanted to vanquish his worries, and did my best not to be a burden on his time and energy. And not just since our return from London, but our entire marriage had been going so well. I had been patient with my emotions, refusing to foist them on Augie before he was ready.

But the time had seemed right. That moment in the tree house had felt like the perfect opportunity to make my feelings known. But his reaction …

Bah! Now I was mad again.

I marched out of the stables and through the gardens to the rear entrance. Making an effort to control my angry stomping, I endeavored to sneak quietly to my former bedroom.

I was grateful in this moment that we'd been slow to transfer all of my belongings to Kensworth Hall. With the eventual move to London for the season, I had been waiting to have my things packed. Procrastination and dragging my feet had proved benefi-cial once again.

I removed my riding clothes and pulled on a nightgown. But then I was out of tasks, and my angry energy hadn't abated. I didn't want to replay our fight and Augie's incredulous words. I didn't want to wallow alone in my childhood bedroom.

Just then I heard a quiet but insistent scratching at my bedroom door. Rushing over, I quickly opened the door to find an aggrieved-looking Gansey on the other side. She brushed past me into my bedchamber. I peeked into the darkened hallway beyond, and when I'd determined that all was clear, I shut my door with a quiet snick.

Gansey had settled herself on top of my coverlet. Blond hair in her nightly plait, she was pulling something out of the basket in her lap.

"What are you doing here?" I asked softly. I was grateful for her presence but unsure how she came to be here.

"Anders found me after Augustus returned home in a temper like he'd never seen. I assumed the worst, and when I didn't find you in residence anywhere, I came here." Her eyes were worried. "I may have also swung by the kitchens and brought some cake with me."

"God bless your cake intuition." I hurried over and joined her on the bed.

Gansey handed me a confection wrapped in a linen napkin. "What happened?"

I placed the fabric bundle on my lap before recounting the disastrous evening in the tree house. Still feeling indignant, I continued heatedly. "Can you believe he refused to listen to me? To even hear me? He not only doubted my sincerity, he refused to believe that I know my own heart and mind. It was unbearable, Gansey."

Did Augie still truly believe our marriage to be a sham? It had been real to me all along. I'd been his wife in mind, body, and soul. And his complete and utter denial tonight had cracked my heart into jagged angry shards.

Gansey looked thoughtful. She broke off a piece of her own cake and chewed carefully before replying. "I'm sorry, Emery."

My friend's quiet acceptance of events cooled my resentful venting. "He lives to be a martyr. I swear, it's as if he thinks himself unworthy of love."

My ire diminished by another degree as I considered Augie and the few examples of love he'd had in his life. His brother had rejected him and diminished him. The Dowager, while affectionate, had enabled and sided with John more often than not. Augie's fraternal relationship with Anders was perhaps the healthiest demonstration of love he had. With the exception of his friendship with me. I sighed.

How could he possibly think it was anything but love growing unchecked between us since that very first kiss?

I frowned, considering. He didn't say it wasn't love. He said he didn't believe it.

Augie who was so cautious and restrained. Augie who never stood up for himself. Augie who put everyone else first. Augie who was unable to see himself clearly. And Augie … who never took what he wanted.

The last of my irritation receded like the tide.

"How do I fight for our happiness when Augie is the one I have to battle against?"

"I don't know, Emery. I don't know how you convince someone that they are worthy of love. And that sacrifice isn't always necessary."

We stopped talking for a time and simply nibbled our respective cakes. Once every crumb was consumed, Gansey asked, "What are you going to do?"

I looked at my friend and said, "I don't know." It was honest and it flayed me open to admit it. "But I'm going to figure it out. For once, I think Augie needs to be rescued."

"So you're not angry with him?"

I scoffed. "Oh, no. I'm definitely angry with him. But what we have is too important not to fight for. I tried doing things Augie's way ... being patient and controlled. And that didn't seem to work at all. Perhaps it's time to approach this problem in my own way."

Gansey's eyes widened.

Flipping the covers back and holding them open for Gansey, I said, "Let's go to bed. I have some plotting to do before tomorrow night."

"Oh, lord," Gansey murmured before climbing in.

Leaning toward the candle on my bedside table, I watched the flame for a long moment before pursing my lips and plunging the room into darkness.

After smoothing the covers, I waited until all was quiet. "So are you ready to tell me what's going on with you and Anders?"

The pillow hit me square in the mouth and shocked a laugh from me. Gansey's mirth joined my own. That was okay. I'd get it out of her eventually.

I was still avoiding Augie the following day. Gansey had returned to Kensworth Hall, but I'd stayed behind and had been lurking around Laurel Park. Mama was visiting neighbors in the village and I'd thankfully evaded a conversation there. She didn't need to know why I was back home in my own bedroom for the time being. I had a plan and part of said plan was to cool off and not approach my husband with anger and condemnation in my heart. And perhaps Augie needed some space to get a handle on his emotions. He'd always been one to take his time to reach a conclusion. I hoped he'd come to realize I was sincere in my affection on his own. But I wasn't counting on it.

That afternoon after having pilfered a few treats from Mrs. Pennyworth, I stumbled upon my father and a guest outside his study. He seemed to be in the process of escorting the man out.

"Emery, what a surprise!" Gesturing to the man now entering the hallway behind him, Father continued, "This is Mr. Palsson. He's new to the area having just purchased the Hawthorn estate. Palsson, this is my middle daughter, Emery. She and the Duke of Kendrick recently wed."

Father's guest was a little older than me, fairly tall with dark brown hair graying at the temples. He wore a close-cropped beard and welcoming smile.

I dropped a small curtsey. "How do you do, Mr. Palsson?"

"Very well, Your Grace." He bowed. "It's a pleasure to meet you."

"I was just showing Mr. Palsson out," my father confirmed. "Would you like to have tea with me, Emery? It's good to see you."

"Of course, Father. Thank you. I'll wait here and let you escort your guest."

The stranger lingered for a moment before turning to my father, "You know, Lord Northcutt, I was quite serious about taking that painting off your hands. My wife is an art lover and I just know she'd love that landscape." He pointed in the open doorway of the study. I didn't have to follow the direction he indicated to know which painting he spoke of.

I stiffened, preparing myself for Father's standard reply. M. Barton would undoubtedly have another commission request within a fortnight.

"I'm afraid I can't part with that one." My father slid me an uncomfortable glance. "You see, Emery painted that for me many years ago. I'm rather attached to it. She's quite talented."

My eyes bulged. What in the bloody hell was he saying?

Rushing to cover my father's admission, I lied quickly. "Father, don't be silly. That one isn't mine." I could feel the strain evident on my face but I willed everyone in the hallway to believe what I was saying. "The painting I gave you is actually in—"

"Is in my study, Emery. It's yours."

Silence descended awkwardly as my father doubled down on his pronouncement. There would be no reinforcing the confused, elderly marquess routine now.

Eventually, Mr. Palsson glanced my way. Eyes friendly but assessing, he said, "Well, how convenient to have the accomplished artist right here, then. Your Grace, if your father cannot find it within himself to part with that painting, perhaps I could commission you to create something new. Something for Mrs. Palsson. Another lovely sunset perhaps?"

"Oh," I exhaled my surprise. In all the times my father had credited the artwork to me … no one had ever cared. They certainly hadn't wanted one of their own after learning the truth. Not an Emery Bartholomew original. I swallowed with some effort before managing a smile. "Yes, I would be happy to. Thank you for your interest."

"Thank *you*, my dear. Mrs. Palsson will be thrilled." He reached into the inner pocket of his waistcoat before producing a calling card. And after extracting a promise from me to call upon the Hawthorn estate soon to discuss details, Father walked Mr. Palsson out. I remained in the corridor with a stupefied expression until my meddling father returned.

"Mrs. Pennyworth is preparing the tea. Come join me, Emery."

I entered the study and sat in the upholstered armchair across from my father's desk. He seated himself behind it, eyes sparkling.

"Well," he said, amusement in his tone.

I laughed lightly. "It's never gone like that before."

Expression dimmed somewhat, he agreed. "No, I suppose it hasn't."

I really looked at Father. His brown eyes were uncomfortable, perhaps a touch remorseful. "Why did you tell Mr. Palsson the truth about the painting? Why not follow the script you've long ago perfected and pass along your solicitor's information for an M. Barton acquisition?"

Father sighed deeply. "You know, I've always loved sharing that secret with you. Whenever we've been at an event or at the dining table and heard about an M. Barton painting, I could always share a knowing look with you. It was something special, something shared between you and I." I nodded my agreement before he continued, "But perhaps in all the secrecy and concealment, I got lost in the game of it. And I think you got lost as well."

Frowning, I asked, "What do you mean?"

Father fidgeted a bit, shuffling some papers around before meeting my gaze. "I think your efforts and your accomplishments got overshadowed, Emery. You assumed this role of mysterious painter and forgot to feel pride in all you'd accomplished. As yourself. I agreed to the secrecy for the fun of it, for the novelty. I've never once been shamed by you. When you were young and overwhelmed by your mother's demands and saddened by Patricia's move to London, I thought you needed this. Something you could call your own. I didn't know it would become a secret art empire." He paused briefly. "I regret lying. I wish that you could own your accomplishments. I would tell the whole world that M. Barton is my daughter. I'm so very proud of you, my dear. Your talents and your strengths and how distinctive you are. And now more than ever—in your new role as a duchess—I think you need to hold on to something for yourself."

I had never felt more childlike in my life, hearing this praise from my father. I wanted to tuck myself in his arms and cry like a baby. Sometimes people don't realize the impact of their words, and how saying something at the perfect time can alter someone's existence. My father couldn't know of my internal struggles, the self-doubt and insecurity I faced in London, as Duchess. But here he was, speaking directly to my heart and lifting me up.

My chin wobbled quite against my will. "Really? You don't think I'm too … much?"

Father smiled gently. "Why would you want to make yourself smaller? Do we ask the sun to dim its light?"

I offered a watery smile in return.

"What's going on, Emery? Not that I am unhappy to see you, but why are you here?" my father asked, looking slightly uncomfortable.

"I just needed some time. Augie and I … we quarreled," I finally admitted.

Father laughed lightly. "Oh well. That does tend to happen between people who love each other. If you didn't care so much, then the other person couldn't possibly make you so angry."

I agreed in a small voice, "I suppose that's true."

"I've been waiting for you and that boy to figure out your future together for a long time. I assumed Augie would approach me for your hand at some point. I did not expect you to announce your betrothal over the vegetable course however." Another small laugh. "But I've known for a long time that your paths were meant to converge. Of course it wouldn't happen the conventional way. I should have known better than to expect that."

Looking down at my lap, I felt foolish for being blind to so much for so very long.

"If you haven't already, I think you should tell Augustus about your painting career," he advised. "I feel certain he would support you. Who we are doesn't have to be a burden to those around us, Emery. Let Augie see the heart of you. You should feel free to be yourself with him."

My father had always been kind and patient. He was often wary of emotions in his daughters, and frankly, there *were* three of us. Emotions were plentiful over the years. He'd always indulged my mother and shown interest in all of us. I felt grateful to have a father who gave me his time and attention. And today his parental advice was timely and meaningful. I hadn't sought it out, but that didn't make the impact any less profound.

I would show Augie my wild and reckless heart. And the place inside, carved out just for him.

259

Seventeen

AUGUSTUS

"Are you going to hide in here all day?" Anders slowly entered the study as if approaching a wild animal. I supposed I did have a feral quality hanging about me. I'd never felt so unfit for polite company.

My foul temper formulated several answers before I discarded all options and simply shook my head.

"She's not here anyway." If this was my friend's attempt to draw me into conversation, it was a poor choice, and I, an even worse conversationalist.

I knew Emery was gone. She hadn't returned last night following the scene at the tree house. I hadn't been ready to face her anyway. I didn't know when I'd be prepared for that. I was restless in my own skin, fighting the pull of her and the need for self-preservation. Perhaps I was hiding in this room in case she *did* return.

However, I knew Emery would be back. She would never let this uneasiness rest between us. She would plan a way to get what she wanted. But what she wanted was impossible. Emery was asking me to believe in something so far outside the realm of possibility. My mind had labeled it forbidden ages ago. The prospect of Emery, or her love, felt terrifying.

Wishing for something unattainable was the quickest way to realize the boundary of hope. It was no longer chasing a dream. It became killing your spirit. One small denial at a time. I'd taken the idea of loving Emery and buried it. My fantasy was in a graveyard somewhere and here she was trying to resurrect it. The notion was unfathomable.

I had confessed the situation to Anders upon my return last night. I'd asked him to find Gansey and ensure Emery was safe—wherever she was.

Anders's advice had been to simply accept what my wife had confessed and be grateful. That input had only furthered my bad temper and Anders had avoided me until now.

How could I follow my friend's guidance? I couldn't possibly just accept getting everything I'd ever wanted without turning over every scenario, questioning all motivations, and considering the sacrifices required. That was who I was.

I didn't want to hurt Emery. And despite her out-of-character patient confrontation last night, she had been hurt. Even in my emotionally overwhelmed state, I'd seen that. I'd hurt her when I'd questioned her feelings. I'd called our marriage an illusion. My stomach turned at my remembered words.

But her admission that she loved me—Christ, I could hardly think it—and how it had manifested was plaguing me. She'd said it was through the changes in our relationship, becoming lovers, and those weeks in the tree house prior to our wedding that made her realize the depth of her feelings. I didn't want to capture her heart by owning her desire. Sharing that sort of intimacy for the first time was likely the cause of her confusion and misplaced emotions. Of course she assumed she loved me when so much physicality was involved. Her revelation was coloring our time together. I felt like I had stolen her affections rather than earned them.

But there was a small part of me that thought *what if*. What if it was true and Emery's heart was waiting on me to get my head out of my ass and live a life we both deserved? A life together in true partnership.

And an even smaller part thought *what does it matter how it came to be?* So what if I'd shown her pleasure and triggered an answering call in her heart?

I didn't know how to remedy my internal strife. Feeling like I was being torn in a thousand directions was growing tiresome.

"Would you prefer I just leave too?" Anders's quiet question, filled with judgement, brought me out of my thoughts.

"I fear I'm not fit for company," I finally admitted. In truth, I felt ill letting so much time and space pass without seeking Emery out. It was unbearable to have our relationship so strained and unresolved. The harshness of my words from the evening prior floated back to me and my chest constricted.

Anders stood for a long moment in front of my desk regarding me. "At some point, Augie, you have to stop standing in your own way. You're going to have to trust someone. If you really loved Emery, you wouldn't diminish her so easily. You dishonor her by casting her opinion aside just because it doesn't align with the lie you've told yourself for so long."

I said nothing.

My friend nodded to himself and then quit the room.

He was right, of course. It was a disservice to any person to discount their thoughts and feelings. I knew the consequences of belittling another. I'd lived with my brother's constant neglect and outright invalidation for years. He'd cast my dreams and ideas for our family's legacy aside, and our relationship along with it.

And here I was, ignoring my best friend, my wife, the love of my life. It wasn't the first time either. I thought back to the weeks following John's death when I tried to end our betrothal and Emery telling me I didn't trust her to know her own mind. I'd apologized then, contrite. But I was doing it again—making the same damn mistake.

My gaze strayed to the window and the evening sun dropping toward the horizon.

I knew this wasn't the end of us. Emery was too stubborn to allow our friendship to fall apart. But after I'd broken us so thoroughly last night, I didn't know if the pieces could be put back together or in what order they'd go.

After Anders's determined speech, that small part of me whispering *what if* was growing louder. What if it was true? What if Emery loved me? What if our happiness didn't require a sacrifice?

She'd always been the brave one. Perhaps it was time for me to show a little courage.

Rising from the desk, I approached the window overlooking the gardens as I watched the sun make its final descent.

Emery wasn't here. I needed to find her and apologize. I needed to do so many things to set us right.

I should find Gansey and ask after her lady. I resolved myself to go and fetch Emery. I wasn't sure what I'd tell her, but I wouldn't shut her out and I wouldn't belittle her with doubts.

If I was smart, I'd beg her forgiveness. Tell her I loved her too. Kiss her and spend the rest of my life being happy. And not consider and analyze it to death.

One step at a time.

Eyes unfocused, I finally took in the scenery before me. The shadows long and the light dimming as the sun sank lower in the sky. And … smoke.

I stepped closer to the glass, fingertips pressing against the pane as I took in the column of smoke drifting over the field behind the estate and out of view.

My heart was beating too fast. It was impossible to tell the origin of the blaze but it looked like it came from the forest, the direction of the tree house. I doubted she'd return to the tree house and the scene of our argument. The tiny structure in the woods felt rife with tension now that I knew we viewed it so differently. I saw our history and friendship and she'd seen our future. The divide felt symbolic and the wounds too fresh to revisit. She'd likely spent the previous night at her family's estate and remained there today. Surely all was well and Emery was safe. She had to be.

I bolted away from the window and made for the stables as fast as my legs would carry me. When I approached the long structure, a groom was returning from exercising one of our thoroughbreds. I took the reins from the startled man and mounted before setting us off at a gallop.

The faster we raced across the countryside, the faster my breaths came. I kept telling myself she was safe. She was at Laurel Park. She was sketching in her notebook. She was cursing me to

Gansey. She was dining with her family. If I filled my head with enough innocuous scenarios then all the others would be forced out.

But as I got closer to the tree house, I could see the smoke getting thicker, taking my fears and giving them shape and conjecture. A blond head bent over a book, reading by candlelight. Emery falling asleep in the tree house. A strong evening breeze through the tattered lace curtains. A candle falling on the blanket we kept there. My heart unable to bear that kind of loss.

I pushed the winded horse faster and before long … there it was, our secret—our hideaway—engulfed in flames and the smoke rising black and nebulous like a specter of tragedy. The single tree stood in front of the tree line, completely consumed.

My horse balked when we reached an invisible wall of heat. I slid from its back and landed upright on the ground, unable to look away from the flames.

My eyes burned and I couldn't tell if it was from the smoke or from despair. I searched the surrounding area frantically. Perhaps … she got out. Maybe she'd never been here in the first place. I refused to let my mind fixate on the worst-case scenario and the last words I'd so callously spoken to her as I listened to the crackle and hiss of the wood. When my gaze swung around again, I took in a startled breath.

There she was. Standing twenty feet away from me watching it burn was Emery. Her hair was loose and wild and she had two buckets at her feet. Then I was running, grabbing her and pulling her roughly into me.

"Are you hurt?" I demanded. I pulled back and let my frantic gaze travel over her form. No soot or smoke marred her. I couldn't detect any burns or singed clothing.

She was clutching my arms in return. "No. No, I'm fine. I wasn't inside."

Wrapping myself around her desperately, I didn't let myself consider the fact that I could have lost her. Emery was here and whole. She hugged me back just as tightly.

"I saw the smoke. I thought ..." I swallowed roughly before continuing. "What happened?"

Emery pulled out of my embrace before clasping my hand and tugging me away. The ground beneath my feet was wet, completely saturated and soggy. I could feel my boots sinking with each step.

Emery walked for a moment and led me far from the fiery tree before answering. "I burned it down."

My feet pulled to a stop as I registered her words. "You what?"

She turned to face me, eyes fierce and unapologetic. "I burned it down, Augie. If all you can see when you look at the tree house is friendship—a symbol of our shared history—then I would gladly sacrifice it. Because we are so much more than that. I don't want our past and everything that goes with it to imprison you and hold you hostage. I want a future with you. That's more important to me than holding on to who we were." She stepped closer and took my face in her hands, smoothing her thumbs over my stunned features before cupping my cheeks. "I love you and I *know* you love me." Her words were defiant and accusatory. She was waiting for me to resist and tell her she was wrong.

My throat was tight with emotion but I could only stare at her determined face.

"I know it, Augie. It's how you indulge me and go along with my every whim. It's how you love my wild even though it's not your style. It's how you roll your eyes at me and know my thoughts as your own. It's our connection and easiness with one another. And it's how you look at me. I'm sorry I didn't see it sooner. I know you better than anyone in the world and I didn't see it, and I'm so sorry, Augie." Emery was crying now and her apology came out broken and stuttering.

I closed the distance between us and kissed her mouth, her chin, and her cheeks lined with tear tracks from the smoky air. Wrapping her up in my arms, I admitted desperately, "You didn't see it because I didn't want you to. I hid it away and never even let myself think on it. I've been so terrified you'd figure it out and I'd scare you away. Or that things would change between us, our easiness evaporating and awkwardness taking its place. You have always been the best thing in my life, Emery. I couldn't lose you. So I kept it from you. And I'm sorry. I would have rather taken my feelings to the grave than sacrifice our friendship."

Full dark settling around us now, she looked at me for a long moment, amber eyes reflecting firelight. "Well, it's a good thing you have me to set it ablaze."

I huffed a surprised laugh. "I've loved you for so long, Em. When you told me you loved me … I just couldn't fathom it in my wildest dreams. I'm so sorry I didn't believe you. The things I said—" Cutting myself off, I stared shame-faced at the earth beneath my boots. "I didn't mean them. I'm sorry I hurt you. I was utterly terrified and completely wrong. I just couldn't accept that I was getting everything I'd ever wanted. To me, people don't just *get* to have happy endings. It's not the way of things."

"No, it's not," Emery agreed hotly. "You have to work for them. You might say it's a dream, but that's some idealized version of me and us together that you've had on a pedestal in your mind. Our marriage will be hard work. It's not a fantasy. It's deciding every day to love one another, to want the best for each other, and to trust. I need you to trust me that I know my own mind. And trust my love, Augie. I'll remind you as often as you need me to, but I need you to believe it."

I nodded, unable to look away. I could do this. I could set aside my worries and fears. For her. For Emery, I would. "I love you," I said for the first time. Allowing the words beyond my lips felt fraught. I wanted to snatch them back lest they do irreparable damage.

But Emery's smile eased the disquiet of my admission. "I love you too."

Eyes finally dry, she stepped out of my arms and turned to watch the remnants of the blaze. We stood shoulder to shoulder, fingers twined together. The smoke still rose, but the flames had burned themselves out for the most part. Only embers remained. The tree itself was charred and dark. The structure it held was a hollowed-out husk, some pieces having broken off and landed on the saturated ground.

"The buckets?" I questioned.

"I watered the area around the perimeter of the tree so that the fire wouldn't spread and that any falling sparks wouldn't light. I knew it was far enough from the tree line that the others weren't in any danger of catching unless it spread over the dry grass."

We were quiet for a time, just watching the smoke dissipate in the clear night sky. This was my future and I was living it. There would be no more hiding. No more sacrificing my own happiness. And Emery was right. It would be an effort, a conscious decision we made. It wouldn't be perfect, but it would be ours. And that was all I'd ever really wanted.

I finally broke the silence. "I can't believe you did that."

Emery turned toward me, one eyebrow raised, smile wicked. "Yes, you can."

I gifted her an indulgent smile before rolling my eyes. "You're right. I can."

Eighteen

EMERY

Two months later

"Do you see the woman with the coal-black hair and lavender gown? That's Tabitha Mooneyham, the Countess Drakefield. She's very soft spoken but tells the bawdiest jokes you've ever heard in your life."

"Truly?" I asked Mary.

"Indeed," Patty confirmed Mary's description. "And curses like a dockworker."

"Well." That sounded like someone I'd like to be acquainted with.

Correctly interpreting my thoughts, my sister replied, "I'll introduce you to Tab this evening."

I smiled my gratitude and she returned it with one of her own.

Those smiles were coming easier. Our interactions were far less awkward and stilted now. Ever since she and Mary had rescued me from Lady Thisby's soiree, I'd seen a new side to my sister. Augie had been right in his advice all those months ago. I needed to stop thinking about the Patty I'd lost. She'd been through so much. That bright-eyed girl didn't exist anymore. But I could have Patty in my life now, as she was. A woman with life experience and a slightly bitter edge. We could still be sisters. I'd simply needed to adjust my expectations. And I think she'd needed to do the same.

We were learning our way around each other. Redefining our relationship.

She and Mary had welcomed me into their circle. I received invitations and insight into every event we attended. They never left me to fend for myself. I'd been warned off making acquaintances with women who they'd had poor experiences with or prior knowledge of their disingenuous behaviors. Mary and Patty made it their goal to see me settled happily in London, and that meant avoiding gossip and vipers in ballgowns. It helped that I was a married duchess and not in competition for the attentions of unmarried gentlemen. For the most part, I fell beneath the notice of unwed young ladies enjoying their first season. Some were eager to make a connection to the Kendrick title, but those girls and their enterprising mamas were easy to spot.

I'd bumped into Miss Gratton several times in the last month since we'd returned to town. She always had a pretty word or friendly smile for me. It helped remind me to never let my guard down. And to remember that appearances were often deceiving. Having Mary and my sister and their vast knowledge of nobles helped beyond measure. I didn't know what I'd do without them.

"Oh, there's Lady Gabriella." Mary indicated a lovely young woman who appeared to be a few years my senior. "We'll introduce you to her as well. She's wonderful and has a brilliant sense of humor."

"And she always serves these little lemon cakes with custard filling that you would appreciate, Emery," Patty added helpfully.

"I do appreciate good cake," I agreed.

"Oh, Patty," Mary groaned suddenly. "Prepare yourself. Here comes Thomas Faulk."

I straightened and turned my head in the direction Mary watched discretely. A rather young-looking gentleman was approaching, determination in his stride.

"Your Grace, good evening," the man—apparently Thomas Faulk—said jovially.

"Hello, Lord Finnigan. It's lovely to see you again." My sister's voice was strained with the effort to maintain decorum. She was painfully uncomfortable—even I could tell. "You know Lady Mary." He nodded warily which I'd noticed was how a great many people approached Mary Lovelace. "And this is my sister, newly in London. Emery Ward, the Duchess of Kendrick."

The man gave a tidy bow over my offered hand before saying enthusiastically, "Your Grace, I am so very pleased to meet you."

"Thank you," I replied, a little struck by his exuberance.

Lord Finnigan turned his pleased expression back to Patty. "Your Grace, I am so happy to meet one of your relations. What a wonderful night!"

I shared a brief look with Mary. Her eyes widened comically before she looked away. I made sure my expression was even before I faced the newcomer again. It wouldn't do to laugh.

With an expectant look for my sister, Lord Finnigan said, "I was hoping I might have the next dance."

"Oh, I do apologize, my lord. I'm taking a brief respite from all the dancing." Despite not having danced at all. "I was just feeling so parched and overheated. My brother-in-law was so kind to retrieve some lemonade for me. I'm sure he'll return shortly." The lord made to speak again, but Patty pressed on, "I appreciate your offer. Perhaps another time."

Lord Finnigan cast a quick glance over his shoulder toward a group of men near the balcony doors before nodding at Patty and bidding us all a good evening.

Taking in my sister's tense expression during the exchange with Thomas Faulk, her relief was palpable when he finally left. I said quietly, "That was very odd. Was it not?"

Mary and Patty shared a look full of meaning, one that once again excluded me while simultaneously offending the most insecure part of myself. It lasted no more than a second before my sister motioned us away from the crush of bodies nearby.

After a protracted glance at those just shy of hearing distance, Patty explained softly, "Lord Finnigan has been persistent in his attentions."

I frowned immediately, disliking the implication. "Is he dangerous? Has he hurt you, Patty?"

"No, Em. No. He … He's in need of a fortune. Specifically an heiress to wed. His family is in debt after decades of mismanagement. And he's very determined to court me."

"He's not the only one," Mary muttered with an eye roll.

"Well, of course. Patty is very desirable. But why did you say it that way?" I inquired.

My sister looked very uncomfortable. Frustration edged her features and I felt helpless in the face of it.

"It means," Mary intoned dramatically. "That every titled lord in need of funds has been after your sister since she came out of mourning. She has refused to court and was overheard publicly claiming she would never marry again." Patty made a grumbling sound at this disclosure, but Mary continued unbothered. "And it seems all the young bucks, and old bucks too, have taken that as a challenge. She receives an invitation to every event and is frequently mobbed with requests for dancing, drinks, conversation, and more."

My eyes widened as I processed this information. "And the circle of men that Lord Finnigan returned to?"

Mary glanced behind me briefly to where Finnigan sulked. Eyes narrowing slightly, she said, "Those also attempting to woo your sister. They're probably ribbing him for his failure. It rotates nightly. Another one of them will be over here before long to try his hand. Patty will shoot him down and the night will continue on. Usually I snag a few dances with her castoffs."

"That's awful," I exclaimed.

"I know," Mary agreed. "I wish I could secure my own dance partners. Alas. I wasn't blessed with your sister's bank account nor her fine looks."

"Oh, do shut up," Patty groused. "There's nothing wrong with your looks. And you don't want any of those wastrels anyway."

"That's not true," Mary argued. "I want part of them."

"What does *that* mean?" I interjected.

Patty sighed but explained on behalf of her friend, as Mary had done for her. "Mary wants a child. The husband … she's less concerned about."

I sought to clarify. "So, Patty, you spend all your time dodging suitors? And, Mary, you are husband hunting so you can have a baby?"

"Essentially."

"For the most part," they replied at the same time.

I didn't know what to do with any of that. "Well, do let me know how I can help."

Mary and Patty both aimed smiles in my direction.

Moments later, Augie approached bearing refreshment for my friends. "Ladies. Are you behaving?"

"Certainly not, Your Grace. You should know that by now." Mary winked at me and earned a smile from my husband.

"Well then, I feel it necessary to steal Emery away lest she get you respectable ladies into any trouble." This time, he winked at Mary and earned a smile from me.

I noticed Patty's gaze on us, warm but a little sad. I reached over impulsively and hugged her. I hated that she felt pursued in every ballroom she entered. And all for disingenuous reasons. She seemed startled by my affection but gave me a brief squeeze before laughing. "I'm sure Augie will return you, Em."

"Oh, surely. He'll tire of dancing soon enough."

I said my farewells as Augie escorted me to the dance floor. He looked rather dashing in his evening attire. As much as I used to protest these kinds of events, I didn't terribly mind the lovely dresses I frequently wore and the handsome husband on my arm.

"You know, I don't think I have you on my dance card, sir." I feigned confusion as I scanned the card about my wrist.

"Is that so, my lady?" Augie moved us into position as I gave him a cheeky grin. His blue eyes regarded me with equal parts amusement and exasperation. A sure sign that all was well. "Because I was fairly certain I was the only one on your dance card for the rest of our lives."

My smile widened as the quartet played the first strains of the quadrille. "I thought you didn't care for dancing?"

Augie's gaze turned warm. "I seem to find dancing enjoyable as long as it's with my wife." He leaned close then and whispered into my ear. "Besides, it allows me to touch you in front of all of these people."

And then he was breaking away from me to follow the momentum of the dancers around us.

His words heated my skin, a blush crawling over my cheekbones as I considered all the ways I wanted his hands on me. And the devil, he knew it too. Flashing me a mischievous grin as he floated between partners before finally making his way back for the final turn with me.

I laughed as he moved to stand before me. "You're a menace," I said. Repeating his words from so long ago.

"You better believe it," he echoed. And I laughed once more.

As the musicians transitioned into the next dance, Augie tucked my hand into the crook of his arm before leading me to the edge of the ballroom. "I never thought I'd see you laughing in a ball-room in London."

I cringed slightly when I thought of how loud I'd likely been in my amusement. It would probably take a while for me to feel completely comfortable among my peers. But things were going well thus far. With the guidance of my sister and Mary, I'd made some new acquaintances. I hadn't yet had to act as hostess for any of my own events in London. Augie said we could wait a while until I was ready.

My husband's expression turned serious. "Are you happy, Em? Truly?"

My instinct was to rush out a reply in the affirmative, to put Augie at ease. I knew he was still troubled by our unexpected path. Guilt still plagued him for necessitating our life here in London. While I wanted to reassure him, I also wanted to consider his question thoughtfully. Was I happy?

I had a home in the country waiting for me in another month. I was building a relationship with my elder sister after years of mourning her loss. I could still paint and do the work that I loved. It turned out they had parks and greenspaces inside of London and the rolling hills beyond the city borders were only a short carriage ride away. And I had Augie. I had the love of a husband in truth. No faking and no arrangement. We were partners in every sense of the word. I had a real husband and a true love.

I fought to keep my voice even when it threatened to wobble from all the happiness I possessed. "Yes, Augustus. I am truly happy."

He nodded once, face still serious and thoughtful.

"But I would be happy with you no matter where we lived," I amended.

"Really?" he questioned. "What about in Scotland?"

"Of course. It's very green there and I should like to paint some sheep."

He snorted but continued. "Would you be happy in America?"

"I don't see why not. I hear they have very fast horses there."

"How about in a house on the ocean?"

"Most definitely. I love swimming. We could race, you and I."

"Hmm," he mused. "Would you be happy in a tree house in the forest?"

Shaking my head sadly, I said, "I'm afraid not. I already burned that idea down."

Augie laughed, as I'd intended.

After a moment, he leaned close and whispered in my ear. "Do you have any regrets?"

I couldn't see his face to read his expression but I could hear the solemnity in his tone. I worried that he feared the honesty and openness of my expression and what he'd see when I answered. But he needn't have worried.

"Just one," I whispered back before pulling away and placing my hand on his cheek. Skin warm under my touch, I turned his head to meet my gaze head-on. Wanting him to see the truth of my words. The conviction in my eyes. "I wish I had demanded you marry me sooner."

Epilogue

EMERY

Some years later

"There you are."

I looked up in surprise as Augie approached on his mare. I'd been busy drawing, in my own little world.

Placing my sketchbook and drawing charcoal aside, I straightened from my hunched position on the blanket. If the protest in my back was any indication, I'd been out here drawing longer than I'd intended.

"Sorry," I called. "I got distracted."

Augie smiled warmly at me before dismounting and joining me on the blanket. He was in his riding breeches and shirtsleeves. It had taken some doing but he now favored being comfortable in place of dressing formally at all times. When it was just us at home in Hampshire, no one cared that he'd foregone a waistcoat. Now, we matched when we went riding together. I smiled to myself thinking of the effect my riding breeches still had on my husband.

"It's okay. I had the afternoon to myself and wanted to see you. Luckily I know most of your haunts." He dropped a sweet kiss on my cheek. "Although admittedly I'm a little surprised to see you here."

We both turned to look at the ruined tree house, claimed by the fire years ago. Truthfully, I rarely came here anymore. But today was special.

The tree containing our little hideaway was little more than a lonely trunk, bark ruined and black, branches and leaves no more.

"I was feeling nostalgic and whimsical today," I explained.

"Ah. Well, perhaps we should put up a plaque. Memorialize the structure." He held up his hands toward the tree forming a frame with his thumbs and forefingers. In a theatrical voice he announced, "The site of Emery Ward's first brush with arson—"

"First?" I squawked. "I don't plan on burning anything else down in my lifetime, thank you very much. That was for dramatic flair and symbolic emphasis. It's not my fault you're terribly stubborn."

I received an eye roll for my comment before he deadpanned, "Yes. I am the stubborn one."

Smothering a laugh, I picked up my notebook. I'd brought this old one with me for a reason. Turning from today's rendering of the destroyed structure, I thumbed back through to a much earlier section. These drawings were completed a handful of years ago. I glanced a simple line drawing of Laurel Park and a quick sketch of Beatrice Two as I turned the pages. Augie's attention had returned to the book in my hands, interested in the imagery. He was still helplessly nosy where my artwork was concerned. I'd caught him in my studio in London many times, observing while I painted my infrequent M. Barton originals as well as a new series of cityscapes by Emery Ward.

It turned out Father's neighbor Mr. Palsson *had* wanted a painting for his wife. He'd commissioned my first painting where I allowed myself to be the artist openly. I hadn't found out until making her acquaintance, but Mr. Palsson had married a wealthy former actress from the London stage. She had many friends and connections within the demimonde. Mrs. Palsson had spread my name—Emery Ward, artist—far and wide among her set. And now I was able to paint for myself, owning my accomplishments and any accolades I received.

A quick peek back toward the notebook showed I hadn't yet reached the page I was looking for, so I continued on. But Augie said, "Wait," and pushed his hand on the page to halt my progress. "Is that ..." He pulled the sketchbook from my lap to better view the drawing he'd discovered.

"That's me," he said quietly, eyes scanning the page. "When did you draw this?"

I thought for a moment. "I suppose I would have been nineteen. The summer you refused to dance with me at the village festival. I couldn't understand the look you'd given me, so I'd drawn it in order to commit it to memory for further analysis. I'd assumed I knew all your looks."

Augie regarded at me softly. I could tell he was remembering too. "It grew to be too difficult at times. Wanting you."

"That was difficult?" I asked.

He nodded, brushing my loose hair back behind my shoulder, as if proving to himself that he was allowed to touch me. That I was his. "The not-letting-on part," he confirmed. "I'd wanted to dance with you. But I'd feared getting too close. I remember it being particularly difficult that day. All I'd wanted was to touch you, and you would have seen it all over my face. This face." He indicated the drawing.

I nodded, taking in past Augie's expression. I could recognize it now and see it for what it was, sketched out hurriedly on the page. Longing and fear.

I returned the book to my lap and continued on to the page I'd been originally searching out. Finally.

Augie leaned over to better see. His warm shoulder brushed my own. Distracted by his nearness, I turned to place a kiss on the underside of his jaw.

He smiled at me before pointing to the drawing. "Back in all its glory."

The drawing was of the tree house, whole and hardy once more. I'd drawn it in autumn several years ago, minimal leaves on the tree so the viewer could take in the whole structure unencumbered by the surrounding foliage. Here, in this moment, I was grateful for the record. It would make this next part so much fun.

"I was thinking," I began slowly. "Perhaps we should rebuild it."

Augie frowned. "I know it holds sentimental value but we're a little old for tree houses, Em. Besides, with Mother permanently in the dowager cottage, we have no reason to sneak away. We can simply adjourn to our bedchamber."

It was his turn to lean in and place lingering kisses along the column of my neck. His progress was slow and lazy.

I smiled preemptively. "Oh, I know. It wouldn't be for us. Though it will be a while yet before he or she is actually big enough to use it."

The lips beneath my ear paused before I felt a gasp against my skin. Augie pulled back suddenly, eyes wide. "Truly?"

My smile grew. "Truly."

He dove forward, clutching me to him and making me laugh. "You're going to be the best father, Augustus. I can't wait."

Pulling back, Augie's eye were bright with emotion. "And you will be the fiercest and most amazing mother. They are going to adore you."

"We still have around six months before little Emery Two arrives."

His groan was a thing of beauty, and I simply could not maintain my straight face. Erupting into giggles at Augie's horrified expression, I collapsed onto the blanket.

"You cannot expect to apply your ridiculous naming system to our child, Emery. Our. Child."

I reached up and used his shirt to pull him to me, body solid and comfortingly draped across me. "Fine!" I relented. "If you're so opposed to Emery Two, I could be swayed to Beatrice Four."

Augie's forehead dropped to my chest as his laughter reached my ears. "It's a good name!" I argued. And then his fingers were digging into my sides and I was squirming and shrieking.

"I will not stop torturing you until you agree to give our child a normal name."

"Fine! Fine! I give up. Just stop tickling me." My breathing was labored from a combination of my husband's teasing treatment and my unbearable joy. I sucked in a gasp as Augie's fingers caressed my side. Beneath my shirt, he was no longer tickling me, rather attempting to rile me in a completely different way.

Our lips met in a furious outpouring of emotion. We kissed for new beginnings and old friendships and for a love that had always been. It had simply changed its face as time went on. My fondest hope was that our love would continue to grow and change with us. For I couldn't wait to see what the future would bring.

I prayed all our days could be like this. Full of laughter and love and the very best friend I could have ever asked for.

*If you want more Emery and Augie? Check out a bonus scene for First to Fall when you sign up for Laney's newsletter **here**!*

If you have trouble with the link for the bonus scene, scan the QR code:

The Bartholomew series continues with Patty's story, Second Chance Dance. You can read it for free in Kindle Unlimited!

Acknowledgments

To my husband: thank you for giving me all the insight I would ever need to write a friends-to-lovers story.

To my ARC readers: thank you for taking a chance on a new author who had no idea what she was doing.

To Nicole: I value your wisdom and experience and your enthusiasm for Anthony Bridgerton. All three are unparalleled.

To Emily: you are stuck reading everything I ever write. From here on out. Apologies.

About the Author

Laney Hatcher is a firm believer that there is a spreadsheet for every occasion and pie is always the answer. She is an author of stories both old and new where the HEAs are always guaranteed. Often too practical for her own good, Laney enjoys her life in the southern United States with her husband, children, and incredibly entitled cat.

Find Laney Hatcher online:
Facebook: https://bit.ly/3s6KnuY
Newsletter: https://bit.ly/3SbXg2v
Amazon: https://amzn.to/3IaOwU7
Instagram: https://bit.ly/3s4IRcS
Website: https://laneyhatcher.com/
Goodreads: https://bit.ly/3BD0Gme
TikTok: https://www.tiktok.com/@laneyhatcherauthor
Threads: https://www.threads.net/@laney.hatcher

Newsletter sign up

Also by Laney Hatcher

Kirby Falls Series

Take It or Leaf It: A Grumpy Sunshine Slow Burn Romance

Leaf It To Me: A Friends to Lovers Small-Town Romance

Leaf and Let Die: A Rivals to Lovers Small-Town Romance

Leaf You Hanging: A Reformed Bad Boy Small-Town Romance

Cozy Creek Collection

Fall Me Maybe

Bartholomew Series

First to Fall: A Friends to Lovers Historical Romance

Second Chance Dance: An Enemies to Lovers Historical Romance

Third Degree Yearn: A Second Chance Historical Romance

Last on the List: A Surprise Pregnancy Historical Romance

Smartypants Romance

London Ladies Embroidery Series

Neanderthal Seeks Duchess

Well Acquainted

Love Matched

Find bonus content, reading order, and other news at my website:

https://laneyhatcher.com/